Up Close and Dangerous

Up Close and Dangerous

A Novel

Linda Howard

**THORNDIKE
WINDSOR
PARAGON**

This Large Print edition is published by Thorndike Press, Waterville, Maine USA and by BBC Audiobooks Ltd, Bath England

ALL RIGHTS RESERVED

LIBRARY OF CONGRESS CATALOGING-IN-PUBLICATION DATA

Howard, Linda, 1950–
    Up close and dangerous / by Linda Howard.
      p. cm. — (Thorndike Press large print basic)
    ISBN-13: 978-0-7862-9651-4 (lg. print : alk. paper)
    ISBN-10: 0-7862-9651-8 (lg. print : alk. paper) 1. Aircraft accidents —
Fiction. 2. Murder — Fiction. 3. Large type books. I. Title.
PS3558.O88217U6 2007
813'.54—dc22
                                 2007023175

BRITISH LIBRARY CATALOGUING-IN-PUBLICATION DATA AVAILABLE

Published in 2007 by arrangement with The Ballantine Publishing Group, a division of Random House, Inc.
Published in the U.K. in 2008 by arrangement with Piatkus Books Ltd.

U.K. Hardcover: 978 1 405 61884 7 (Windsor Large Print)
U.K. Softcover: 978 1 405 61885 4 (Paragon Large Print)

Printed in the United States of America on permanent paper
10 9 8 7 6 5 4 3 2 1

Up Close and Dangerous

ACKNOWLEDGMENTS

My deepest thanks go to two men who went out of their way to answer a *bunch* of questions: Jim Murphy and Major Marc Weintraub, USMC. Thanks, guys, for telling me how to crash a plane. Any mistakes are mine, either because my imagination ran away with me or I didn't know the right questions to ask.

1

Bailey Wingate woke up crying. Again.

She hated when she did that, because she couldn't see any reason for being such a wuss. If she were desperately unhappy, if she were lonely or grieving, crying in her sleep would make sense, but she wasn't any of those things. At worst, she was pissed.

Even being pissed wasn't a full-time attitude; that came only when she had to deal with her stepchildren, Seth and Tamzin, which, thank God, usually happened only once a month when she signed off on the allotted funds they received from their inheritance from her late husband. They almost always contacted her then, either before to make their pitches for more money, which she had yet to approve, or afterward to let her know, in their individual ways, what a scummy bitch they thought she was.

Seth was by far the most vicious, and more times than she cared to count he'd left her emotionally bruised, but at least he was forthright with his hostility. As tough as he was to take, Bailey preferred dealing with him to having to wade her way through Tamzin's passive-aggressive crap.

Today was the day their monthly funds were released to their bank accounts, which meant she could look forward to either their phone calls or actual visits. Oh, joy. One of Tamzin's favorite punishments was to visit, and bring her two young children. Tamzin alone was tough enough to take, but when her two whiny, spoiled, demanding children were added to the mix, Bailey felt like running for the hills.

"I should have asked for combat pay," she grumbled aloud as she threw back the covers and got out of bed.

Then she mentally snorted at herself. She had nothing to complain about, much less cry in her sleep over. She'd agreed to marry James Wingate knowing what his children were like, and how they would react to their father's financial arrangements for them. He had, in fact, banked on those reactions and planned accordingly. She had gone into the situation with her eyes open, so she had no grounds for complaining now. Even from the grave, Jim was paying her well to do her job.

Going into the plush bathroom, she

glanced at her reflection — something that was difficult *not* to do when the first thing she faced was a floor-to-ceiling mirror. Sometimes, when she saw herself, she had a moment of almost complete disconnect between the person reflected and what she felt like inside.

Money had changed her — not inside so much as outside. She was slimmer, more toned, because now she had both the time and the money for a personal trainer who came to the house and put her through hell in the private exercise room. Her hair, before always a sort of dirty blond, was now so artfully streaked with different hues of blond that it looked completely natural. An expensive cut flattered her face, and fell into such graceful lines that even now, fresh out of bed, her hair looked pretty damn good.

She had always been neat, and she had dressed as well as she could on her salary, but there was a world of difference between "neat" and "polished." She had never been beautiful, and certainly wouldn't qualify for that level of good looks even now, but she did sometimes reach "pretty," or even "striking." Skillful application of the best cosmetics available made the green of her eyes more intense, more vibrant. Her clothes were tailored to fit her and only her, instead of millions of other women who were the same general size.

As Jim's widow, she had the full and unquestioned use of this house in Seattle, one in Palm Beach, and another in Maine. She never had to fly on a commercial airline unless she wished to; the Wingate corporation leased private jets for its use, and a plane was always available to her. She paid only for her personal possessions, which meant she didn't have to worry about bills. That was undeniably the biggest bright spot of the deal she'd made with the man who had married her and, in less than a year, made her a widow.

Bailey had been poor, and though amassing wealth had never been her life's focus or ambition, she had to admit that having money made life much easier. She still had problems, the main ones being Seth and Tamzin, but problems felt different when they didn't involve paying bills on time: the sense of urgency was gone.

All she had to do was oversee their trust funds — a duty she took very seriously even though they would never believe that — and otherwise fill her days.

God, she was bored.

Jim had thought of everything regarding his children, she thought as she stepped into the round, frosted-glass shower. He had safeguarded their inheritances; insofar as he was able he'd also ensured that they would always be financially secure, and very skillfully read their personalities while doing so. His plans, however, hadn't included how her life would play out after he was gone.

He likely hadn't cared, she thought ruefully. She'd been the means to an end, and even though he'd been fond of her and she of him, he'd never made any pretense of feeling anything more than that for her. Theirs had been a business arrangement, one he'd initiated and controlled. Even if he'd known beforehand, he wouldn't have cared that his friends, who had dutifully invited her to their social events while Jim was still alive, had dropped her from their guest lists like a hot potato as soon as he was in the ground. Jim's friends had mostly been in his age group, and a lot of them had known and been friends with Jim's first wife, Lena. Some of them had also known Bailey from before, in her capacity as Jim's personal assistant. They were uncomfortable with her in the role of his wife. Hell, *she* had been uncomfortable, so how could she blame them for feeling the same way?

This wasn't the life she'd wanted for herself. Yes, the money was nice — very nice —

but she didn't want to spend the rest of her life doing nothing but growing money for two people who despised her. Jim had been certain that Seth's humiliation at having his inheritance controlled by a stepmother who was three years his junior would shock him into stepping up to the plate and behaving like a responsible adult, instead of an older male version of Paris Hilton, but so far that hadn't happened and Bailey no longer had any faith it ever would. Seth had had plenty of chances to apply himself, to take an interest in the corporations that funded his lavish and lazy lifestyle, but he hadn't seized any of them. Seth had been Jim's hope, because Tamzin was completely disinterested in and unsuited for the type of financial decisions huge amounts of money demanded. All Tamzin was interested in was the end result, which was cash at her disposal — and she wanted all of her inheritance *now,* so she could spend it as she wished.

Bailey winced at the thought; if Tamzin had control of her inheritance, she would blow through the money within five years, tops. If Bailey herself didn't control the funds, someone else would have to.

The phone rang just as she turned off the shower and reached for a champagne-colored towel to wrap around herself. Wrapping another around her wet hair, she stepped out and picked up the cordless phone in the dressing room, looked at the Caller ID, and set the unit back down without answering. The number had been blocked; she had registered all her numbers on the national do-not-call list, so the blocked number wasn't likely to be a telemarketer. That meant Seth was probably up bright and early thinking of insults he could use, and she refused to deal with him before she had her coffee. Her sense of duty extended only so far, and this was beyond those boundaries.

On the other hand, what if something was wrong? Seth partied hard, seldom getting to bed before dawn — at least not his own bed. It wasn't like him to be calling this early. Feeling her boundaries stretch a little, she grabbed the phone again, punching the "talk" button even though the answering machine would have already picked up and started its spiel.

"Hello," she said over the recorded message made with the canned male voice that was the system's default. She had kept it instead of recording a message of her own because the canned one was more impersonal.

The answering system halted in midsentence when she picked up, then beeped, and clicked off.

"Hi, Mom."

Sarcasm was heavy in Seth's voice. Mentally she sighed. Nothing was wrong; Seth was just trying out a new way of annoying her. Being called "mom" by a man who was older than she didn't bother her, but dealing with him at all certainly did.

The best way to handle Seth was to show no reaction at all; eventually he'd get tired of his needling and hang up. "Seth. How are you?" she responded in the cool, even tone she'd perfected while working as Jim's PA. Neither her tone nor her expression had ever given anything away.

"Things couldn't be better," he responded with false cheer, "considering my money-hungry whore of a stepmother is living large on *my* money, while I can't touch it at all. But what's a little theft between relatives, right?"

Usually she let the insults roll off her back. "Whore" was one he'd pulled out the second he'd heard the provisions of his father's will. Seth had gone on to accuse her of having married his father for his money, and taken advantage of Jim's illness to persuade him to leave even his children's money in her control. He had also promised, threatened, to contest the will in court, at which time Jim's lawyer had sighed heavily and advised

16

against such action as a waste of time and money; Jim had capably handled the reins of his empire up until the last few weeks before his death, and the will had been signed almost a year before that — the day after his marriage to Bailey, in fact.

Learning that, Seth had turned dark red, said something so filthy to her that everyone else in the room had sucked in a breath, and then he'd stormed out. Bailey had schooled herself by then not to show any reaction, so a simple "whore" now wasn't likely to get a rise out of her.

On the other hand, being called a thief was beginning to get under her skin.

"Speaking of your inheritance, there's an investment opportunity I want to investigate," she said smoothly. "In order to maximize the gain, I'll need to put as much as possible into the venture. You won't mind if your monthly allowance is cut in half, will you? Temporarily, of course. About a year should do it."

A split second of silence greeted that proposal, then Seth growled in a voice thick with rage, "You bitch, I'll kill you."

This was the first time she had countered his insults with a threat of her own, shocking him out of his own set pattern. The threat didn't alarm her. Seth was big at making threats he didn't carry out.

"If you have other investment proposals you'd like me to consider I'll be happy to look at them," she said as politely as if he'd asked the particulars instead of threatening to kill her. "Just research them fully, and put your proposals in writing. I'll get to them as soon as possible, but that will probably be a few weeks. I'm going on vacation day after tomorrow and expect to be gone for a couple of weeks."

Her answer was a phone slammed down in her ear.

Not a great way to start the day, she thought, but at least her monthly encounter with Seth was now behind her.

Now, if she could just avoid Tamzin . . .

2

Cameron Justice gave the small airfield and parking lot a swift, encompassing glance as he pulled his blue Suburban into his allotted slot. Though it wasn't yet six-thirty in the morning, he wasn't the first to arrive. The silver Corvette meant his friend and partner, Bret Larsen — the L of J&L Executive Air Limo — was already there, and the red Ford Focus signaled the presence of their secretary, Karen Kaminski. Bret was early, but Karen made a practice of getting into the office before anyone else; she said it was the only time she could get any work done without being constantly interrupted.

The morning was bright and clear, though the weather report called for increasing cloudiness during the day. Right this minute, though, the sun shone brightly on the four gleaming J&L planes, and Cam paused for a moment to enjoy the sight.

The custom paint job had been expensive,

but worth the cost in the image presented by the shining black slashed by a thin line of white curving upward from the nose to the tail. The two Cessnas — a Skylane and a Skyhawk — were paid for, free and clear; he and Bret had busted their asses the first couple of years, working side jobs as well as flying, to get them paid off as fast as possible and to improve their debt ratio. The Piper Mirage was *almost* theirs, and after it was paid for they planned to double up on payments on the eight-seater Lear 45 XR, which was Cam's baby.

Though in reality the Lear was fairly close in length and wing-span to the F-15E Strike Eagle that Cam's partner had flown while in the air force, Bret had since become accustomed to the much smaller Cessnas and the midsize Mirage, preferring their agility. Cam, who had flown the huge KC-10A Extender during his time in the service, preferred having more aircraft around him. Their favorites illustrated the basic differences between them as pilots. Bret was the fighter-pilot, cocky and with lightning-fast reflexes; Cam was the steady Eddie, the guy whose hands you wanted on the yoke when a plane needed refueling thousands of feet in the air, at hundreds of miles an hour. The Lear needed every available inch of runway the small airfield provided in order to take off, so Bret was more than glad for Cam to be in the pilot's seat on those flights.

They'd done well for themselves, Cam thought, while doing something they both loved. Flying was in their blood. They had met in the Air Force Academy, and though Bret had been a year ahead of Cam they'd become friends, and remained friends through different deployments, different career tracks, different postings. They had seen each other through three divorces — two for Bret and one for Cam — and a number of girlfriends. Almost without really planning it they had somehow, through phone calls and e-mails, decided to go into business together when they left the military; what type of business was never in question. A small air charter service had seemed tailor-made for them.

The gig had turned into a good one. They now employed three mechanics, one part-time pilot, a cleanup crew consisting of one full-time and one part-time, and Karen the Indispensable, who ruled them all with an iron fist and a total lack of tolerance for bullshit. The company was solvent, and both of them made a good living from it. The day-to-day flying didn't provide the thrills and chills of military flight, but Cam didn't need an adrenaline rush to enjoy life. Bret, of course, was a different type; fighter pilots *lived* for the burn, but he'd adjusted, and got his occasional doses of drama by joining the Civil Air Patrol.

They had lucked out on the location, too. The airfield was perfect for their needs. It was convenient, most of all, to the corporate headquarters of the Wingate Group, J&L's main client. Sixty percent of their flights were with Wingate, for the most part ferrying high-ranking executives to and fro, though sometimes the family used J&L for private excursions. Other than convenience, though, the airfield offered good security and an above-average terminal building in which J&L had a three-room office. It was Bret's connections that had got them the Wingate business, and he usually flew the family members, while Cam took care of ferrying the corporate suits around. The arrangement suited both of them fine, because Bret got along with the family better than Cam did. Mr. Wingate had been a nice guy, but his kids were assholes, and the trophy wife he'd left behind was as warm and friendly as a glacier.

Cam climbed out of the Suburban. He was a tall, broad-shouldered man, and the big vehicle suited him, giving him the leg- and headroom he needed. Crossing the parking lot in his loose-limbed, unhurried stride, he let himself in the private door on the side of the terminal building, swiping his ID card to unlock it. A narrow hall led to their office, where Karen sat industriously tapping away on her computer keyboard. Fresh flowers sat in a vase on her desk, the fragrance mingling with that of coffee. She *always* had flowers, though he suspected she bought them herself. Her boyfriend — a black-leather wearing, motorcycle-riding, bearded pro wrestler — didn't seem like the flower-buying kind. Cam knew she was in her late twenties, he knew she liked to dye black streaks into her short red hair, and that she made the office run like oiled silk, but beyond that he was afraid to ask. Bret, on the other hand, had made it his life's mission to flap the unflappable, and teased her relentlessly.

"Morning, Sunshine," Cam greeted her, because, what the hell, he wasn't above teasing her either.

She gave him a squinty-eyed look over the top of her monitor, then returned to her typing. Karen was as far from being sunshiny in the mornings as Seattle was from Miami. Bret had once voiced the theory that she moonlighted as a guard dog in a junkyard, because she was as mean as one and didn't turn reasonably human until around nine a.m. Karen hadn't said anything, but Bret's personal mail had disappeared for over a month, until he got a clue and apologized, whereupon his mail began being delivered again, but he was a month behind in all his bills.

Opting for caution over valor, Cam didn't say anything else to her; instead he helped himself to the coffee and wandered over to the open door of Bret's office. "You're early," he said, propping a shoulder against the door frame.

Bret gave him a sour look. "Not willingly."

"You mean Karen called and told you to get your ass down here?" Behind him, Cam heard a sound that could have been either a chuckle or a growl. With Karen, it was hard to tell the difference.

"Almost as bad. Some idiot waited until the last minute to book an eight o'clock."

"We don't call them 'idiots,' " Karen said automatically. "I sent you a memo. We call them 'clients.' "

Bret was taking a sip of coffee when she spoke, and he half choked, half laughed. " 'Clients,' " he repeated. "Got it." He indicated the sheet of paper he'd been scribbling on, which Cam recognized as a schedule form. "I've called Mike in to take the

Spokane run this afternoon, in the Skylane" — Mike Gardiner was their part-time pilot — "and that'll free me up to take the Mirage to L.A. if you want to take the Eugene run in the Skyhawk — or we can swap if you'd rather do the L.A. run."

Whoever got into the office first was the one who had to start on the paperwork, which was one reason why Bret was seldom there so early. He was matching the range of the planes to the length of the flights, which was only common sense because it saved time if they didn't have to stop for refueling. Normally Cam would have preferred the L.A. run, but he'd already flown a couple of long trips this week and he needed a little break. He also needed a few hours in one of the Cessnas; he flew so much in the Lear and the Piper Mirage that he had to make an effort to get his hours in on the smaller planes. "No, it's fine the way it is. I need the hours. What's on for tomorrow?"

"Just two. Tomorrow's an early day for me, too; I'm taking Mrs. Wingate to Denver for a vacation, so I'll be deadheading back unless I can pick up something. The other one is . . ." He paused, looking through the papers on his desk for the contract sheet Karen had written up.

"A cargo run to Sacramento," Karen said

from the outer office, not bothering to pretend she wasn't eavesdropping.

"A cargo run to Sacramento," Bret echoed, grinning, as if Cam hadn't heard her perfectly well. The growling sound came again. Bret scribbled a note and pushed it across his desk; Cam ambled forward to put one finger on the piece of paper and twirl it around.

Ask her if she's had her rabies shot, the note read.

"Sure," he said, and raised his voice. "Karen, Bret wants me to ask you —"

"Shut up, you asshole!" Bret lunged to his feet and punched Cam on the shoulder to stop him from completing the sentence. Laughing, Cam left the room to go to his own office.

Karen gave him the squinty-eyed look again. "Bret wants you to ask me what?" she demanded.

"Never mind. It wasn't anything important," Cam said innocently.

"Yeah, I'll bet," she muttered.

The phone rang as he sat down, and though technically it was Karen's job to answer calls, she was busy and he wasn't, so he punched on line one and answered.

"Executive Air Limo."

"This is Seth Wingate. Does my step-

26

mother have a flight booked for tomorrow?"

The man's voice was abrupt, raising Cam's hackles, but he kept his own tone neutral. "Yes, she does."

"Where to?"

Cam wished he could tell the jerk that Mrs. Wingate's destination wasn't any of his business, but when it came down to it, jerk or not, he was a Wingate and would have a lot to say about whether or not J&L kept the Wingate Group's business. "Denver."

"When is she coming back?"

"I don't have the exact date in front of me, but I believe it's around two weeks."

The only reply was the line being disconnected, without a "thank you," "kiss my ass," or anything else.

"Bastard," he muttered as he clicked the receiver down.

"Who?"

Karen's voice floated through the open door. Was there anything she didn't hear? The hell of it was, the tap-tap of computer keys never stopped, never hesitated. The woman was downright scary.

"Seth Wingate," he replied.

"I'm with you on that, boss. He's keeping tabs on Mrs. Wingate, huh? I wonder why. There's no love lost between those two."

No surprise there; the first Mrs. Wingate,

whom he'd known briefly but really liked, had died barely a year before Mr. Wingate married his personal assistant, who was younger than both his children. "Maybe he's going to throw a party in the house while she's gone."

"That's juvenile."

"So is he."

"That's probably why Mr. Wingate, the old one, left her in charge of the money."

Surprised, Cam got up and went to his office door. "You're kidding," he said to her back.

She glanced over her shoulder at him, her fingers still flying over the computer keys. "You didn't know?"

"How would I know?" Neither any of the family members nor the executives in the Group talked personal finances with him, and he didn't believe they confided in Karen either.

"*I* know," she pointed out.

Yeah, but you're scary. He bit back the words before his mouth got his ass in big-time trouble. Karen had her ways of finding out stuff. "*How* do you know?"

"I hear things."

"If it's true, no wonder there's no love lost between them." Hell, if he was in Seth Wingate's shoes, he'd probably be acting like a bastard toward his stepmother, too.

"It's true, all right. Old Mr. Wingate was a smart guy. Think about it. Would *you* have left either Seth or Tamzin in charge of millions and millions of dollars?"

Cam had to think about it for maybe one thousandth of a second. "No way in hell."

"Well, neither would he. And I like her. She's smart."

"I hope she's smart enough to have changed the locks on the doors when Mr. Wingate died," Cam said. And to watch her back, because he wouldn't trust Seth Wingate not to put a knife in it, if he had the chance.

3

The phone jarred Cam awake the next morning and he fumbled for it without opening his eyes. Maybe it was a wrong number; if he didn't open his eyes, he'd be able to go back to sleep until the alarm on his wristwatch went off. He knew from experience that once he opened his eyes he might as well get up because sleep wasn't gonna happen. "Yeah."

"Boss, get your pants on and get down here."

Karen. Shit. He forgot about keeping his eyes shut and bolted straight up, a shot of adrenaline clearing his brain of cobwebs. "What's wrong?"

"Your idiot partner just showed up with his eyes swollen almost shut, barely able to breathe, and he thinks he's capable of flying to Denver today."

In the background Cam heard a thick, hoarse voice that didn't sound at all like Bret saying something unintelligible. "Is that Bret?"

"Yeah. He wants to know why I call you 'boss' and him 'idiot.' Because some things are just evident, that's why," she snapped, evidently replying to Bret. Returning her attention to Cam, she said, "I've called Mike, but he can't get here in time to take the Denver flight, so I'm giving him your flight to Sacramento and you have to get your butt in gear."

"I'm on my way," he said, disconnecting and dashing for the bathroom. He showered and shaved in four minutes and twenty-three seconds, threw on one of his black suits, grabbed his cap and the overnight bag he always kept packed because things like this sometimes happened, and was out the door in six minutes. He backtracked to turn off the coffeemaker that was programmed to begin brewing in about an hour, then, because he didn't know if he'd have time to stop for breakfast he snatched some trail mix bars from the cabinet and dropped them in his pocket.

Shit, shit, *shit.* He swore under his breath as he wove through the early-morning traffic. His passenger today was the frosty Widow Wingate. Bret got along with her, but Bret got along with almost everyone; the few

31

times Cam had been unlucky enough to be around her, she'd acted as if she had a stick up her ass *and* he was a bug on the windshield of her life. He'd dealt with her type before, in the military; the attitude hadn't set well with him then and it sure as hell didn't now. He'd keep his lip buttoned if it killed him, but if she gave him any lip he'd give *her* the roughest ride of her life; he'd have her puking her guts out before they got to Denver.

He made good time; he lived on the outskirts of Seattle, plus he was heading away from the city instead of toward it, so his side of the road was relatively clear while the other side was a solid ribbon of vehicles. He pulled into his parking slot a mere twenty-seven minutes after hanging up the phone.

"That was fast," Karen said when he entered the office, overnight bag in hand. "I have more bad news."

"Lay it on me." He put down the bag to pour a cup of coffee.

"The Mirage is in for repairs, and Dennis says it won't be ready in time for the flight."

Cam sipped in silence, thinking through the logistics. The Mirage could have made it to Denver without refueling. The Lear obviously could, but they used it for groups, not just one person — and though he could fly the Lear by himself, he preferred having a copilot. Neither of the Cessnas had the range, but the Skylane had a service ceiling of about eighteen thousand feet, while the Skyhawk's ceiling was thirteen five. Some of Colorado's mountain peaks topped fourteen thousand, so the choice of aircraft was a no-brainer.

"The Skylane," he said. "I'll refuel in Salt Lake City."

"That's what I figured," Bret said, coming out of his office. His voice was so hoarse he sounded something like a frog with sinus congestion. "I told the crew to get it ready."

Cam looked up. Karen hadn't exaggerated Bret's condition at all; if anything, she had understated it. His eyes were red-rimmed and so swollen just a narrow slit of blue iris showed. His face was blotchy, and he was breathing through his mouth. All in all, he looked like hell, and if his miserable expression was any indication he felt like it, too. Whatever it was he had, Cam didn't want it.

"Don't come any closer," Cam warned, holding up his hand like a traffic cop.

"I've already sprayed him with Lysol," Karen said, glaring across the office at Bret. "A considerate person, with half an ounce of common sense, would have stayed home and *called,* instead of coming to work to spread his germs around."

"I can fly," he croaked. "You're the one who insists I can't."

"I'm *so* sure Mrs. Wingate would want to spend five hours cooped up in a little plane with you," she said sarcastically. "I don't want to spend five minutes in the same office with you. *Go. Home.*"

"I second that motion," Cam growled. "Go home."

"I took a decongestant," Bret wheezed in protest. "It just hasn't kicked in yet."

"Then it isn't going to kick in in time for you to fly."

"You don't like flying the family."

Especially Mrs. Wingate, Cam thought, but aloud he said, "It's no big deal."

"She likes me better."

Now Bret sounded like a sulky kid, but then he always pouted when something interfered with his flight time. "She can tough it out for five hours," Cam said, unrelenting. If he could, she definitely could. "You're sick, I'm not. End of discussion."

"I pulled up the weather reports for you," Karen said. "They're on your computer."

"Thanks." Going into his office, he seated himself at his desk and began reading. Bret stood in the office doorway, looking as if he didn't know what to do with himself. "For

God's sake," Cam said, "go to a doctor. You look as if you've been Maced. You may be having an allergic reaction to something."

"All right." He sneezed violently, then went into a coughing fit.

From where Cam was seated he couldn't see Karen, but he heard a hissing noise, then Bret was enveloped in a mist. "Oh, for God's sake," the sick man wheezed, flapping his arms to drive the mist away. "Breathing this can't be good."

She simply sprayed more. "I give up," he muttered after a futile few seconds of flapping, because he was losing ground against the cloud. "I'm going, I'm going. But if I develop lung failure because you've Lysoled me to death, *you're fired!*"

"If you're dead, you can't fire me." She got in the last shot, delivered to his back as he slammed out of the office.

After a moment of silence, Cam said, "Spray some more. Spray everything he touched."

"I'll need a new can. This one's almost empty."

"When I get back, I'll buy you a whole case."

"For now, I'll spray the doorknobs he's touched, but other than that stay out of his office."

"What about the bathroom?"

"I'm not going in the men's john. I used to think men were human, but I went in a jock john once and almost passed out from shock. Going into another one would probably throw me into psychotic episodes. You want the bathroom sprayed, you'll have to do it yourself."

He pondered for a moment on the faintly unbelievable detail that *she* worked for *them,* then he also considered the probability that the office would fall into complete chaos if she weren't there. Probability, hell; she'd make damn certain it did. When he weighed those two viewpoints against each other, he concluded that bathroom spraying wasn't on her list of duties. "I don't have time right now."

"The bathroom isn't going anywhere — and I use the ladies'." Meaning she didn't care if the men's got de-germed or not.

He stared through the open door, only now realizing how many of their conversations were carried on with her in the outer office and him in his office, and most of the time he couldn't see her at all. "I'm going to put up a big round mirror," he said. "Right there next to the outer door."

"Why?"

"So I can see you when I talk to you."

"Why do you want to do that?"

"To tell if you're grinning."

Cam stowed his bag in the luggage compartment then inspected the Skylane, circling it, looking for anything that was loose or worn. He tugged, he pushed, he kicked. He climbed into the cockpit and ran through the preflight procedures, checking each item off on a list on his clipboard. He knew this procedure by heart, he could do it in his sleep, but he never relied on his memory alone; one moment of distraction, and he might miss something crucial. He went by the list so he knew he covered everything. When he was two miles high was the wrong time to discover something wasn't working.

Checking his watch, he saw that it was almost time for Mrs. Wingate's arrival. He started the engine, listening to the sound as it caught and smoothed out. He checked the instrumentation display on the monitors, double-checked that all the data was normal, then checked the area traffic before idling toward the chain-link gate in front of the terminal where he would pick up his passenger. Out of the corner of his eye he saw a flash of movement in the direction of the parking lot, and he glanced that way just long enough to verify that a dark green Land Rover was pulling into the closest available slot.

Seeing her in the Land Rover always surprised him. Mrs. Wingate didn't look like a utility-vehicle or SUV type of woman; if he'd been meeting her for the first time, he'd have pegged her for someone who preferred a big luxury model — not a sporty type, but one of those that someone else drove while she sat in the backseat. Instead she always drove herself, wheeling the four-wheel-drive around as if she intended to take off across a field at any moment.

He'd cut it too close. Normally Bret would already be at the gate, and he'd help her get her luggage out and stowed. Cam saw the way she stood for a moment, eyeing the Skylane coming closer, then she closed the door and went around to the back to begin hauling out her luggage herself. He was still a good sixty yards from the gate; no way would he get there in time.

Great. She'd probably start the flight already pissed, because no one was there to help her. On the other hand, at least she hadn't stood there waiting, with her nose in the air, until someone did show.

Once he was in position he cut the engine and climbed out. As he turned toward the gate he saw her coming out of the terminal building, pulling a suitcase behind her with one hand while she carried a large tote bag with the other. Karen, of all people, was with her, rolling two more suitcases along.

Mrs. Wingate watched him stride closer, and turned to Karen. "I thought Bret was supposed to be my pilot," she said in her cool, even tone.

"He's sick," Karen explained. "Trust me, you wouldn't want him anywhere near you."

Mrs. Wingate didn't shrug, or let her expression give away even a hint of what she was thinking. "Of course not," she said briefly, her eyes completely obscured by the black sunglasses she wore.

"Mrs. Wingate," Cam said in greeting as he reached them.

"Captain Justice." She stepped through the gate as soon as he opened it.

"Let me take your bags."

Silently she relinquished her hold on the suitcase before his hand got anywhere near the handle. Following her lead, he didn't speak as he stowed it and the two other bags in the luggage compartment, wondering if she'd left any clothes behind in her closet. The bags were so heavy she'd never have made it on a commercial airliner without paying a hefty fee.

When there was only one passenger he or she often opted to sit beside him rather than in one of the four passenger seats behind the cockpit, partly because talking to him was easier while wearing the copilot's headset. He helped Mrs. Wingate into the plane, steadying her as she stepped on the strut and then inside; she took the seat behind him, making it evident she didn't want to talk to him.

"Would you take the seat on the other side, please," he directed, his tone of voice making it a demand rather than a request, despite the "please" he'd tacked on.

She didn't move. "Why?"

He'd been out of the air force for almost seven years, but the military habits were so deeply ingrained that Cam almost barked at her to move her ass, *now,* which would likely have resulted in their contract being canceled within the next hour. He had to grit his teeth, but he managed to say in a relatively even tone, "Our weight will be balanced better if you sit on the other side."

Silently she moved into the right-hand seat, buckling herself in. Opening her tote bag, she pulled out a thick hardback and immediately buried her nose in it, though her sunglasses were so dark he doubted she could read a word. Still, her message was received, loud and clear: *Don't talk to me.* Fine. He didn't want to talk to her any more than she wanted to talk to him.

He climbed into his seat, closed the door, and donned his headset. Karen waved before returning inside. After starting the engine and automatically checking that all the data reads were normal, he taxied from the ramp onto the runway. Not once, even during takeoff, did she look up from her book.

Yep, he thought wryly, it was going to be a long five or so hours.

4

Great, Bailey thought as soon as she saw Captain Justice climb from the cockpit of the Cessna and walk toward the gate. There was no mistaking his taller, leaner, broad-shouldered form for that of Bret Larsen, the pilot who usually flew her on her trips. Bret was cheerful and gregarious, while Captain Justice was grim with silent disapproval. Since marrying Jim Wingate, she'd become acutely attuned to when that attitude was directed at her, and though she would never characterize herself as thin-skinned, it still pissed her off.

She was damned tired of being looked at as a coldhearted gold digger who had taken advantage of a sick man. This whole situation had been Jim's idea, not hers. Yes, she was doing it for the money, but damn it, she *earned* the salary she was paid every month. Seth's and Tamzin's inheritances were not only safe under her directorship, but growing at a healthy rate. She wasn't a financial whiz by any means, but she had a good head for investing and she understood the markets. Jim had thought she was a little too conservative in her personal investments, but when it came to preserving trust funds that was exactly what he'd wanted.

She supposed she could take out an ad in the paper explaining all that, but why should she have to justify herself to people? Screw 'em.

That was an easy philosophy to take with Jim's old friends who were now too good to socialize with her, and she was glad she didn't have to spend time with them — she'd never thought of them as *her* friends anyway. She did, however, have to spend several hours cooped up in a small plane with Mr. Sourpuss, unless she wanted to cancel the flight and wait until Bret was well again — or book a commercial flight to Denver.

The idea was tempting. But she might not be able to get on the next flight out, assuming she could even get to the airport in time to make the flight, and her brother and sister-in-law were already on their way to Denver from Maine. Logan was supposed to have a four-wheel-drive rental waiting and ready to go by the time her flight landed. By eight this evening they were due at the outpost they'd selected, for two weeks of river rafting. The whole idea sounded like heaven to Bailey: two weeks of no cell service, no cold or disapproving looks, and most of all no Seth or Tamzin.

White-water rafting was Logan's thing; he and Peaches, his wife, had even met while rafting. Bailey had done a little rafting in her college days and liked it, so this had seemed an ideal way to spend some time with them. Her family was scattered and had never been big on get-togethers, so she didn't see them a lot. Her father lived in Ohio with his second wife; her mother, whose third husband had died almost four years ago, lived in Florida with her second ex-husband's sister, who was also widowed. Bailey's older sister, Kennedy, was ensconced in New Mexico. Bailey was closest to Logan, who was two years younger, but she hadn't seen him since Jim's funeral; he and Peaches were the only members of her family who had attended. Peaches was a sweetheart, and Bailey's favorite of all her in-laws or step-whatevers.

The whole trip was Peaches's idea, and e-mails had been flying for several months as they worked out the details. The plan was they would rent the bigger items, such as the tents and camp stoves and lanterns, that they would need for two weeks of camping on the banks of the river, and they would pick up food and water and other essentials — such as toilet paper — in Denver, but still Bailey's suitcases were jammed with things she thought she might need.

Her limited experience with rafting had taught her that she'd rather have something and not need it than need it and not have it. On the second of her two previous excursions, she'd gotten her period a few days early, and she'd been completely unprepared. What should have been fun had instead been misery, because she'd had to use her extra socks as pads, which meant she'd endured cold, wet feet for almost the entire trip. *Not* fun. This time she had pored over travel-oriented mail-order catalogs beforehand, and ordered everything she could imagine using, such as a pack of disposable sponge toothbrushes, waterproof poker cards, and a book light.

Logan would tease her about overpacking, but she'd have the last laugh if he happened to need anything from her cache. She even had a small roll of duct tape in case her tent sprang a leak, which had *also* happened on that last, miserable trip. She liked rafting, and when she was in the raft being wet and cold was part of the fun, but when she wasn't actually in the raft she wanted all the comforts of home. Okay, so she was being a girly-girl, but she was sure Peaches would also prefer the aloe body wipes over the joys of washing with a bucket of river water and a bar of soap.

She'd been looking forward to this trip so much that she couldn't bear the idea of a delay, even if being on time meant she had to endure the company of Captain Justice. She wanted to snort in derision every time she heard the name. *Captain Justice,* for God's sake. It sounded like the title character of a comic book.

He'd hefted her three bags into the luggage compartment without even a grunt, but though his expression looked set in stone she'd known what he was thinking; that she'd packed her entire closet. If he'd been human he'd have at least looked a little incredulous, or asked her if she had rocks in there; Bret would have grunted and acted as if the suitcases weighed even more than they did, made a joke out of it. Not Mr. Stone-face, though; she'd never seen him so much as smile.

When he helped her into the plane, the firm grip of his hand had been so unexpected she'd almost faltered. Bret didn't help her, she realized; for all his easygoing camaraderie, he was very careful not to encroach on her personal boundaries, which admittedly had expanded a lot since she'd married Jim. She simply didn't trust most people now, which made her stiff and unapproachable. Captain Justice either hadn't noticed her "do not touch" signs, or he simply didn't care. His grip was strong, his hands harder and rougher than those of the business executives and stockbrokers with whom she usually associated. The shock of being touched, the heat of his hand, actually made her heart lurch.

She was so dismayed she barely registered his order to move to the other seat. As soon as she'd belted herself into the seat he'd indicated, she dug out her book and pretended to be absorbed in it, but mentally she was kicking herself.

How pitiful was she that she would respond so easily to the simple touch of a man's hand? Not just any man, either, but one who clearly disliked her. Okay, so her love life was currently nonexistent; it would remain that way as long as she had to deal with Jim's children, because she refused to give them either ammunition or a target. Yes, there were times when she felt incredibly horny, but she hoped she had enough pride not to ever reveal that to someone like Justice, to allow him to think she had such a low opinion of herself that any man would do.

The hell of it was, physically, he *was* an attractive man — not handsome, not a pretty boy at all because his face was too rugged for that, but definitely . . . attractive. There was something compelling about gray eyes, and his were a lighter shade than usual, with just a faint hint of blue. The expression in those eyes was usually cold and remote, as if he had no feelings at all.

He and Bret were evidently good friends, though she couldn't imagine him in any sort of real friendship with anyone. When Bret talked about him, though, he sounded as if he really liked and respected Justice. "A pilot's pilot" was how Bret had once described him. "Completely cool. I swear, there's not a nerve in his body. He could hold a KC-10 steady in a hurricane, and not break a sweat."

Bailey had been curious enough, later, to go online and find out exactly what a KC-10 was.

It was easy, now, to imagine him in the cockpit of the huge supertanker, holding it steady while plane after plane swooped up behind him to be refueled. She hadn't read exactly how that worked, but she didn't think it could be easy, not at hundreds of miles an hour, being buffeted by high winds.

She surfaced from her thoughts to realize she'd stopped staring at her book and was instead staring at his hands, so sure and steady on the controls. Mortified, she snapped her gaze down again. Thank God she had on sunglasses, so he couldn't tell she'd been staring at him — though he probably wondered how she could read through the dark lenses. She couldn't, but he didn't need to know that.

She felt self-conscious and uncomfortable, which wasn't like her at all. She needed to relax and get her mind on other things. If she pulled off her sunglasses she would actually be able to read, and the book was a good one, but when she reached up to remove the glasses she didn't get them all the way off before shoving them back in place again. They were a good shield, and she felt as if she needed one.

Okay, reading was out. A nap, maybe?

It was too early in the day, barely mid-morning. She could pretend to nap, the way she'd been pretending to read, but that wouldn't redirect her thoughts.

If she'd brought her laptop she could have played some games, but she'd left it at home. She wouldn't have Internet access for the next two weeks, so after its battery died the computer would have been useless weight she'd have to lug around, unless she'd also wanted to carry spare batteries, which she hadn't, not when she was already taking so much stuff. Their guide was supposed to have vehicles that took their camping gear and personal items from site to site, but there were three rafts, each with six people, so that meant the gear and paraphernalia of eighteen people had to be carted around. She hoped the guide had some damn big vehicles.

The prospect of the next two weeks filled her with excitement. Some of the rafting would be fun, some would be exciting, some of it downright dangerous, but for two weeks she wouldn't have to watch every word she said, and she wouldn't be surrounded by people who either openly despised her or looked askance at her. She would be able to relax, to laugh and have fun, to be *herself*. For two weeks, she was free.

She looked out the window for a while, watching Washington's vast expanse beneath them. Commercial airliners were fast, but she preferred flying in smaller craft because she could see so much better at the lower altitudes. The loud drone of the engine was hypnotic and she actually did doze a little, her head resting against the back of the leather seat. The morning sun hit the windshield, warming the interior of the plane until she began to feel too warm and removed her lightweight silk jacket. She wouldn't wear silk again for two weeks, she thought drowsily; the silk bed-sack she'd brought, in case her sleeping bag got too hot or too cool, didn't count.

When she glanced at her watch, she saw with surprise that they'd been in the air almost an hour and a half; time had seemed to be crawling, but maybe she'd dozed longer than she'd thought. "Where are we?" she asked, raising her voice so he could hear her.

He lifted one earpiece of his headset and glanced over his shoulder at her. "Ma'am?" he asked; his expression was cold, but his tone was polite. Barely.

"Where are we?" she repeated.

"Coming up on Idaho."

She looked through the windshield and saw enormous white-capped mountains looming straight ahead. Her heart jumped and she couldn't contain a gasp; they were on a collision course with the mountains unless this little plane could go higher — a *lot* higher.

He replaced the earpiece, but she thought she saw a flicker of satisfaction in the set of his mouth. From her angle she couldn't really tell, but if he'd heard her gasp she had no doubt he was amused. Of course the plane could go higher; they wouldn't be in this one if it couldn't. *Jerk,* she thought irritably.

Settling back in her seat, she stared at the mountains. They were still a good distance away, but their size was so overwhelming that they seemed to be crouching right in front of her, like huge prehistoric beasts, waiting for her to get closer before they rose up and pounced.

What was it about mountains? They had always tickled her imagination. In reality they sat there, big wrinkles in the earth. From the air they reminded her of a piece of paper that had been badly crumpled, then halfheartedly straightened. Unless they were volcanoes, the mountains never actually *did* anything, so why did they always seem so alive to her? She didn't mean "alive" as in they had trees growing on them, or animals both small and large prowling around, but alive as in the mountains themselves seemed to live and breathe, to each have a personality, to communicate with one another. When she was little, she had thought hills were a mountain's children, that when the hills grew up they would become mountains, and as they grew all the houses that had been built on them would go sliding off. She could remember being terrified any time she visited a home on even the teeniest slope, thinking that at any minute the ground would start rising beneath their feet and they'd begin sliding to their deaths.

By the time she was ten she knew better, but she never quite lost the feeling that the mountains lived.

Gray clouds were building ahead, butting and surging against the mountains as some weather system tried to build enough momentum to make it up and over. The old ladies were dressing up, she thought; the clouds draped around the mountains' shoulders like a dirty boa, with the snowcaps jutting above and the broad green bases below.

As they droned closer to the mountains, Justice began taking them to a higher altitude. The pitch of the engine changed as the air grew thinner. Thin wisps of clouds wrapped around them, then blew away; the aircraft hit a few bumps in the air, jolting her.

Leaning forward, she tried to make out the altitude reading, but they hit another rough patch and she couldn't focus on the numbers.

"What's our altitude?" she asked loudly.

"Thirteen-five," he said without taking his hands from the controls or looking at her. "I'm taking us up to sixteen."

The air smoothed out as they climbed above the bumpy thermal layer. She looked down, doing the math in her head. They were two and a half miles high. The *Titanic* had sunk almost that deep in the ocean, about two and a quarter miles. That was a long way down, she thought, thinking of the glittering ocean liner with its lights extinguished, drifting down, broken and dark, all life gone. She shivered, suddenly cold, and reached for her jacket. She paused before putting it on, though, watching the first giant earth-wrinkle slide past beneath them.

The engine coughed.

The bottom dropped out of her stomach as if she were on a roller-coaster ride. Her heartbeat was suddenly thumping hard in her chest. Bailey leaned forward again. "What was that?" Her tone was a little tight, edged with alarm.

He didn't answer. His posture had changed, going from relaxed to completely alert in a millisecond. That alarmed her more than the slight break in the engine's monotonous drone. She gripped the edge of the seat, her nails digging into the leather.

"Is something wrong?"

"All the readings are normal," he replied briefly.

"Then what —"

"I don't know. I'm taking us down a little."

A little was right, she thought numbly, staring at the enormous, jagged mountains that abruptly seemed way too close beneath them, and coming closer. He couldn't take them down very far or they'd be skimming the mountaintops. But the engine seemed to have smoothed out; if that little hiccup had signaled anything serious, wouldn't it have continued?

The engine coughed again, hard enough that the airframe shuddered. Bailey sat frozen, watching the blur of the propeller blades, listening to the motor as she willed the sound to even out again. "Keep going, keep going," she urged under her breath. "Just keep going." She imagined the steady sound, pictured the propeller turning so fast she couldn't see it. In her mind the plane lifted up and over the mountains, if she just concentrated fiercely enough it would actually happen —

The engine sputtered a few times . . . and stopped.

The silence was sudden, and complete. In wordless shock she watched the blur of the propeller slow, become distinct blades, and then it . . . stopped.

5

"Shit!"

Captain Justice spat the word through clenched teeth; his hands moved swiftly as he tried to restart the engine, tried to keep the nose up. They were so close to the mountains that if the nose dropped, they would go straight in. The landscape below was a study of stark, inhospitable contrasts: snow-covered crags and boulders, the snow so white it was almost blue, the shadows so dark they were black. The slopes were steep and jagged, dropping away in sharp, almost vertical angles. There was nowhere to land, nowhere even remotely flat.

Bailey didn't move, didn't breathe. She couldn't. The awful paralysis of absolute terror and helplessness seized her body, her voice. There was nothing she could do to help, nothing she could do to change the outcome. She couldn't even scream a protest; all she could do was watch, and wait to die. They *were* going to die; she saw no way out of it. In a few minutes, maybe even a few seconds, they were going to crash on the rocky, snow-covered top of this mountain. For now, for a precious frozen moment, they seemed to float in place, as if the plane hadn't quite given in to the laws of gravity — or the mountains were playing cat-and-mouse games with them, letting her feel a faint, unreasonable hope before snatching it away.

"Mayday, Mayday, Mayday!"

Dimly she heard Justice on the radio, calling out the distress signal, their plane designation, and current location, then he cursed viciously and fell silent as he fought the inevitable. The plane dropped suddenly, a move that sent her stomach climbing into her throat, and she squeezed her eyes shut so she couldn't see the rocky peaks rushing at them. Then the left wing rose as the right one dipped and they rolled to the right, a nauseating maneuver that made her swallow convulsively. A few seconds later the right wing rose and for a brief — very brief — time they were level. Then the left wing dipped and they swung to the left.

Her eyes popped open. For a moment she couldn't focus on anything; her vision was narrowed, dim, and her chest hurt. Distantly she realized she was holding her breath, and with an effort she exhaled, then sucked in oxygen. Another breath, and her vision cleared a little, enough to let her see him. He was *all* she could see, as if his image were magnified and everything else remained lost in the fog. She could see his right jaw, see the clenched muscles working, the sheen of sweat, even the curl of his eyelashes and the faint shadow of newly shaved whiskers.

An agonized thought shot through her brain: he was the last person she would see! She caught another breath, pulling it deep. She would die with him, this man who didn't even like her; a person should at least die with someone around who cared. The same could be said of him, though, and she felt a deep sadness for both of them. He was . . . he was . . . The thought splintered, her attention caught. What the hell was he doing? Realization dawned, sharp and incredulous. He was *guiding* the plane, with the rudder and skill and ruthless determination, and also every prayer he knew, probably. The engine was dead, but he was still *flying* the damn plane, somehow keeping it under rudimentary control.

"Hold on," he said harshly. "I'm trying to

get down to the tree line, but we might not make it."

Bailey's brain felt like sludge, barely able to move, to function. Tree line? What did that matter? But she shook off the terror-induced brain fog enough to pull her seat belt tighter, press her head against the back of the leather seat, and hold on tight to the sides of the bottom cushion.

She squeezed her eyes shut to block out the sight of oncoming death, but she could feel the plane tilt first one way, then the other. *Thermals,* she thought, the single word swimming into focus. He was using the movement of the air currents to give them some lift, buy them precious seconds. The plane was too heavy to function like a glider, but the layers of air were slowing their descent somewhat; whether it would be enough to make a difference, she didn't know, but Captain Justice must have something in mind, mustn't he? Why else would he be fighting so hard to control the plane? If the end result was the same, then why bother?

With a sense of doom she waited for the overwhelming crush of impact, the last split-second of awareness. She hoped dying wouldn't hurt much. She hoped their bodies were found fast, so her family wouldn't suffer through a long search. She wished . . . she wished for a lot of things, none of which would happen now.

She felt as if an hour had passed since the engine stopped, though logically she knew mere minutes had gone by . . . no, not even minutes. Less than a minute, surely, though that minute seemed endless.

What was taking this damn plane so long to crash?

Him. Justice. He was the reason this was dragging out. He was still fighting the laws of gravity, refusing to give in. She felt an irrational urge to punch him, to say "Stop prolonging this!" How much terror was she supposed to take before her heart gave out under the strain? Not that it made any difference, under the circumstances —

WHAP!

The jolt jarred her teeth; it was followed instantaneously by a horrendous, deafening roar of screeching metal and thunderous cracks, more of those weird *whapping* sounds, and an impact so hard everything went black. The seat's shoulder strap jerked almost unbearably tight. On some level she was aware of tilting to the right, then dropping, falling; the seat belt held her in place though her arms and legs were flopping like those of a broken doll. Then the right side of her head cracked against something rigid, and she was swallowed by darkness.

Bailey coughed.

Her brain faintly registered the involuntary response. Something was wrong; she wasn't getting enough oxygen. She felt a vague sense of alarm and tried to move, tried to get up, but neither her legs nor arms worked. She concentrated, hard, her entire being focused on moving, but the effort was too much and she drifted back down into nothingness.

The next time she surfaced, she struggled and concentrated and was finally able to twitch the fingers of her left hand.

At first she was aware only of small things, immediate things: how hard it was to move, how her right arm felt as if something was cutting into it, the need to cough again. Saturating all of those small things was pain, insistent and unwavering. Her entire body hurt, as if she'd fallen —

Falling. Yes. She'd been falling. That was it. She remembered hitting —

No. The plane . . . the plane had crashed.

Realization filled her, a realization mixed with both wonder and trepidation. The plane had crashed, but she was alive. She was alive!

She didn't want to open her eyes, didn't

want to see the extent of her injuries. If she was missing any body parts she didn't want to know about it. If she was, she would die anyway, of shock and blood loss, on this isolated mountaintop both miles and hours from any possible rescue. She wanted to just lie there with her eyes closed and let whatever would happen, happen. Everything hurt so much she couldn't imagine moving and risking pain that was more intense.

But it was annoying, the way something was interfering with her breathing, and her right arm really hurt where something sharp was digging into it. She needed to move, she needed to get away from the wreckage. Fire. There was always the danger of a fire in a plane crash, wasn't there? She had to move.

Groaning, she opened her eyes. At first she couldn't focus; all she could see was a brownish blur. She kept blinking, and finally the blur became some sort of fabric. Silk. It was her silk jacket, covering most of her head. Laboriously she lifted her left arm and swiped at the jacket, managing to drag it away from her eyes. Pieces of glass made small tinkling sounds as the motion dislodged them.

Okay. Her left arm worked. That was good.

She tried to push herself upright, but something was wrong. Nothing was where it should be. She made a few more feeble, futile efforts to sit up, then made a low sound of frustration. Instead of struggling like a worm on a hook, she needed to take stock of the situation, see exactly what she was dealing with.

Concentrating was difficult, but she had to focus. Taking deep breaths, she looked around, trying to make sense of what she saw. Mist, trees, occasional glimpses of blue sky. She saw her own feet, the left one sans shoe. Where was her other shoe? Then, like a bolt of lightning, another thought shot through her brain. Captain Justice! Where was he? She lifted her head as much as possible, and immediately saw him. He was slumped in his seat, his head dropped forward. She couldn't make out his features; they were covered by what looked like a sea of blood.

Urgently she tried to surge upright, only to fall back once more. Her position confused her. She was lying on the floor of the cabin — no, that wasn't right. Fiercely she concentrated, forcing her brain to make the adjustment from what it expected to the reality of her position, and abruptly things made sense. She was still buckled in her seat, and she was lying against the right side of the plane, which was resting at a fairly sharp angle. She couldn't sit up because she needed to haul herself up and to the left, and she couldn't do that unless she could use both arms, but her right arm was trapped and she couldn't free it unless she first got her weight off it.

If Justice wasn't already dead, he soon would be if she didn't get in a position to help him. *Get out of the seat.* That's what she needed to do. With her left hand she fumbled for the seat belt, popped the clasp open. When the belt released, her lower body rolled off the seat and dropped with a painful thud that made her groan again, but she was still tangled in the shoulder strap. She struggled free of it, and managed to get to her knees.

No wonder her right arm had felt as if something was cutting into it: something *was*. A triangular shard of metal protruded from her triceps. Feeling irrationally insulted by the injury, she jerked the shard out and threw it away, then scrambled forward until she could reach Justice. The angle at which the plane was resting made balance difficult even if she hadn't been woozy and dealing with her own aches and injuries, but she braced her right foot against the side of the plane and hauled herself up so she could reach the scant space between the two pilots' seats.

Oh, God, there was so much blood. Was he dead? He'd fought so hard to bring the plane down at a survivable angle, she couldn't bear it if he'd saved her life and died in the attempt. Her hand shaking, she reached out and touched his neck, but her body was too outraged by the abuse it had taken to stop trembling and she couldn't tell if he had a pulse or not. "You can't be dead," she whispered desperately, holding her hand under his nose to see if she could feel his breath. She thought she did, and stared hard at his chest. Finally she saw the up-and-down movement, and the relief that swamped her was so acute she almost burst into tears.

He was still alive, but unconscious, and injured. What should she do? Should she move him? What if he had spinal injuries? But what if she did nothing, and he bled to death?

She leaned her aching head against the side of his seat, just for a moment. Think, Bailey! she commanded herself. She had to do something. She had to deal with what she knew was wrong with him, not what might be wrong, and she knew for a fact he was losing a lot of blood. So, first things first: stop the bleeding.

She looked up, searching for something to

hold on to while she clambered forward into the cockpit, but nothing, literally, was there. The left wing and most of the fuselage on that side were just gone, ripped away as if a giant can opener had opened up the aircraft. There was nothing to grasp except the razor-sharp edges of mangled metal. Part of a broken tree limb stuck through the gaping hole.

There was nothing else to use, so she gripped the top edge of Justice's seat and pulled herself up, slithering between what was left of the roof and the top of the copilot's seat. The best position she could get in was a crouch, with her feet braced against the right door. "Justice," she said, because she'd read somewhere that unconscious people sometimes could still hear and respond a little to their names. Whether or not that was true, she didn't know, but what could it hurt?

"Justice!" she said again, more insistently, as she grasped his shoulders and tried to pull him upright. It was like pulling on a log. His head lolled to the side, blood dripping from his nose and chin.

Pulling on him wasn't going to work. His seat belt was holding him in place, but she was working against gravity. She needed to release the belt and get him out of the seat, try to get him out of the plane.

Like she had, he would fall out of the seat as soon as the belt was released, but it was a small plane; the distance was a couple of feet, at best. Still, the fuselage had been crushed inward on the copilot's side, and a tree branch had punctured all the way through the metal skin like a wooden stake through a vampire's heart. The sharp end of the tree branch was angled toward the back, rather than pointing upward, but she didn't want to take the chance he might be impaled, so she looked around for something to put over the branch.

The first thing she thought of was her tote bag, but she didn't see it. It had been lying on the left side of the bench seat, so it may have gone flying when that side of the plane was torn open. All that was available was her bedraggled, bloodstained silk jacket. Twisting around, grunting with the effort, she managed to grasp one sleeve and drag it to her. The garment was thin, almost weightless. Silk was strong, but what she needed in this situation was bulk to cover the sharp end of a tree branch, not tensile strength.

Inspiration struck. Swiftly she bent forward and removed her remaining shoe, a very expensive designer loafer, and jammed it over the jagged point of wood. Then she folded her jacket and placed it over the tree branch, as a bit of extra padding.

"Okay, Justice, let's get you out of this seat," she said gently. "Then I'll see about getting you out of the plane, but first things first. When I undo your seat belt you're going to fall a little ways, just a foot or so. Ready?" He'd probably fall on *her,* given the severely limited space, and then she'd be pinned with no wiggle-room for escape. She was in a really bad position. Sighing, she crawled over the top of the seat into the back again.

A low moan sounded deep in his throat.

She jumped, so startled by the sound she almost screamed. "Oh, thank God," she whispered to herself as she scrambled into an upright position. In a slightly louder than normal voice she called his name again. "Justice! Wake up if you can. I can't get you out of the plane by myself; you need to help me if you can. I'm undoing the seat belt now, okay?" As she talked she reached up and around, searching for the release, sliding her fingers along the woven fabric of the belt until she found the metal. A quick flip of the catch, and he dropped out of the shoulder restraint like a rock, onto his right side with his head and shoulders resting on the floor, his long legs still draped over the console and tangled with the controls.

"Damn it!" she groaned. This position wasn't any better; his back was to her, and she still couldn't see much of his bloody face. Nor was there room for her to wedge herself in front of him to see where all the blood was coming from.

Bailey took a few more deep breaths, wondering how she was going to manage this. The air she sucked in was cold, and sharp with the scent of evergreens. The effect was almost like a slap in the face. Once again she took stock of their situation. She couldn't drag him up — he was far too heavy, and the slope of the plane was too severe. On the other hand, if she could get the copilot's door open, then she could pull him out through it. Examining the protruding tree branch, she saw that it had actually entered the cabin in front of the door's hinge, so the branch wasn't an impediment. But the way the plane was tilted, the door might be blocked. She peered at the tinted windows on the right side, which were so badly scratched she could barely see through them, much less tell if anything was blocking the door.

The copilot's window was hinged. If she could push it open — Action followed hard on the heels of the thought, but the frame was buckled just enough that the window hinge didn't work, and she couldn't get herself braced to apply any leverage to it. In frustration she lifted her fist and used the side of it to pound the window, which accomplished nothing except making her hand hurt.

"Damn it, damn it, *damn it!*" She blew out a frustrated breath. If she couldn't open the window, she likely wouldn't be able to open the door. "On the other hand," she said out loud to herself, "why am I wasting time with the window when I need the *door* open?" If she could open the door, she wouldn't need to open the window.

She felt as if she were missing several obvious points, that her brain was working at only half speed, but she was doing the best she could under the circumstances. Her entire body felt as if she'd been severely beaten, her head ached, and her arm was bleeding. She would think of things when she thought of them, and anyone who didn't like it could take a hike.

Take a hike. Very funny. Ha ha. And there was no one here to like or not like her decisions — other than Justice, and he was in no condition to comment — so her little pity party was wasted.

Legs. Legs were much stronger than arms, and she was stronger than most women thanks to all those hours of working out. She could lift four hundred pounds with these legs. She wasn't a weakling, and she shouldn't think like one. If the door was stuck, maybe she could push it open with her legs.

Justice's tall body was in the way, but she thought she could get some leverage. Before she went to all that trouble, though, she leaned around and tugged on the handle to see if the latch would release. She felt resistance, like metal scraping on metal, but she'd expected that and tugged harder. Finally the latch gave, but the door didn't open. Again, not surprising.

She had to find some way to hold the handle in the release position, or she'd never be able to kick the door open. There was nothing to tie it to, assuming she had anything to tie it *with,* which she didn't. She'd have to jam something under it, and at the moment she was woefully short of jamming material, too.

Maybe there was something under one of the seats. People stuck things under seats all the time. Stretching, she patted around under each seat. Nothing.

Maybe a sock would do. Peeling off one of her thin trouser socks, she twisted it into a rope and looped it around the handle, twisting again to hold it secure. Squirming around, she folded herself into the copilot's seat in as tight a tuck as she could manage and braced both feet against the door. The position was incredibly awkward, but using the sock to hold the handle gave her a precious few inches. Straining her shoulder and arm, she pulled up on the sock, once again feeling the protesting metal as it gave. With her other hand she gripped the forward edge of the seat so she wouldn't simply shove herself backward, accomplishing nothing. "Please," she whispered, and slowly began pushing. Her thigh muscles tightened; the smaller muscles around her knees turned rock hard as she exerted pressure on them. Her fingers, digging into the edge of the seat, began to protest, and then to slip. Furiously she hung on, and with a final effort did everything she could to straighten her legs.

The door creaked open, her hand slipped off the seat, and she fell backward from the momentum. Quickly she scrambled up, her heart pounding with elation. Yes! Untwisting her sock from the handle, she pulled it back on, then braced her feet against the door and pushed some more, gaining an opening about a foot wide. She could get through that, she thought in triumph, leaning forward to see if there was anything in the way, like a tree or a boulder. She didn't see any obstructions, so she maneuvered until she was lying on her stomach, then slithered past Justice and, turning on her side, worked her way out the door. Metal scraped her back, her hips, but she made it through and onto the snow-covered ground.

The freezing cold bit through her thin socks. She needed to put on shoes and dry socks, almost immediately, to stave off the danger of frostbite. Her feet would have to wait, though, until she'd seen to Justice.

Examining the opening, she considered Justice's size. He wouldn't fit; his chest was probably too deep. She'd have to open the door wider. Taking hold of the edge, she tugged until she'd gained another few inches from the crumpled, protesting metal. That would have to do, she thought, her breathing faster than she liked. At this altitude, she had to be careful and not overexert herself, or she would be asking for a killer case of altitude sickness. She was already sweating a little, and that was dangerous in the cold. She was wearing only a pair of thin, fluid trousers and a silk tank, plus her underwear and the socks, none of which was doing much to keep her warm. She had plenty of clothing in her suitcases, but getting them out would be an effort, and she had to get Justice out first.

Justice groaned again. Remembering how slowly she'd regained her senses, how difficult even the smallest response had been, she began talking to him as she crouched in the open door and reached in, seizing him under the arms. "Justice, try to wake up. I'm going to pull you out of the plane now. I don't know if you have any broken bones or anything, so you'll have to let me know if I'm hurting you, okay?"

No response.

Bailey tightened her leg muscles and pushed backward. From her crouched position she couldn't gain much leverage, but she was pulling him downhill, so gravity helped. When his head and shoulders were through the opening she shifted position until she was more fully under him; he was deadweight, completely limp and unable to help himself, so she'd have to protect his head. She paused a minute to catch her breath, then pulled her knees up, dug her heels into the ground, and pushed herself backward once more, dragging him with her. His weight slid forward and he flopped out of the plane, landing on top of her and pinning her to the icy earth.

Oh, God. She could see his face now, see the horrific cut that began about three inches back in his scalp, angled all the way across his forehead, and ended just above his right eyebrow. She didn't know much about first aid, but she did know a bad cut on the scalp could result in severe blood loss. The proof of it obscured his features, saturated his shirt and pants.

He weighed a ton. Panting, she wiggled from beneath him and wrestled him onto his back. Her energy was fading fast, and she sat for a moment, her head down as she tried once more to catch her breath. Her feet were in agony, they were so cold, and now her clothes were caked with snow and rapidly becoming wet. The crash itself hadn't killed her, but the altitude and hypothermia might well do the job pretty soon.

Justice began breathing more heavily, his throat working. Bailey said, "Justice?"

He swallowed, and thickly mumbled, "What th' fuck?"

She gave a quick, breathless, laugh. Their situation wasn't any less dire, but at least he was regaining consciousness. "The plane crashed. We're both alive, but you have a bad cut on your head and I need to stop the bleeding." Slowly she got to her knees and reached into the cockpit, fumbling for her one shoe and her jacket. She was freezing, but even though the jacket was thin it was better than nothing. She started to put it on, then stopped, and drew her arm out. Instead she turned one sleeve so she could attack the seam, and began tugging at it. She needed something she could use as a pad to place over the cut and apply pressure, and this was all she had.

He coughed, and said something else. She paused. She hadn't understood everything he'd said, but part of it had sounded like "first-aid kit."

She leaned over him. "What? I didn't understand. Is there a first-aid kit?"

He swallowed again. He hadn't yet opened his eyes, but he was winning the war against unconsciousness. "Glove box," he mumbled.

Thank God! A first-aid kit would be a lifesaver — if she could open the glove box — she thought. She crouched down and wriggled her way back inside the open door. The glove box was in front of the copilot's seat. Slipping her fingers under the latch, she tugged on it, but the glove box wasn't as cooperative as the door latch had been. She banged it with her cold fist, and tugged some more. Nothing.

She needed something sturdy, with a sharp edge, to pry the box open. She looked around for what felt like the thirtieth time. There should be something in the wreckage she could use, like . . . like that crowbar held to the lower front edge of the copilot's seat by a pair of brackets. She stared at it in disbelief. Was she already hallucinating? She blinked, but the crowbar was still there. She touched it, and felt the cold, rough metal. The bar was a short one, just about a foot long, but it was real, and it was just what she needed.

Removing the crowbar from the brackets, she jammed the sharp end in at the middle, where the lock mechanism was, and pushed up. The lid buckled a little, then sprang open.

She grabbed the olive-drab box with the red cross on it, and once more worked her way out. Going down on her knees beside him in the snow, she fumbled with the latches on the box. Why did everything have to have a damn latch? Why couldn't things just *open*?

His eyes opened, just a slit, and he managed to lift his hand toward his head. Bailey grabbed his wrist. "No, don't touch it. You're bleeding a lot, so I have to put pressure on it."

"Suture," he rasped, closing his eyes against the blood that seeped into them.

"What?"

He took a few breaths; talking was still difficult. "In the box. Sutures."

She stared at him, aghast. She could put pressure on the wound. She could clean the cut, she could fashion butterfly bandages from tape to hold the edges of the cut together. She could put salve on it. But he wanted her to *sew him up?*

"Oh, shit!" she blurted.

6

Arguing with a semiconscious man made no sense, but Bailey couldn't seem to stop herself. "I don't have any medical training, unless you count watching *ER*. No one in his right mind would want me sewing on him, but, hey, you aren't in your right mind, are you? You have a head injury. On the theory that it isn't smart to let someone with possible brain damage make the decisions, I'm going to ignore that suggestion. Besides, I don't sew."

"Learn," he muttered. "Make yourself useful."

She ground her teeth together. Useful? What did he think she'd been doing while he lolled about unconscious? Did he think he'd made it out of the plane under his own steam? She was wet and freezing because she'd been lying in the snow, pulling him out of the plane. Her hands were turning blue, and she was shaking so hard it would serve him right if she *did* try to sew him up.

The cold made her think: the jacket. She'd forgotten about the jacket, which was even more evidence that shock, or cold, or both, had slowed down her mental processes. She pulled it on, grateful for even that thin protection from the cold, but she was so wet she wasn't certain anything could get her warm unless she first got dry.

Silently she tore open a pack of sterile pads and placed two of them over the cut on Justice's head, using her hands to hold them in place and apply pressure. A rough sound of pain rattled in his throat, then he bit it off and lay perfectly still.

She should probably talk to him, she thought, help keep him conscious and focused. "I don't know what to do first," she confessed. A fit of convulsive shaking seized her and she stopped talking, her teeth chattering so hard she couldn't have said a word anyway. When the shaking passed, she concentrated fiercely on holding the sterile pads in place. "I have to stop this bleeding. But we're in the snow" — another episode of shaking interrupted her — "and I'm so cold and wet I can barely move. You'll go into shock —"

He took a few breaths, as if gearing himself up for the ordeal of speaking. "Kit," he finally managed. "Blanket . . . in bottom of kit."

The only kit at hand was the first-aid kit. Leaving the pads in place on his head, she began taking things out of the kit and setting them in the open lid. Under everything, neatly folded in a sealed pouch, was one of those thin silver space blankets. Opening the pouch, she shook the blanket open. How much good it would do she didn't know, having never used one before, but she wasn't about to question anything she could use as a barrier between them and the cold. She was tempted to wrap it around herself and curl into the tightest ball possible until she felt a little less miserably cold, but he'd lost a lot of blood and needed it more than she did.

Which should she do, put the blanket under him for protection from the snow, or over him to help hold in what body heat he had? Could he warm up at all, lying in the snow? Damn it, she couldn't think! She'd have to go on instinct. "I'm spreading the blanket beside you," she said, suiting action to words. "Now I'm going to help you shift onto it, so you won't be in the snow. You'll have to help me. Can you do that?"

"Yeah," he said with effort.

"Okay, here we go." Kneeling on the blanket, she slid her right arm under his neck, seized the front of his belt with her left hand, and lifted. He helped as much as he could, using his feet and his right arm; the biggest help was that he wasn't deadweight any longer. Straining every muscle, she shifted him so that most of his torso, at least, was lying on the blanket, and decided that was good enough. Quickly she folded the rest of the blanket over him, tucking it in where she could.

Suddenly dizzy and nauseated, she sank to the ground beside him. *Altitude sickness,* she thought. She was almost at the end of her rope. If she pushed herself much harder, she'd find herself lying in the snow, unable to get up, and she'd die before the next morning — probably even before sunset today.

Still, she had to get to their suitcases, put on dry clothing, and lots of it — now. She had to function, or both of them would die.

She schooled herself to take slow, deep breaths to feed her oxygen-hungry body. Slow — that was the key. She should move slowly, when she could, and not let panic lure her into rushing around until she collapsed. That meant she had to plan every move, think through what she was going to do so no effort was wasted.

The luggage was loaded into the plane

through the baggage compartment door, and secured by a cargo net that kept the bags from flying around the cockpit during rough weather, though she thought her suitcases would probably be too thick to fit in the space between the roof and the high seat backs. The problem was, though most of the roof was now gone and the suitcases would fit through the gaping hole, they would have to be lifted almost straight up, and they were very heavy, and she was so weak and cold and exhausted she didn't think she could manage the task. She'd have to open them while they were still in the baggage compartment, and get out what she needed.

She'd have to unclip the cargo net. She was sure she could reach the clips, but she wasn't sure she could manage if the clip was a particularly strong one. If that was the case, then she would need some other way of getting through the net.

"We have to get warm. I need to get more clothes out of my suitcase," she told him. "If for any reason I can't get the cargo net unclipped, do you have a knife I can use to cut it?"

His eyes opened a little, then closed again. "Left pocket."

Getting to her knees, she untucked the blanket she'd just tucked around him and slipped her right hand into his pocket. The warmth was startling, and so delicious she almost moaned, but her fingers were so cold they were numb and she couldn't tell if she was touching the knife or not. She grasped at whatever was there.

"Careful," he murmured. "Good Time Charlie's down there, and he's attached."

Bailey snorted. "Then keep him out of the way, or he might get unattached." Men. Here they were on the verge of dying from hypothermia and, in his case, blood loss, but he was still protective of his penis. "*Good Time Charlie,* my ass," she muttered, pulling her hand out of his pocket to see if she'd snagged the knife.

A tiny smile curved his mouth for a moment, then faded.

She paused, her gaze on his bloody face. That was the first hint of humor she'd ever seen him display, and it struck at her heart because, despite everything she could do, they might not make it out of this situation alive. He hadn't given up, he'd gotten them down alive, and she couldn't bear the thought that he might still die because she made the wrong decision or didn't do enough. She owed him her life, and she would do everything she could to safeguard his — even sew him up if she had to, damn it.

85

The pocketknife and a dollar or so in change lay in her palm. Picking up the knife, she slid the change back into his pocket, then put the blanket in place again. "I'll be back in a few minutes," she said, giving him a comforting touch on the chest.

The plane loomed in front of her, a crippled bird with the right wing crumpled and the left one completely gone. They were downslope of it, which wasn't the safest place if the wreckage began sliding, she realized. She didn't think it would, with the crumpled wing digging into the mountainside the way it was, plus the tree branch impaling the fuselage was another anchoring point, but she'd rather err on the side of safety and move out of its path, after she'd changed clothes and gotten warmer, and felt more capable of making the effort.

She didn't have any pockets, so she held the knife in her teeth as she climbed back into the cockpit, then clambered to the back. Kneeling on the bench seat, she stretched over the luggage compartment, reaching for the cargo net clips at the rear of the cabin. To her relief, the net easily released. Pushing it to the side, she tugged one of her suitcases around and unzipped it; the suitcases were identical, so she didn't know what was in which case, but she didn't really care. She wanted to be dry, she wanted to be warm, and the clothes she put on didn't matter.

Justice's bag was there, too, but it was the typical pilot's overnight bag, just big enough for a shaving kit and change of clothes. She dragged the bag up and over the seat, because there was no sense leaving it in the plane even though he likely wouldn't need anything in there just yet. For now, she had plenty of clothes with which she could cover him; it wasn't as if he needed to actually *wear* them, since he couldn't even stand up. He would need clothes, yes, but she thought she'd save the clothes that actually fit him until later.

She began pulling clothes out of the suitcase she'd opened. When she came to a flannel shirt, she stopped right there and peeled off the silk jacket and tank. Her bra was damp, too, so it came off. Shuddering from the cold, she put on the flannel shirt and buttoned it up before resuming systematically emptying the bag. As she came to warm items she could use right then, she stopped and put them on. Socks. Sweatpants. Another pair of socks. A thick down vest, with handwarmer pockets; she put Justice's knife in one of the pockets. She needed something to cover her head, too, but the only thing she'd packed that had a hood was a cotton knit hoodie. Not wanting to wait until she came across it, she used the next long-sleeved shirt she came across, folding it and tying the sleeves under her chin as if it were a bandanna.

Already she felt better, if simply not feeling quite as miserable qualified as "better."

She found the plastic trash bags she'd packed to use as dirty-clothes bags, and began stuffing clothes into them. After she emptied one suitcase, she pushed it to the side and hauled another one around so she could get to the zipper. In that bag she found the pair of insulated hiking boots she'd packed, and gratefully she stopped to pull them on. Getting her feet warm *before* she put on the boots would have been nice, but she didn't have that luxury.

She had enough clothes to cover him, now, so she stopped and left the second suitcase partially unpacked, and the other one un-opened. Tossing his overnighter through the open door, she followed it with two trash bags full of clothes, then she followed the bags. As she crawled out, her gaze fell on the vinyl floor cover in front of both the pilot's and copilot's seats. Taking Justice's knife from the vest pocket, she opened it and went to work.

He was lying deathly still, his eyes still

closed. The pads covering his forehead were soaked through with blood.

"I'm back," she said, putting the piece of vinyl down beside him and kneeling on it; getting dry had been important, but staying dry ranked right up there with it. "I brought clothes to cover you with, as soon as I can get the bleeding stopped and get you out of these bloody clothes."

"Okay," he murmured.

Thank God, he hadn't lost consciousness again, but his voice was weaker. Taking two more sterile pads from the first-aid kit's supply, she placed them over the bloody ones, and pressed down. This time she stayed in position, talking to him the whole time, telling him everything she'd done and why she'd done it. If he disagreed with anything he could speak up, but he remained silent.

She hadn't thought to time how long she'd been maintaining pressure, but the third time she lifted the edge of the pads to check, the bleeding had slowed dramatically. She pressed down once more, held the pressure for about five minutes, then checked again. No new trickle of blood welled from the ugly gash.

"I think that's done the trick," she breathed. "Finally."

The next step was to wash any dirt and debris from the cut, but for that she needed water. She'd put a bottle of water in her tote bag, wherever it was. It had to be around here somewhere. It had probably gone out of the plane when the left wing snapped off, so if she located the missing wing, the tote bag should be between the wing and the rest of the plane.

"I'm going to look for some water," she told him.

"I'm not going anywhere."

No, he wasn't; she doubted he'd be able to stand on his own.

Standing, she began examining the area immediately around the plane. When she didn't spot the tote bag, she followed upward, with her gaze, the path the plane had taken, marked with broken and splintered trees and limbs.

Her eyes widened. The mountains loomed around her, silent and shrouded with snow. The only sound was the occasional sighing of the wind in the trees. No leaves rustled, no birds sang.

The mountains were immense, looming high above her on all sides, so tall they would soon block the afternoon sun. Slowly, disbelieving, she turned in a circle. There was nothing but mountains, and more mountains, as far as she could see. They spread out below, massive bases that were veiled by gray clouds. Deep, incredibly rugged folds in the earth created black shadows where sunshine seldom touched. The plane was nothing more than a dot on the steep mountainside, already half-covered by the limbs of the trees into which they had crashed, and those black shadows were spreading toward it.

She felt dwarfed, insignificant to the point of nothingness. She and Justice *were* nothing, she realized. They were completely, totally insignificant to these mountains. Any rescue could conceivably take days to reach them. They were alone.

7

Bailey looked for the tote for as long as she could without exhausting herself, but an extensive search would have involved climbing up the steep, sometimes vertical mountainside, and she simply wasn't capable of that. Finally giving up, she slowly made her way back to Justice. He looked dreadful, she thought, and it wasn't just the blood; he was lying so still, as if life were seeping out of him even though she'd gotten the bleeding stopped. What blood loss hadn't accomplished on its own, cold and shock were finishing. The bottom dropped out of her stomach at the thought. "Justice, are you awake?"

He made an "um" sound in his throat.

"I can't find the bottle of water I brought. There's snow, but I don't have any way to make a fire to boil it. If I sew up this cut without washing it out first, there's a big risk it'll get infected. I'll clean it out as best I can with the alcohol wipes, in a little while, but first I'm going to do what I can to get you warm." She cast a worried glance over her shoulder at the plane. She still didn't think it would shift, but she couldn't discount the possibility. Moving him, though, was something else that would have to wait.

"Good," he said, the word only a thin thread of sound.

Working quickly, she lifted his feet and stuffed one of the trash bags of clothes under them, to help with the shock. Opening the other bag, she took out another flannel shirt and folded it, then gently tucked it around his head to help keep him from losing even more body heat. Then she pulled the space blanket aside and started layering clothes over him, starting at his feet and working up. When she got to his shirt, cold and wet with blood, she opened his knife and simply sliced the shirt off him, then wiped the blood off his chest as best she could with the first garment that came to hand, which happened to be a pair of her underwear.

When he was as dry as she could get him, she layered more clothes over his chest and shoulders. Finally she lay down beside him, snuggled under the layers of clothes until she was against him and could get her arms around him, and as a last covering pulled another shirt completely over their heads so the air they breathed would be warmer. The shirt didn't block out all the light, but the effect was sort of like being in a cave. Their breathing almost immediately made the air feel warmer against her face, and the small comfort was so welcome she could have cried in relief.

He felt like ice against her. He needed something hot to drink, or something sweet to eat, to help him combat the shock and cold. She still wasn't thinking as clearly as she needed to be, because while she couldn't provide anything to drink she had put a stash of candy bars and some chewing gum in one of the suitcases — evidently the one suitcase she hadn't opened. She should have thought of them, and taken a few minutes to find them.

Her own shivering was lessening, but he wasn't shivering at all. That couldn't be good.

"Hey, Justice," she said. "Stay awake. Talk to me. Tell me if you can feel any warmth coming from me."

For a long moment he didn't answer, making her fear he'd lost consciousness again, but finally he said, "No."

Maybe she had on too many clothes for her body warmth to seep through to him. Wiggling around under the pile of clothing, she removed the down vest, and worked it over him so that it was the first layer next to his body. She was colder without the vest, but she snuggled close enough that she was partially covered by it, too. The down had absorbed some of her body heat, because she could feel it against her icy hands.

"Feel that," he murmured in a drowsy tone.

"Good. You have to stay awake, so keep talking to me. If you can't think of anything interesting to say, just make a noise every now and then so I know you're still conscious."

She began running her left hand over his chest and shoulders and arms, to stimulate his circulation. "There are some candy bars in one of my bags. When you get warmer, I'll dig them out and get some sugar down you; that'll make you feel better." She paused. "Now you say something."

"Something."

"Smart-ass." Despite the fact that the word was slurred and his voice incredibly weak, her heart lifted. If he could still be a smart-ass, then maybe he wasn't as far gone as she feared.

Cam listened to Mrs. Wingate talking. He felt as if his consciousness was split in two and part of him drifted away into fog, tethered only by her occasional demands that he respond. On a far closer level he was also aware of his complete physical misery; he was so cold that he had a whole new appreciation of the word. Why couldn't the two parts trade places, and the physical awareness float out there in the ether? The one thing he didn't want to happen, right now, was for the two to merge, but at the same time he knew he couldn't let himself drift any further away.

Hearing her voice gave him something to focus on, helped keep him from floating away into darkness. He knew he was hurt and he even knew why, though he was fuzzy on how. He'd crash-landed the plane, evidently successfully since they were both alive. He remembered the engine inexplicably quitting, and he remembered trying to get the plane to the tree line so the vegetation would help cushion the impact. That was it; nothing about the actual crash at all. His next memory was of his head feeling as if someone had used a baseball bat on it — hell, his entire body felt like that — and nothing making sense except Mrs. Wingate calling his name.

He had to concentrate hard to hold on to the thread of what she was saying, and sometimes his thoughts drifted and he'd lose touch, only to be brought back by a sharp question or a jab of pain. Sometimes every word was crystal clear; sometimes they were just sounds that he knew were supposed to mean something but didn't. There was no clear line of demarcation between what was real and what wasn't, and he floated in that no-man's-land.

Now she was touching him. That, at least, was real, because he could feel her. He was vaguely surprised; she didn't want to speak to him, but she'd touch him? Strange. She'd covered him with something, he didn't know what, but it felt nice and heavy. Then she'd lain down beside him, put her arms around him, and begun briskly rubbing his chest and arms. A faint warmth began to seep into him.

The warmth, as faint as it was, felt great. What also felt great was her breast against his arm, which he guessed proved that, even if he was half dead, a man was still a man and a breast, any breast, was always worthy of attention. Lulled by the comfort of both breast and warmth, he began drifting to sleep.

His relaxation shattered when his entire body suddenly tensed and shook. He'd been cold before, teeth-chattering, body-shaking cold, but had experienced nothing like this. Shudders racked his entire body, clenched every muscle, rattled every bone. He shook so hard he thought he might break his teeth, and clenched them together. Mrs. Wingate tightened her hold on him, murmuring something he couldn't understand. After a few minutes the convulsive shaking stopped and, exhausted, he felt his muscles go limp.

He'd barely relaxed when another spasm seized him.

He didn't know how long the excruciating spasms lasted, just that they were agony, and he was helpless to control them. She stayed right there the whole time, holding him, stroking him, talking to him. He fastened onto the sound of her voice as if it were a lifeline, even though most of the time he couldn't understand what she was saying, because as long as he could hear her that meant he wasn't dead. His own body was trying to kill him, but to hell with that. Fuck dying. He didn't intend to give up, though he was so exhausted giving up would be easier than battling through this.

He just wanted to rest for a while. Sleep. But even during the brief periods when the shaking stopped and he could relax, he couldn't sleep because she kept talking. At some point his brain reconnected and the words made sense again. "— good," she was saying. "You're shivering, and that's good."

Shivering? She called these brutal, muscle-locked spasms *shivering?*

In a moment of clarity he managed to say "Bullshit."

He heard a low sound that was almost like a laugh. Mrs. Wingate, laughing? Maybe he was hallucinating.

"No, it is good," she insisted. "It's your body generating heat. I know *I* feel warmer, now. Even my feet aren't as frozen."

He did a laborious mental inventory of his body. Maybe she was right. He couldn't say he was toasty, but he was definitely warmer. He tried to open his eyes, but they'd been glued shut. Slowly, every movement needing every ounce of concentration and strength he had, he lifted his right hand toward his face.

"What are you doing?"

"Eyes . . . trying to open my eyes." Fumbling clumsily at his eyelids, he could feel a thick crust under his fingertips. "What's . . . this crap?"

"Dried blood. I guess your eyelids are stuck together," she said matter-of-factly. "You're a mess. When you're a little warmer and I've gotten some chocolate down you, I'll clean your face and get your eyelids unstuck. Then I'll see if I can manage some stitches, though I warn you the results won't be pretty."

Stitches? Yeah, he remembered now. His head was cut. The first-aid kit had sutures in it, and he'd told her to sew him up.

He didn't want to wait for her to clean his face; he wanted to see *now.* He wanted to get up and assess the situation for himself. He needed to see how much damage the plane had sustained. Maybe he could still make radio contact.

Another spasm grabbed him and shook him. The interval this time had been longer, but the spasm itself was just as intense. She held him tightly, as if she could ease the shaking by controlling it. The tactic didn't work, but he appreciated the effort.

When the spasm left and he could relax again, he was so tired he gave up on any idea of getting up and assessing anything. He wanted to just lie there. Besides, he thought vaguely, if he got up, he wouldn't be able to feel her breasts against him and he was really liking that. Okay, so he was a dog. He liked breasts. Throw him a bone and call him Fido.

It occurred to him, in his floating, fuzzy way of thinking, that he could feel her breasts even better if they were lying facing each other.

100

"What are you *doing*?" She sounded a little alarmed, or maybe that was annoyed. "If you throw these clothes off after all the trouble I went to to get you covered, I'll leave your butt in the snow to freeze."

Annoyed. Definitely.

"Get closer," he muttered. He was trying to get his left arm up so he could roll onto his left side, facing her, but she was lying against his arm and he couldn't manage the necessity of first pulling away from her, then lifting his arm, then rolling onto his side.

"All right, but be still. Let me do it."

She moved around some, heaving and wiggling, then she lifted his left arm and slid under it, pressing against his side. He almost sighed with pleasure, because now he could feel both of those soft/firm mounds. She draped an arm across his stomach and cuddled closer.

"Better?"

She had no idea how much. He made a sound in his throat. Let her interpret it any way she wanted.

"I guess this is warmer. In a few minutes I'll get up and get to work. If I stay here any longer, I might go to sleep, and that won't be good. I have a lot to do, but I have to take my time doing it or the altitude gets to me."

He wanted to ask what she had to do, but

he was so sleepy and tired, and he was feeling much warmer — almost comfortable, in fact, that staying awake was fast becoming almost impossible. He made another sound, and that seemed to satisfy her noise requirements. She kept talking, and he tuned her out and went to sleep.

8

Carefully Bailey crawled out from under the enormous pile of clothing. Justice was asleep, and though she thought she was supposed to keep him awake, because of the head injury, she also thought sleep might be the best thing for him. He had to be exhausted from all that shaking and shuddering.

She felt better, herself. Her feet were still cold, but overall she was much warmer — though she did miss the down vest that was now covering Justice. To make up for its loss, she fished a third shirt from the pile and put it on.

Lying down for a while had helped her headache and nausea, too. If she were careful and didn't forget to move slowly, maybe the altitude wouldn't bother her so much.

Even though she knew what she would see, she took a moment to look around again, at the massive mountains with the white peaks soaring high above her. But for Justice, they would have crashed on those bare expanses of jagged rock, with little or no chance of survival. Once again she felt the immensity of the wilderness surrounding them and an overwhelming sense of being alone.

She listened for the distinctive *whap-whap* sound of a helicopter or the distant drone of a plane, looked for smoke that might indicate a campsite, but . . . there was nothing. Shouldn't someone be searching for them by now? Justice had sent out that Mayday call, surely someone had heard it and contacted the FAA, or whatever agency needed to be contacted. She didn't care if the ASPCA was contacted, so long as *someone* was searching for them.

The utter silence was unnerving. She didn't expect car horns or flares arching overhead, but some indication there were other human beings on the planet would be welcome.

The lack of sound and movement, of activity that would have given her hope, only reinforced her profound sense of isolation. How would they survive the night up here, with no water, no way of making a fire?

By continuing to do what she was doing, that was how. She had a ton of clothes they could use as cover, they had at least a little food to eat, and there was moisture in the snow. She also had Justice's knife —

Oh, crap. Where was the knife?

Still in her pocket, she thought, relieved. With it, she could manage to rig together some sort of shelter for them, enough, at least, to keep them out of the wind. The first item on her to-do list, though, was to feed Justice.

Climbing back into the plane, she finished removing all of her clothing from the suitcases, setting aside the candy bars when she finally found them, as well as the packs of wet wipes she'd packed. When her suitcases were finally empty and the trash bags containing her clothes were on the ground, by flipping the lids back she had enough clearance to drag the opened cases over the tops of the seats. The bags could be put to some use; she'd figure out later exactly what that use would be.

Going back to Justice, she knelt beside him and thoroughly examined the contents of the first-aid kit. Besides the space blanket there were scissors, which would come in handy; lots of gauze pads and adhesive bandages; a roll of tape; cotton balls and cotton tips; a tube of antibacterial salve; both alcohol and iodine wipes; antiseptic towelettes; plastic gloves; OTC painkillers; and — oh, joy —

sutures. There was a bunch of other stuff, like finger splints and a twelve-hour light-stick, but her immediate concern was that the kit contained the basics to treat the cut on Justice's head. It did, which meant she had no excuse if she chickened out. To further seal her fate, there was a First Aid Guide.

She flipped through the guide, looking for any instruction on setting stitches. There was, complete with illustrations. Unfortunately, the first line said *"Thoroughly flush wound with water for five minutes, then gently wash with soap."*

Yeah, right; she didn't even have water to half-ass flush the wound with, much less "thoroughly." She'd have to do the best she could, and pray there was no debris in the cut.

Wait a minute. She had mouthwash!

Quickly she pulled open the trash bag containing her toiletries and pulled out the zipped plastic bag in which she'd put her shampoo and mouthwash. Taking out the mouthwash, she turned it over and read what was in it, from which she learned nothing because she wasn't a chemist. On the front, however, it said it killed germs. It was wet, it killed germs, and she had almost a pint of it.

She also had the plastic bag in her hand. Quickly she filled the bag with snow, zipped it closed, and placed it on a rock. If she was lucky, while she was dealing with Justice's injury, the sun would warm the rock enough to melt the snow, and they would have water. Not much of it, true, but every little bit counted.

With everything she needed laid out on one of the trash bags, she was about to wake Justice when she realized that he probably had mouthwash, too. Going to his bag, she unzipped it and found his shaving kit stuffed on top of, as she had expected, a single change of clothing and underwear. The kit had two zippers; the one on the left opened to reveal a hairbrush, a travel-size bottle of shampoo, and about a dozen condoms. Men. The right side held a toothbrush, a tiny tube of toothpaste, a disposable razor, and a travel-size bottle of mouthwash.

"Damn it," she said, sighing. He'd already used the mouthwash at least once; about half of it was gone, and there hadn't been much to start with. Half an ounce wasn't going to make any real difference, so she left the little bottle in place, zipped up the shaving kit, and replaced it in his bag.

She'd have to do the job with what she had. She just hoped what she had was sufficient to keep him from developing a raging infection.

First, though, she needed to get some sugar into his system, and then, well, a couple of preemptive painkillers were probably called for.

Carefully she removed the shirt that covered his face; even though she knew what he looked like, she almost flinched when confronted by the reality. His entire face was covered with dried blood, caked in his eyes, his ears, his nostrils, the corners of his mouth. Even worse, his forehead was swelling, pulling the edges of the cut wide. She hadn't anticipated the swelling, and winced at the idea of stitching him now. The swelling would probably get worse, though, so waiting wasn't an option either.

"Justice," she said, reaching under the layers of clothes to touch him. "Wake up. It's showtime."

He inhaled, a quick, deep breath. "I'm awake."

His voice was stronger, so maybe she'd made the right choice to get him warm before she tried to do something about that cut.

"I have a candy bar here. I want you to eat a couple of bites, okay? In a little while, if we're lucky, we'll each be able to have a swallow or two of water. Then I want you to take two ibuprofen. Can you swallow them without water? If you can't, I'll put some snow in your mouth, but we can't eat much snow because it'll lower our body temps. Uh, on second thought, maybe you should take the ibuprofen first, let it get started working."

"I'll try."

She opened the sealed square containing two generic ibuprofen tablets, and slipped one between his lips. She saw his jaw working a little as he maneuvered the pill around, worked up some saliva, and swallowed. She gave him the other pill; he repeated the process, then said, "Mission accomplished."

"Good. Now for the food." Tearing open the candy bar wrapper, she pinched off a small piece of the Snickers bar and held it to his lips. Obediently he took it in his mouth and began to chew.

"Snickers," he said, identifying the taste.

"You got it. Normally I take my chocolate straight, but I thought the peanuts were a good idea, for the protein, so I brought Snickers. Smart, don't you think?"

"Works for me."

She waited a minute, to see if the chocolate made him sick. She was on unfamiliar ground here, so she didn't know if he was likely to start vomiting or not. She did know that, after donating blood at the Red Cross, the donors were given something to drink to help replace their lost liquid, and some crackers or cookies to stave off shock. With the Snickers, she figured she had half of the bases covered.

After a few minutes she gave him another bite of candy. "I wish I had something to numb your scalp and forehead," she murmured. "Even teething gel for babies would be better than nothing, but the first-aid kit doesn't seem to be geared toward babies."

He chewed, swallowed, and said, "Ice."

The first-aid kit did have one of those instant ice packs, but she was hesitant to use it. "I don't know. If you weren't already a little shocky, if the cold wasn't already a problem, I wouldn't worry. But an ice pack on your head will cool you all over, and I don't want to do that." She chewed on her lip a moment, thinking. "On the other hand, pain causes a shock to the system, too. If the effect's going to be the same, why make you go through the pain?"

"I vote for less pain."

She got the ice pack from the kit, read the directions, and began kneading the plastic tube. The pack wasn't large enough to cover the entire cut, but if she positioned it just right she could get it over most of the swelling, and over the scalp where the laceration was deepest. When the pack was so cold she could barely stand to hold it, she cut some gauze from the roll and covered the cut with a single layer, then gently placed the ice pack on top of the gauze.

He sucked in his breath at the cold. She imagined it made his head hurt like blue blazes, but he didn't complain.

"While that's doing its thing, I'm going to clean some of this dried blood off you. Bet you'd like to open your eyes, huh?"

She kept up a running commentary as she opened a pack of her premoistened, aloe-treated wipes, extracted one, and set to work around his eyes. Dried blood, she discovered, wasn't easy to remove. A washcloth, with its rougher surface, would have worked better. Blood was caked in his eyebrows and eyelashes, two areas where she couldn't scrub; she didn't want to cause the cut to begin bleeding again so she had to be gentle around his eyebrows, and she couldn't scrub around his eyes even if he hadn't been cut. So she swabbed away, and when the towelette was completely red, she put it aside and got a fresh wipe.

When she glanced back at him, the new wipe in her hand, his eyes were slitted open and he was watching her. The pale bluish-gray color of his irises was startling in contrast with the darkness of his lashes.

"Well, hello. Long time no see," she said.

Another of those faint smiles quirked his mouth. Slowly, as if moving his eyes hurt, he looked around as much as he could while lying flat on his back and not moving his head at all. When he looked past her and saw the mangled plane, his eyes widened a little and he said, "Holy shit."

"Yeah, I know." She definitely agreed with the sentiment. The fact that they were alive and all in one piece, though not completely without damage, was a bit startling when compared to the structural hit the plane had taken. She handled the shock by not looking at the big picture, instead focusing on the details of survival and the tasks ahead of her. Details, by definition, were little things. She could handle the little things, one by one.

Gradually she worked her way down his face, behind and in his ears, down his neck, over his shoulders and chest. Even his arms and hands were bloody. She kept him covered as much as possible, uncovering one section at a time and re-covering it as soon as she had it clean. His pants were bloody, too, but they could wait until he could manage for himself, she thought. The first layer of clothes she'd laid over him were already stained; the blood had dried, and there was nothing she could do about that. She did need to get his feet clean and in dry socks, though, to ward off frostbite.

Moving down to the bottom of the heap, she folded the clothes back, worked his bloody shoes and socks off, and as quickly as possible cleaned and dried his feet. Cleansed of the rusty stains, they were white with cold. Bracing herself against the shock, she raised the hems of her multiple shirts and shifted forward so his feet were against her stomach. They were so cold she shuddered at the contact but didn't jerk away. She began chafing his toes through the layers of cloth. "Can you feel this?"

"Oh, yeah." There was a deep note in his voice, a sort of subtle purr; he sounded like a tiger getting a massage.

It took her a second, but then she realized his cold toes were tucked against her breasts — her bare breasts. There was no help for it because his feet were big, probably size elevens or even larger, and she couldn't make her torso any longer, so, logically, his toes were going to be on her breasts. She swatted his leg. "Behave," she said sharply, "or I'll let you get frostbite."

"You aren't wearing a bra," he said, instead of responding to what she'd said — or maybe that was his response, as if the fact that she wasn't wearing a bra was excuse enough for the fact that he was wiggling his toes, just a little.

"It got wet when I was dragging you out of the plane, through the snow, so I took it off." She kept her tone severe.

He got the inference that she was braless only because of what she had done to rescue him, and he winced a little. "Okay, okay. But, damn, bare tits. You can't blame me."

"Want to bet?" It occurred to her that the icy, unfriendly Captain Justice wouldn't normally be talking this way to her, that he almost certainly had a concussion and was woozy and in pain. She couldn't see him being roguish and plainspoken, but from the moment he'd regained consciousness his language had been as informal as if he were talking to another man. It said something, she thought, that a concussion had improved his personality. "And I don't like the word 'tits.' "

"Boobs, then. Is that better?"

"What's wrong with 'breasts'? "

"Not a damn thing, as far as I can tell." His toes wiggled again.

She swatted his leg again. "Be still, or you can get your own feet warm."

"I don't have any boobs to tuck them

114

against, and even if I did I wouldn't be able to get my feet up to my chest. I'm not into yoga."

He was definitely feeling better, and was more awake; he was speaking in sentences instead of one- or two-word answers. Chocolate had to be a miracle drug.

"Well, tell you what: get some breast implants, take up yoga, and you'll be set for life." Judging that he'd had enough fun, she removed his feet from under her shirts, tugged his clean pair of socks on him, and tucked the layers of clothing around him again. "Fun's over. Is your forehead frozen yet?"

"Feels like it."

"Let me finish reading the instructions, and we'll get this over with." She picked up the booklet again. "By the way, since we don't have any water to flush out the wound, I'm going to use mouthwash. It might sting."

"Great." A world of irony was in the single word.

Bailey hid a smile as she read. "Okay . . . yada yada . . . I got that part. *'Grasp the needle with pliers so the point curves upward.'*" She looked at the curved suture needle, then the rest of the contents from the first-aid kit. No pliers were included. "That's great," she said sarcastically. "I need pliers. Normally I

115

have a pair in my makeup bag, but, gee, it never occurred to me I'd need them on vacation."

"There's a small toolbox in the plane."

"Where?"

"Secured in the baggage compartment."

"I didn't see it when I was getting the bags out," she said, but got to her feet to recheck. "How big is it?"

"About half the size of a briefcase. It's just a few basic tools: hammer, pliers, a couple of wrenches, and screwdrivers."

Feeling as if she'd been in and out of the wreckage so often she was wearing a groove in the earth, Bailey maneuvered her way back into the plane, clambered into the passenger seat, and looked over the back into the baggage compartment. The floor of the plane was buckled from the impact so everything back there had been tossed around, but the cargo net had been in place to keep anything from flying out the way her tote bag had. Just as she opened her mouth to tell him nothing was there, he said, "It should be in brackets against the back wall, just inside the baggage compartment door. See it?"

She looked where he'd said and there it was, safely secured. Duh. She'd been looking on the floor of the plane, not on the walls. "Yeah, I've got it." Toolbox in hand, she backed out of the plane.

She felt a little light-headed when she stood, so she remained still for a moment. Was it altitude sickness again, even though she'd been careful to move slowly? Or did she need some of that candy bar? After a moment the dizziness passed, so she voted for the candy bar.

"I think I need to eat, too," she said, going to her knees beside him and breaking off a bite of the Snickers bar. "I don't want to pass out while I'm jabbing a needle into you." At this rate, she'd be doing good to have him stitched up by sunset.

Thinking of sunset reminded her of time, and she realized that not once had she checked her watch. She had no idea how long ago she had regained consciousness, or how long it had so far taken her to accomplish her tasks, much less how much time she had left in the day. Automatically she pushed up the cuffs on her left arm, and stared at her bare wrist where her watch had once been.

"My watch is gone. I wonder how that happened."

"Probably you banged your arm against something and a pin snapped, or a link broke. Was it expensive?"

"No, it was a cheap waterproof deal I

bought for vacation. I'm going — I *was* going — white-water rafting with my brother and his wife."

"You can catch up with the guide party tomorrow, or the day after."

"Maybe." Slowly she chewed the candy, not sharing with him her terrible sense of isolation, as if rescue was a long time away.

She allowed herself only one bite, to stave off the dizziness, then forced herself back to the matter at hand. After carefully folding the wrapper over the remaining portion of candy and putting it aside, she removed the cold pack from his forehead.

"I have to shift you around, so you're lying with your head downhill, at least until after I rinse the cut — unless you want mouthwash all over your face and running under you."

"No thanks. I can do this myself, though; just tell me what you want me to do."

"Slide toward me, first; I don't want you to get off the blanket into the snow. Okay, good. Now rotate on your butt — wait a minute, let me get this piece of vinyl under your head. That's it." His gyrations had caused part of the mound of clothes to fall off and she took a minute to replace them.

To keep the mouthwash out of his eyes, he tilted his head back as far as it would go. "Okay. Here goes," said Bailey, using her left hand as a barrier against any stray splashes, and began carefully pouring the mouthwash over the cut. He twitched, once, then held himself very still.

She watched for any trash or dirt that may have gotten into the wound, but all she saw was blood being washed away. The instructions had said not to dislodge any obvious clots, so she tried not to let the mouthwash splash directly into the cut. When all the mouthwash was gone, she put the cap back on the empty bottle and set it aside, then opened one of the alcohol prep pads and began cleaning around the cut.

She didn't let herself think about the seriousness of the gash, or how easy it would be for him to pick up an infection in these less than sterile circumstances. Instead she concentrated on what she had to do, step by step. She wiped her hands, the needle, and the pliers with another alcohol pad. Then she put on the disposable plastic gloves and wiped everything again. She wiped his forehead with an iodine pad. When she had done everything she could possibly do to kill every germ, she prepared a suture, took a deep breath, and began.

"The instructions say to start in the middle," she murmured as she punctured his skin with the curved needle and forced it on around to the other side of the cut. "I guess that's so you don't end up with a big lump of skin at one end, if I don't sew you up evenly."

He didn't answer. His eyes were closed and he was taking very measured breaths. Even with the ice pack and ibuprofen, Bailey knew this had to hurt, but evidently it wasn't the agony she'd feared she would be inflicting on him. He wasn't tensing every time she jabbed him, at any rate. She went slowly, afraid of making a mistake. Every stitch had to be tied off and clipped, so one stitch was independent of all the others, and the instructions had said to make certain the knot was lying on the skin, not directly on the cut. She made herself think of it as hemming a pair of pants, which didn't help a lot because sewing was *so* not her favorite thing to do — and she wasn't very good at hemming pants, either.

The gash was a good six inches long. She had no idea how many stitches per inch she was supposed to put in, so she simply worked from the middle and put in as many as looked right to her. When she was finished, her hands were shaking, and she was sure she'd taken at least an hour to get the stitching done. She carefully blotted the line of black stitches, wiping away the dots of blood where the needle had punctured his skin, then hesitated. Should she apply antibiotic salve before putting a bandage over the wound? She didn't think doctors did that now, but then they normally did their stitching in a sterile environment, with all the drugs and paraphernalia they needed. She and Justice were stuck on the side of a mountain, in the snow, with very little food. She thought his immune system might need all the help it could get.

She carefully applied the salve, which also contained a mild analgesic; that had to be a good thing. Then she covered the wound with sterile pads and wrapped gauze around his head; when she was finished with that, she used the Ace bandage to wrap around his head and cover the gauze. The finished product was rather neat, if she did say so herself, and the Ace bandage would help keep dirt away from the wound.

"There," she finally said, collapsing on her butt beside him. "That's done. Next on the agenda: shelter."

9

Damn, she was sexy.

Cam had never thought so before, but he definitely did now — and not because of the way she looked, either, because right now she looked like hell. Her hair was a mess, her face sported both blood and dirt, as well as bruised areas under both eyes that would probably be black tomorrow. Her current state of dress made her look like a cross between a mountain man and a bag lady. And despite the fact that she'd just spent an hour punching holes in his head — or maybe because of it — he wanted to kiss her.

He inwardly snorted at the last thought. Kiss her, my ass. He wanted to do a hell of a lot more than that, so he guessed it was a good thing his current physical condition wasn't the greatest, or he'd have already risked having his head handed to him on a platter by making a heavy, serious-as-a-heart-attack pass at her.

He'd always wondered what made a male praying mantis court death by mating with the deadly female, whether they didn't have functional brains so the poor saps had no idea they were literally fucking themselves to death or if something had short-circuited in their evolution. After all, a process that ended in death for the male couldn't be good for the species. At the same time, he'd sort of admired the little bastards; it took a dedicated male to keep on humping while his head was being torn off and eaten. For the first time, he sort of understood the motivation. He'd risk a hell of a lot to get her naked and under him.

Not that Mrs. Wingate — Hell, what was her first name? He knew it, but he was in the habit of thinking of her as Mrs. Wingate and it didn't immediately spring to mind. Right now his brain wasn't exactly firing on all cylinders anyway. Remembering seemed important, though, as if it wasn't right to think about getting her naked if he couldn't remember her first name.

Thus motivated, he concentrated on the task of recall. Something unusual . . . like a brand of booze. He began running names through his head: Johnny Walker, Jim Beam, J&B, Bailey's . . . Bailey. That was it. He felt triumphant. Now he could fantasize with a clear conscience.

Anyway, it wasn't as if Mrs. Wingate — Bailey, damn it! — would tear his head off, but he sensed she wouldn't be easy, in any sense of the word. She was a challenge both physically and mentally. She'd built a wall around herself and he suspected few people ever saw past it to the woman barricaded within. Only the emergency conditions thrust on them by the crash had made her emerge from that fortress and let him see the real woman.

But he had seen her, and he liked what he saw.

If he'd ever wondered what it would be like to be marooned with her, which he hadn't, he'd have been certain she would be either a whiny, useless, royal pain in the ass, or a bitchy, demanding, royal pain in the ass. Either way, she'd have been a PITA. Instead she'd been so calm and competent, tackling every problem and situation with both common sense and ingenuity, that he never would have believed it if he hadn't seen it himself. She'd done whatever was necessary, and had likely saved his life. She hadn't hesitated to warm his icy feet against her warm body, nor had she blushed or been upset when he'd discovered she wasn't wearing a bra.

He liked that kind of composure, and the inner surety of self it revealed. His divorce had taught him some truths about himself, and he hadn't forgotten them in his subsequent dealings with women. He was a former military officer and a pilot, two groups that pretty much excluded the shy and retiring types. He himself was self-confident and authoritative; he was accustomed to taking command, making decisions, and having most people do what he told them to do. It took a strong woman to deal with him on an equal basis, but now, in his late thirties, an equal relationship appealed to him a lot more than one in which he had to hold himself back to keep from hurting a woman's feelings or overwhelming her. He didn't like playing games, and he didn't want a woman who tried to make him jump through hoops.

Maybe women like that were thin on the ground, or maybe he'd been looking in the wrong places, but he hadn't found many women who combined that kind of mental appeal with a strong physical appeal. Karen, for instance, was strong and forceful, but he felt zero sexual attraction for her. In Bailey's case, his distaste for what he'd thought was a permafrost personality had overridden any physical interest he might have felt.

Things were different now. He didn't know

why she'd built such a tall, icy wall around herself, but she had temporarily relaxed and let her guard down, let him inside the walls, and he damn sure intended to stay there. This crisis had forged a bond between them, a bond of survival. When this was over, when rescue reached them, she would try to put matters between them back on their original footing. He wouldn't let that happen. Somehow, between now and then, he had to win her trust for good.

He was handicapped by being flat on his back, and judging from the way he felt, he was likely to be that way for at least the next day or two. He was concussed, as well as suffering from serious blood loss. He doubted a rescue party would be able to reach them before nightfall, and any search parties in these mountains were always suspended during the night hours because continuing would simply be too dangerous for the searchers. That meant he and Bailey had to survive tonight, when temperatures would drop like a rock and dying from hypothermia was a real possibility. On the one hand, they were in serious trouble. On the other, the rest of the day and tonight would likely be all the time he had to make any lasting headway with her.

He couldn't move his head much without

triggering lightning bolts through his brain, but by carefully cutting his eyes to the left he could keep her within his field of vision. She was picking up something and looking at it, but he couldn't tell what the something was.

"This kind of half-worked," she said, coming back to his side and squatting down. In her hand was a zipped clear plastic bag, in the bottom of which was what looked like slush. "I tried to melt some snow for us to drink by leaving the bag on a rock. It's definitely mushy and runny, so I guess with more time in the sun we'd have real water, but this will have to do for now because you need some fluids in you." She looked around. "You wouldn't have a drinking straw handy, would you? Or a spoon?"

He was a little amused by the question. "Afraid not."

He watched her brow furrow and her lips purse as she looked around, as if she could conjure up either item with sheer force of will. Now that he was aware of her ingenuity, he could almost hear the wheels turning as she searched for a solution to the dilemma of the moment. Then her brow cleared and she said "Ah ha!" in a tone of satisfaction.

"Ah ha, what?" he asked, his curiosity tickled, as she straightened and stepped out of his sight.

"You have a can of spray deodorant. I know because I went through all your stuff."

"And?" He didn't care that she'd gone through his bag; under the circumstances, *not* going through his stuff would have been stupid — and stupid was one thing she definitely wasn't. She'd needed to know what resources she had at hand.

"And that can has a cap on it."

Ah ha, indeed. The spray can cap was essentially the same as the cap on a thermos bottle, just smaller. He should have made the connection himself.

He heard the familiar sound of a plastic cap being removed from a spray can. "The taste might be a little weird," she said. "I'll wash the cap out with snow, that should help some in case you've hit the nozzle and sprayed some deodorant on the inside of the cap. Is there anything in deodorant that wouldn't be good to have in your water?"

"Probably everything," he said casually. "Did you bring any hair spray?" Hair spray was probably less toxic than deodorant. Deodorant had some sort of aluminum in its chemical makeup, didn't it? He didn't know what was normally in hair spray, other than alcohol, but alcohol had to be better than aluminum.

"Nope," she said from behind him. She

sounded a little absent, as if she was concentrating on something other than conversation. "I was going rafting, remember? What would be the point of hair spray? Hmm. I guess I could rig up a funnel and pour this into the mouthwash bottle, if you don't want to take a chance with the deodorant cap."

"Just wipe it out with snow; it should be okay." Now that she'd mentioned water, he was abruptly aware of how thirsty he was, and he didn't want to wait while she searched for something she could fold into a funnel. He'd take his chances with deodorant residue.

"Okay, then."

He listened to her crunch around for a minute, then he heard the crisp rustle of plastic. A few seconds later she squatted beside him, the blue cap in her left hand.

"Don't try to sit up," she instructed. "If you pass out and fall over, you might make me drop the water." As she spoke she eased her right arm under his neck, the position cradling the side of his face against her breasts. He could feel the firm resilience, smell the warm, faintly sweet scent of a woman's skin, and the sudden urge to turn his head and bury his face against her was so fierce that only a sudden stab of pain deflected him.

"Be careful," she murmured, holding the cup to his lips. "It's just a couple of swallows, so try not to spill even a drop."

As soon as he took a sip she moved the cup away. The partially melted snow had a sharp mineral taste, mingled with that of plastic, and was so cold that it almost made his teeth hurt. The liquid washed over the swollen, scratchy tissues of his mouth and throat, being absorbed almost as fast as he could swallow. When she started to put the cup back in place for another swallow, he forestalled her by giving the merest shake of his head, which was all he could manage. "Your turn."

"I'll eat some snow," she replied. "I'm moving around, so eating snow won't lower my body temperature as much as it would yours." She frowned. "How long do you think it will be before a search party finds us? It's been several hours since your Mayday call, but I haven't even heard a search helicopter, much less seen one. If you think it'll be much longer, I'll have to find a better way to get some drinking water. Melting snow isn't very efficient."

No, because it took a lot of snow to make a little water, and vice versa. In answer to her question he said, "Likely it will be tomorrow before a search party can reach us, at the earliest."

She didn't look surprised, just worried — and annoyed. "Why so long? It's been hours since your Mayday call." As she talked she held the plastic cap to his lips, and he took another sip of water.

"Because no one will have even started searching for us yet," he said when he'd swallowed.

The look of annoyance grew stronger. "Why not?" she asked, her tone sharp.

"When we don't make our scheduled fuel stop in Salt Lake City, that's when the alert will go out. If we don't check in somewhere within a couple of hours after we miss that stop, a search will be organized."

"But you sent out a Mayday call! You gave our location."

"Which may or may not have been monitored. Even if it was, a search wouldn't be initiated then. Searches are damned expensive, and search teams have limited resources; they have to be certain the Mayday wasn't bogus, that some idiot didn't think it would be funny to send out a Mayday call when nothing was wrong. So they wait until a plane doesn't show up where and when it's supposed to before initiating a response. Even after an alert is issued, organizing a search takes time. This is June, so the days are long, but even so I doubt a search team could locate us before dark. They would stop for the night, and start again tomorrow morning."

He watched her as she processed that information, her gaze searching the massive landscape around them. After a few minutes she sighed. "I hoped I could get by with just finding some way to keep the wind off us, but we'll need a lot more than that, won't we?"

"If you want to still be alive tomorrow morning, yes."

"I was afraid of that." She gave him the last of the water, then carefully lowered his head to the blanket and eased her arm from beneath him. Her smile was rueful as she reached under the pile of clothing covering him, finally withdrawing her arm with his pocketknife in her hand. "I'd better get started, then. This will take time."

"Don't try for anything elaborate. It needs to be small enough that our body heat can warm the air around us a little, so the smaller the better, as long as there's room for both of us. Salvage what you can from the plane: the leather from the seats, any wiring you can use to lash poles or sticks together, things like that."

She snorted at his instructions. "Elaborate? Dream on. Just so you know: I really suck at construction."

10

Having Justice confirm what she'd instinctively known, that no one was searching for them, rattled Bailey more than she wanted to reveal. She had really, really needed to hear that they'd be rescued soon, because managing any sort of shelter would tax her little remaining strength to the limit. She simply didn't know how much longer she could keep going.

Resting beside Justice and warming herself while she warmed him had helped, but the least bit of exertion now seemed to bring an onslaught of dizziness, which wasn't good considering the steepness of the slope she was having to negotiate. The smallest misstep or stumble could send her tumbling down the mountain, and in this rugged terrain that would almost guarantee a broken leg or arm, at the least. The only bright spot she could see was that while her headache was nonstop, it didn't seem to be intensifying. Some bright spot; it wasn't exactly giving her hope.

Both of their lives depended on her, so she'd have to be extremely cautious. Caution took time, though, and time was almost as limited as her strength. The temperature, which she doubted had been above thirty degrees all day, would plummet like a rock even before the sun completely set. As soon as the sun slipped below the summit of the mountains looming over them, and that could happen a couple of hours before sunset, the temperature would begin falling. She had to have water for them before then, and she had to have at least a rudimentary shelter rigged.

Seizing the empty mouthwash bottle, she crouched and began packing snow into the bottle's narrow mouth. The process wasn't a fast one, precisely because the mouth was so narrow. Her hands were cold even before she began; within a minute, the pain in her fingers was agonizing. She had to stop and tuck her hands in her armpits, closing her eyes and rocking back and forth as the pain slowly ebbed and warmth seeped into her flesh. She needed something to cover her hands, and she needed it fast.

Automatically she began running through her options. She had brought two pairs of waterproof gloves for handling oars, but they had no fingertips, so while they'd be good for preventing blisters they wouldn't help keep her fingers warm. She could put socks on her hands as makeshift mittens, but they would be clumsy and they'd get wet, which would make her fingers even colder. The socks would come in handy later.

Forget gloves; she needed a fairly efficient method of getting snow into the bottle that didn't involve getting her hands in it. What could she use as a makeshift rake, or a scoop?

Leaving the bottle lying in the snow — it wasn't as if the snow already inside would melt and pour out — she moved over to the trash bags that now contained the remainder of her clothing and supplies, sat down on one bag, and began methodically removing from the others everything that wasn't clothing. She considered each item, trying to think of a use other than its intended one.

Her stick deodorant was pretty useless for anything other than keeping her underarms from getting smelly. She supposed if she needed anything waxy the deodorant would do, but right now no possible reason for that sprang to mind. Hairbrush, basic makeup — mascara, sunscreen, lip gloss — the books and magazines she'd brought to read could be used in a variety of ways, but none of those ways would help her get snow into a mouthwash bottle. She had her book light — again, handy to have, but not right now. She had a couple of pens, a small notebook, a roll of duct tape that she set aside because she'd definitely need it when working on their shelter, a deck of cards, insect repellent, a poncho that she also set aside, tissues and tush wipes — also set aside — as well as four microfiber towels and a bunch of the little sponge disposable toothbrushes.

Damn it, she thought fretfully. Why hadn't she packed something useful, like a box of matches? Her teeth might be clean and her mouth fresh when her frozen body was found, but what good was that?

She looked over the motley collection of things she'd thought would be good to have on a two-week rafting trip, sighed in disappointment . . . then looked again at the deck of cards. They were brand-new cards; the box was still sealed in plastic. She picked up the cards, caught an edge of the plastic with her teeth, and began tearing it open. Then she opened the box and took out a card. It was plastic coated, so it would stand up to a lot of use.

Good enough, she thought with a little ping of satisfaction.

The card was just stiff enough, and just limber enough, that she could roll it into a slight scoop and push snow into the bottle mouth. By shaking the bottle and tapping the bottom hard against a rock she made the snow pack down, so she could get more into it. When the bottle was full of snow, she put the lid back on and screwed it down tight.

"This isn't going to feel good," she warned as she carefully made her way back to Justice. He'd been lying there with his eyes closed while she dealt with the water situation, and he slowly opened them when she spoke. His face was pale, which wasn't surprising, but the corners of his mouth kicked up in a wry smile.

"So what else is new?"

She showed him the bottle of snow. "It won't be much water when it melts, but this is the best I can do. The trick is to get the snow to melt. I have to put the bottle somewhere warm, and guess where that is?"

"I'm betting it isn't going under your shirt." The smile took a sardonic twist.

"That would be a safe bet." She ignored his reference to the way she'd warmed his feet. The fact that he'd felt her bare breasts didn't embarrass her, but on the other hand she wasn't exactly comfortable with this abrupt sea change in their relationship, if cold unfriendliness could be called a relationship. Now they were suddenly best friends, just because they'd survived a plane crash together? She didn't think so. On the *other* other hand, hostility had no place between them now; they still needed each other in order to survive. And if there was a third other hand, well, after seeing his herculean effort to control the crash and make it survivable, her foremost feelings for him were respect and admiration. Let's face it: he was her hero.

She mentally sighed. All in all, she didn't know what she thought, or felt. Making herself focus on the matter at hand, which was more important than what she did or didn't feel, she slid the bottle under his coverings, against the side of his hip. "I hope this doesn't make you start shivering again. Is it miserably cold?"

"No, it's okay. I have two layers of clothes between me and it. You're working your ass off, so the least I can do is serve as a snow-melter."

"That's true."

This time the smile became a real one, showing a flash of teeth and a tiny dimple just above the left corner of his mouth. Only then did she realize how less than gracious her reply had been, and she gave her head a rueful shake. "Sorry. That was rude."

"But truthful." He held his head very still, understandably, but his eyes were crinkled with amusement, and that little dimple flashed again. It was amazing how a smile changed him from Captain Sourpuss to a very attractive man, bandaged head, bruised face, and all.

"Well . . . yes."

"Thank God you said yes. If you hadn't, I'd have thought you'd completely lost touch with reality."

"I have a fairly firm grip on reality," she said wryly, and sighed. "Unfortunately, reality is telling me I'd better get my butt in gear, or we'll freeze to death tonight. The altitude is really getting to me, so I have to be slow and careful."

His gaze suddenly sharpened as he studied her face. "You have altitude sickness?"

"Headache, dizziness — yeah, I'm pretty sure. The headache could partly be from banging my head, but overall I think it's the altitude."

His expression turned grim. "And I can't do anything to help you. Bailey, don't push yourself. It's dangerous if you do. Altitude sickness can kill you."

"So can hypothermia."

"We can get through the night. There are

enough clothes here to cover ten people, and we can share our body heat."

They'd have to do that anyway; she had no illusions about her ability in the shelter-building department. She also had no illusions about how cold these mountains could get at night, or how precarious his condition was. Weighed objectively, hypothermia and altitude sickness weren't equal dangers — not for her, and certainly not for him. Considering how much blood he'd lost, he was in far more danger of dying during the coming night than she was.

"I'll be careful," she said, getting to her feet. She looked up at the plane, tilted almost on its side on the slope above her. Just thinking of climbing those few yards again made her feel exhausted, but she needed the cargo net, as well as the leather from the seats. Oh, yeah, and the wiring, too. She could see lots of wiring, hanging from the broken wing and the gaping hole where the left wing and part of the cabin had been.

The enormity of the job she faced almost made her panic. She was hungry, she was thirsty, and she was cold. She ached all over. The puncture wound in her right arm, which she'd almost forgotten, was making its presence felt. Even if she'd had a decent meal in her, plenty of water, and the proper clothing

— as well as a nice, toasty fire — she wouldn't have liked knowing she was responsible for building them a shelter that would actually hold together. Architecture bored her. She'd never even built sand castles.

All she had to rely on were some episodes on survival that she'd watched on the Discovery channel, the details of which hadn't really stuck with her. She knew they'd be warmer with a layer of something between them and the ground; she knew she had to get a roof of some sort over their heads to protect them from possible rain or snow. Beyond that, all she could think of was that they had to be protected from the wind, too. All of this she was somehow supposed to accomplish with sticks and leaves.

Worming her way into the wreckage, she finished unhooking the cargo net and let it drop through the door to the ground. That task wasn't physically demanding, and neither was removing the leather from the seats. To keep the leather in the largest pieces possible, she painstakingly used the point of the knife to cut the stitches. The backseat was a single bench, with two individual seat backs and arms; the bench would provide the largest piece. Wind couldn't get through leather; that's why motorcyclists wore leather clothing.

Cutting all those stitches took time, longer than she'd anticipated. Some of the leather she had to cut out anyway, because it wouldn't pull free even after she'd sliced all the stitching. Removing the leather from the seats revealed the thick foam that provided cushioning; she could easily see a need for that, so the pads of foam followed the cargo net and the pieces of leather. The floorboard provided more vinyl. The bounty salvaged from the airplane that had almost killed them, she thought, might save them yet.

11

"Guess what?" Bret practically sang early that afternoon as he bounced into the J&L office with his jaunty stride. "Turns out Cam was right about the allergic reaction. It was —" He stopped in midsentence, the humor fading from his face, his sharp blue eyes locking on Karen's face. "What's wrong?"

Karen stared wordlessly at him. Her face was paper white, her expression drawn and stark. She was holding the telephone receiver, and slowly she replaced it. "I was just about to call you," she said. Her voice was thin, toneless.

"What?"

"It's Cam."

Bret looked at his watch. "He called already? He's made damn good time."

"No, he . . . hasn't called." Karen spoke as if she was barely able to move her lips. She swallowed. "He didn't make the fuel stop at Salt Lake."

144

A tiny muscle in Bret's jaw began to twitch. "He stopped somewhere else," he said flatly, after a moment. "Before Salt Lake. If there was any trouble, he'd put down —"

Slowly, wobbling a little, Karen shook her head.

Bret hung there, staring at her while he absorbed what she was telling him. Then he bolted for his office, grabbed his trash can, and vomited into it. "God," he said in a strained voice, when he could talk. He pressed both fists over his eyes. "God in heaven. I can't — I can't believe . . ."

Karen hovered in the office door. "An alert has been issued."

"Fuck an *alert*," he said savagely, swinging around. "A search —"

"You know the protocol."

"They're wasting time! They have to —"

Her only answer was another agonizingly slow shake of her head.

Furiously he kicked his chair, sent it slamming into the wall. "Shit!" he bellowed. "Shit, shit, shit!"

Then he picked up the phone and began calling people, only to be told over and over that protocol would be followed, that if Cam hadn't checked in somewhere within a couple of hours, a search would be initiated.

Slamming down the phone for the last time, he went over to the map on his wall and traced a line from Seattle to Denver, marking the route Cam would have taken. "Over a thousand miles," he muttered. "He could be anywhere. Anything could have gone wrong. Have you talked to Dennis? Did Mike write up the Skylane yesterday for anything?"

The two questions were directed at Karen, who had been listening to his calls, hoping against hope that he could kick-start the search. "I've already checked," she said. "There wasn't anything. Dennis said there hasn't been anything on the Skylane except normal maintenance." She hesitated. "Whatever happened . . . didn't have to be mechanical. A bird could have hit them, or he could have gotten sick and passed out . . ." Her voice trailed off.

Bret was still staring at the map. Cam's route had been over some of the most rugged, remote terrain in the country. "He could have set it down," he insisted. "In a field, a canyon, on a dirt-bike trail — anywhere. If it can be done, Cam can do it."

"They're doing a communications search," she said. "If he could land it, he'll radio in. An FSS will pick up his transmission." Her voice wavered a little as she said,

"All we can do is wait."

Flight Service Stations were air-traffic facilities that performed a lot of different functions; among them was the constant monitoring of the aircraft emergency frequency. Cam had filed a Visual Flight Rules flight plan, which placed him in the FSS system of graduating emergency levels. When Cam hadn't arrived in Salt Lake at his estimated time, the system went into a distress phase. A communications search notified all the communication sites and airports along his route that he was late in arriving and asked for any information.

The protocol was that, after an hour, if the plane hadn't been found, the communications search was intensified and expanded, and all possible landing sites were checked. After another hour of no results, the FSS would hand the search over to Search and Rescue. Cam's friends and relatives would be called. Only after three hours was an actual, physical search initiated; a satellite would pick up the Emergency Locator Transmitter on the plane and lead the Search and Rescue team to it, but depending on how remote the location was, that could take several more hours.

Karen was right. All they could do was wait.

Bret paced. Karen returned to her desk and sat staring at nothing, stirring only to answer the phone whenever it rang. The minutes ticked by so slowly that time might have been a variation of Chinese water torture.

Then Karen answered the phone one last time, in a strangled voice said, "Yes, thank you," hung up, and burst into tears.

Bret dragged in deep, ragged breaths. He stood frozen, his fists knotted. "They found wreckage?" he asked hoarsely.

"No." She wiped her eyes and firmly set her jaw. "No distress calls were received, no radio contact made. If he'd made an emergency landing somewhere —" She didn't have to say it. If Cam had *landed,* he'd have radioed in, but landing and crashing were two very different things. "SAR has been initiated."

Brett's color had gone gray and his shoulders were slumped. "I'd better . . . I guess I should call Seth Wingate." Returning to his desk, he dropped heavily into his chair and fumbled with the phone book. Karen quickly pulled up the family's file on her computer and called out the number to him.

"Yeah, what's up?" a slightly slurred voice greeted him. A television played loudly in the background.

148

He was already drunk? It was the middle of the afternoon. "Seth?"

"The one and only."

"Bret Larsen, of J and L." Bret propped his elbows on his desk and covered his eyes with one hand.

"I thought you were taking the step-bitch — sorry, my dear, *dear* stepmommy — to Denver today."

"Cam, Captain Justice, took the flight at the last minute." He felt as if he were running out of air so he sucked in a quick breath. *Get this over with.* "We've lost contact with the plane. They never arrived at the refueling stop in Salt Lake."

Incredibly, Seth laughed. "You're shitting me."

"No. Search and Rescue has been initiated. They —"

"Thanks for calling," Seth said, and laughed again. "I guess some fucking prayers do come true, huh?"

Bret found himself listening to the dial tone. "Asshole!" he roared, fighting the urge to throw the phone across the office. "Shithead! Bastard!"

"I gather he isn't upset," said Karen. She was still pale, but her eyes were dry and she had the drawn, numb look of someone who was functioning through a massive shock.

"The son of a bitch *laughed*. Said his prayer has come true."

"Maybe with some help from him," she said with fierce loathing.

The first thing Seth did was mute the television and call his sister, Tamzin. When she answered he could tell by the shrieking and splashing in the background that she was sitting by the pool watching her two brats. He didn't like his nephew and niece. He didn't much like his sister, but on this front, at least, they were united.

"You won't believe this," he purred in satisfaction. "Seems like Bailey's plane crashed on the way to Denver."

Like him, her first reaction was laughter. "You're kidding me!"

"Bret Larsen just called. He was supposed to be her pilot but the other one, the tall one, took the flight instead."

"Oh my God, this is great! I can't believe — I mean, I know we shouldn't *celebrate,* but she's been so — How did you manage it?"

Instant fury roared through him. She was so fucking *stupid.* She had Caller ID; she knew he was calling on a cell phone, which were notoriously unsecure, and she said something like *that?* Was she trying to get him arrested?

"I don't know what you're talking about," he said coldly.

"Oh, come on. Madison! Don't do — I'll have to cancel your play date if you —" She shrieked suddenly. "Now look what you've done! Mommy's all wet! That's it! You can't have anyone over for a *month!*"

Even over the phone Seth could hear the obnoxious whine of his niece, a particularly grating sound, as she immediately launched into a campaign to wear her mother down and get her privileges reinstated. Tamzin never made good on any of her threats, as her children knew all too well. All they had to do was whine long enough, and Tamzin would give in just to shut them up. He pinched the bridge of his nose. "Can't you shut her up? She sounds like a steam whistle."

"They're driving me *insane* today."

Short drive, he thought, cynically.

"So, what do we do?" Tamzin asked. "Do we have to claim the body, or anything like that, because I don't care if she's buried or not. I'm not spending a penny on her funeral."

"We don't do anything yet. They're searching for the plane."

"You mean they don't even know where it is?"

"Why else would they be searching for it?" He pinched harder.

"How do they know it crashed if they don't know where it is? You'd think someone would have noticed if a plane just disappeared off the radar screen."

He started to explain to her that general aviation flights didn't occupy the same altitudes as commercial aviation and weren't tracked by radar until they approached controlled air space, but decided to save his breath. "It didn't show up at their scheduled refueling stop."

"So it might not have crashed? They don't know for certain?" Disappointment laced her voice.

"They're as certain as they can be."

"So when do we get control of our money?"

"When the bodies are found and a death certificate issued, I suppose." He really had no idea; the legal issues might take some time to settle.

"How long will that take? It's ridiculous that we don't have control over our own money. I hate, I absolutely *hate,* Dad for doing this to me. I have to pretend to all my friends that we let her live in the house out of the goodness of our hearts, and that I'm careful with money when the truth is she doles out every penny as if it's hers."

"I don't know," he said impatiently. "Call your lawyer if you have to find out this minute."

"Furthermore, I'm not wearing black, and I'm not pretending to be sorry."

"Yeah, yeah, I'm not either." Suddenly he couldn't bear to talk to her another minute. "I'll let you know when I find out something more concrete."

"You could have called earlier. I've had a shitty day, and if you'd told me this first thing this morning I'd have been in a much better mood."

Seth disconnected the phone and in a fit of anger threw it across the room. What had started out as sheer satisfaction now left a bitter taste in his mouth. Going into the bathroom, he gulped down a glass of water and stared in the mirror as if he'd never seen himself before, wondering if other people looked at him and saw someone who would kill to achieve his own ends. His mouth thinned as he compressed it, and he whirled away from his reflection.

Going back into the living room, he picked up the scotch he'd been drinking, his third of the day, and brought it to his mouth. Then, without sipping, he set it back down. He needed a clear head, so that meant no more scotch right now.

He'd have to be very, very careful, or his stupid sister's loose mouth would land him in prison.

12

Bailey stepped back to survey the fruits of her labor, and not because she was overwhelmed by its beauty. The "shelter" — she hoped it was sturdy enough to qualify — was such a motley collection of odds and ends, and so weirdly shaped, that a third-world country might have disavowed it. Her knees were wobbly — after all the work putting the shelter together she was on the verge of falling on her face.

Her head was throbbing with pain. She was so thirsty her mouth felt like cotton, and melting snow in her mouth provided only short-term relief, plus it made her even colder. She was hungry. She ached all over, her muscles protesting every move. And she was so dizzy that, toward the end, she'd been forced to crawl, which meant her sweatpants had gotten wet with the snow and now leeched even more of her body heat away.

But the thing was finished, and she and

Justice had a place to sleep that, if it didn't fall down on top of them, would provide at least some protection from the icy wind. And that wasn't easy.

With only Justice's pocketknife for cutting, she had to use what broken limbs and branches she could find. The plane had broken a lot of limbs, but not all of them had been sheared completely off. Some of those that hadn't been completely broken off she'd been able to hack free, if they were hanging by a few shreds, but she couldn't afford to spend a lot of energy or time on them. Picking up two broken limbs from the ground, even if they weren't as sturdy as one left still hanging, was much easier than performing an amputation with a pocketknife.

After picking out a sort of oblong spot among a fairly tight grouping of trees, tucked against the slightly concave side of a boulder and recommended mostly because the spot was fairly level, as well as by the lack of large roots protruding from the ground, she had scraped away as much snow as she could and lined the cleared spot with a crosshatch pattern of the most limber branches. All of the trees seemed to be evergreens and firs, so the branches with their bristling of needles would make a good, cushioned layer between them and the ground.

Maybe she went about it backward, but for her own thought patterns she needed to make their bed first, then build the shelter around it so she could better visualize how large the shelter should be. As he'd said, the smaller the better. Because she was concerned about getting the shelter long enough so he could stretch out his legs, she stood beside him and carefully measured him by the heel-to-toe method. He was a little longer than seven of her heel-to-toe steps.

He watched her do this, a quizzical little frown on his face. "Are you practicing for a sobriety test, or something?"

"I'm measuring you. You're an inch or so longer than seven feet — my real feet, not the twelve-inch kind. I don't want to make the shelter too short for you."

She tried to make their bed maybe an inch longer than that — rather, she tried to make one side of it longer than that, because overall the thing was kind of lopsided because of how the trees were positioned. She figured she'd take the short side.

Over the crosshatch of limbs and needles, she put the foam pads she'd removed from the plane's seats. She had six short pads and one long piece from the bench seat, and she figured that would give more cushioning than they'd have in sleeping bags. Given her druthers, though, she'd have taken the sleeping bag — at least that way she'd be warm. Staying warm tonight, without a fire, would be a real challenge.

When she had the pads positioned, she went to work with the bigger limbs. Obviously she needed some sort of frame, and just as obviously her roll of duct tape was called for to lash the limbs together, but she was oddly reluctant to use it. The roll was a small one, and wouldn't go far. If she used strips of cloth to tie the skeleton frame together, at least the strips could be reused if she didn't get it right the first time, whereas the tape, once it was used, was gone.

The ruined silk jacket was perfect for cutting into pieces.

At first she tried making an inverted V-shaped thing, but that was evidently beyond her building skills, which wasn't surprising. After the rudimentary frame collapsed for the third time, she made an executive decision and stopped wasting time on that method.

Returning to where Justice lay under the mound of clothing, she crouched beside him and said, "Remember when I said I suck at construction?"

He cracked his eyes open. "Is this your way of telling me we're sleeping in the open tonight?"

"No, this is my way of asking for help. Help! Just give me some instructions. Pointers. Anything. If you have *any* experience at this, you know more than I do."

"I thought you'd been rafting before."

"I have. I'd like to point out that you don't raft on top of a snow-covered mountain."

"Didn't you set up a tent?"

She made a scoffing noise. "I was a college student. Of course not. We slept in sleeping bags, around a campfire."

"Okay." He thought a moment. "What type were you trying to build? An A-frame, or a lean-to?"

"A-frame. I can't get it to stand up."

"Make the base first. Lay out the long sides with two parallel long branches, then lay the cross braces on top, one on each end, and secure all four corners."

That sounded easy enough. Returning to the site of collapse, she sorted out the variety of limbs, sticks, and branches into the two best fits for the length of the bed, which she then placed, one on each side. Then she positioned two shorter limbs, one on each end, and used the strips of silk to tie each short limb to the two longer ones. When she finished she wiggled the frame to see how sturdy it was, cautiously pulled each knot tighter, and wiggled the frame again. Good enough.

"What now?" she called.

"Now you need to establish the height. Get four branches that are taller than you want the height to be."

That was easy, but all four branches still had a lot of limbs and needles attached. Using the knife, she trimmed off what she could. "Got it."

"Take two and make a rough X with them. The point where they cross will be the height of the shelter. You want to tie the second pair where they cross at the same height as the first pair. Then get two shorter pieces and put them below the crossing point of the Xs, as braces."

Hmmm. She thought she saw where he was going with this. She got busy with her silk strips, and when she was finished she had what looked like two letter As, with horns sticking out the top. "Now I tie these to the base, right?"

"First get another long limb and put it in the notches of the two Xs, and tie it off on both ends so the upper frame is as long as the base. Then you attach the whole thing to the base."

Even with his instructions, the shelter's frame sort of listed to the left and sagged at the back, but when she looked for the sun she saw that it had slipped behind the mountains, and time was too short for her to try to improve her handiwork. Instead she tied bracing pieces of limbs wherever the thing seemed to need it most, which was pretty much all over. When she judged it sturdy enough to stand, at least for one night, she moved on to the roof.

Technically, she supposed big black trash bags draped over the top didn't qualify as a real roof, but they were the closest thing to a tarp that she had. She taped the trash bags to the wooden frame, then threw the cargo net on top of that to anchor them in case the wind got up, and for added weight and insulation wove the pliable tree branches, needles intact, through the webbing of the net.

The trash bags didn't completely cover the sides of the A-frame, but she didn't have enough of them to do the job. She attached more limbs to cover the gaps, then even more limbs, then began sticking clumps of needles everywhere she could stick them. With one eye on the steadily decreasing light and part of her attention focused on the dropping temperature, she forgot to keep her movements slow and easy. Instead, a sense of urgency drove her faster and faster, until her breath was coming in audible gasps.

As she stood up to reach for yet another limb to cover a tiny gap she'd just noticed, her vision went black. She stumbled, reaching out in panic to grab something, anything, but her hand waved uselessly in the air as she pitched headlong into one of the trees.

When her vision returned she was on her knees in the snow, one arm wrapped around the slender evergreen, her heart hammering in panic. Not wanting to risk falling, she stayed on her knees, gritting her teeth as she clumsily covered the small gap. Nausea, oily and bitter, rose in her throat, and she swallowed it back.

She still had to enclose the ends, and her only way to do it was by crawling. After standing the limbs and branches to cover the back, she piled snow against them; heaven knew the snow wasn't going to melt, and it made an effective barrier against the swirling wind. The front end could be only partially enclosed, because they had to get inside somehow; more branches, starting at the sides and working in, leaving barely enough open space for him to crawl through. To cover the entrance, she clumsily tucked the biggest piece of leather into the inside of the frame and let the flap hang down; it didn't completely cover the entrance, but it didn't have to. The gap that remained she could fill by pulling one of the trash bags containing her clothes into it.

The biggest problem facing her now was getting upright, staying upright, and somehow getting Justice into the shelter. She couldn't drag him, because she was dragging herself. Carefully she pulled herself to a standing position, gripping one of the trees for support. Her knees threatened to buckle beneath her, and her head gave such a vicious throb that she almost blacked out again. When the threat passed, she stared tiredly at the ramshackle, lopsided structure. It would do because it had to do; they had no other options.

Wobbling, staggering, she made her way down the slope to where Justice lay. In actual distance it wasn't far, no more than thirty feet — just far enough to get out of the path of the plane if it should start sliding. Still, for the effort it took her to go those thirty feet, it might as well have been a mile.

"It's ready," she gasped, staggering to her knees beside him. Her hands were numb and clumsy with cold, the mountains were doing a slow swirl around her, and she was fighting off nausea again. "I don't know how you're going to get there, though, unless you can crawl."

His eyes opened, the irises pale amid the dark bruises that had already formed. "I think I can stand. If I can't, then I'll crawl." He took in the pallor of her skin, the way she was shaking and shivering, the dampness of her sweatpants from the knees down, and his brows lowered. "What the *hell* have you done to yourself?" he asked sharply. "Never mind; I know. You've been half killing yourself trying to make a shelter for us. Damn it, Bailey —"

She felt ridiculously hurt, as if what he'd thought mattered to her, and because that hurt made her angry her own tone was sharp. "You know, you don't have to sleep in it. You can freeze your ass off out here, if you want."

One muscular, bare arm shot out from under the clothes, a hard hand gripped her forearm, and the next thing she knew she was flat on the survival blanket. It infuriated her that, as weak and wounded as he was, she was so weak herself after all her exertions that she was about as effective as a rag doll in resisting him.

His gray eyes had gone frosty. "We're sleeping together, whether it's in the shelter or out here. First, though," he said grimly, "you're going to get under these clothes with me and lie down for a little while, before you pass out." As he spoke he was slowly, laboriously shifting onto his left side to face her.

Lying down felt like heaven to her achy body and swimmy head; the idea of being warm was such a delicious dream that she almost cried at the thought of it. Anger and hurt made her want to wrench away and stomp off to lie in the shelter in glorious solitude, but the reality was that she didn't feel capable of stomping anywhere. Denied the satisfaction of physical resistance, she resorted to words. "You ungrateful jerk. I've always thought you were an ass, and now I'm sure of it. I'll be damned if I give you any more of my chocolate."

"Yeah, yeah," he said, tugging her closer to him and struggling with the heavy layers of clothing so he could get them over her. Once that was accomplished, he pulled her even closer until she was nestled in his arms, against his half-naked body.

What felt like a blast furnace of heat enveloped her. Realistically she knew it wasn't, that at best he was only moderately warm, but she was so cold in comparison she might as well have been on fire. Her cold face pressed into the warm crook of his neck and shoulder, his arm was around her back pressing her even closer, and the sensation of heat on her icy, throbbing hands was at once so painful and so wonderful that she almost burst into tears. Instead she shoved her hands against his naked sides in search of more warmth. He flinched and swore, but he didn't remove them.

Bailey continued her litany of unhappiness, mumbling it against his warm throat. "When you go to sleep, I'm going to rip all those stitches out of your head. See if I don't. And I'm taking my clothes, too; you can keep warm with your own clothes, all three pieces of them. *And* I want my mouthwash bottle back."

"Shh," he murmured. His hand was moving in slow strokes over her spine, up and down, up and down. "Rest now. You can finish giving me hell when you feel better."

"I'll give you hell on my own schedule, not yours. Are you *smiling?*" she asked furiously, jerking her head up to see because she could have sworn she heard that telltale note in his voice.

If he had been, he managed to wipe the evidence away before she could see it. "Who, me? Not in this lifetime. Come on, put your head down," he said, moving his hand to the back of her head to apply a little pressure. "Get closer."

Closer? The only way she could get closer was if she pulled off her clothes as well. She gave in to the insistence of his hand, once again pressing her face to the warmth of his skin. "Stop humoring me. I absolutely hate that, and it won't work."

"Never thought it would."

Damn him, he was still doing it. She thought about pinching him, but that would require effort, and complete lassitude was washing over her. She wanted nothing more than to lie right there for the foreseeable future, her aching head on the warm pillow of his shoulder.

She didn't dare go to sleep. Darkness was coming at them like a runaway freight train, and she still had so much left to do. "I need to get up. It's getting dark —"

"We have a good hour of daylight left. We can afford five minutes for you to rest and get a little warmer. I've been adding snow to the mouthwash bottle as it melted, so we have about a pint of water if you need a drink."

Did she ever. She hadn't noticed him moving around, but she'd been kind of occupied so that wasn't surprising. He pulled the bottle out from beneath the covers.

She could see some tiny dark specks of dirt floating in the melted snow, but she frankly didn't give a rat's patootie. She was so thirsty she could have drank all the water, but she allowed herself only three sips, swishing the wonderful liquid around in her mouth until it warmed before swallowing it. "That was good," she said on a sigh, recapping the bottle. He returned it to its place under the covers, then once again tugged her close.

Wrapped tightly in his arms, surrounded by his heat, Bailey let all the tension seep out of her muscles. What the hell; as angry as he'd made her, the hard truth was that they were in this together. Faced with the brutal cold of a night at high altitude, they could either live together or die separately. It was just for one night; tomorrow they would be rescued. She would join up with Logan and Peaches, who by now must be crazy with worry, and maybe they could join the rafting party farther down the planned route. White-water rafting seemed kind of tame after being in a plane crash, she thought drowsily. There was adventure, and then there was *adventure;* nothing like a life-and-death situation to get the adrenaline pumping.

Gradually, another hard truth dawned on her.

Justice was half-dead from blood loss, his head was sliced open, and he undoubtedly had a concussion. He'd already been close to life-threatening hypothermia, and God only knew what other injuries he'd sustained. He'd been through all that — and the damn man had a hard-on.

13

"Crap," Bailey said guiltily, exaggerating only a little. "You need to pee, don't you? I'm sorry, I should have asked a long time ago."

A couple of seconds ticked by before he said, "I'm okay. I can wait."

"Well, if you're sure . . ."

"I'm sure." His tone was faintly annoyed.

She didn't allow even a hint of a grin, because with her face pressed against him the way it was he'd feel her facial muscles move. If he'd had any thoughts of some convenient sex — she was convenient, so he'd have sex with her — attributing his erection to a bodily function instead of a manly one was sure to tell him that *she* certainly wasn't thinking of him in terms of sex. How on earth he thought he could possibly do anything was beyond her, but she'd noticed that men often had no sense of reality when it came to their penises.

Her sense of reality, however, was strong, and it had told her they were in dire circumstances. Even if he hadn't been injured, she didn't have time or room on her to-do list for a play session. And besides, there was always the classic reason for saying no: she had a headache — a real one, so severe that only the urgent need to fashion a shelter for the night had kept her going.

Speaking of which . . . *Up and at 'em, girl,* she told herself, pushing her physical complaints aside. "If you're sure you don't need to pee —"

"I'm sure," he growled. Now he sounded definitely testy.

"Then let's get this show on the road, Captain Justice."

More than an hour later, she literally dragged herself into the ramshackle shelter beside him and collapsed on the pieces of foam rubber, which she'd covered with the space blanket on the theory that heat rose, so they'd be warmer lying on top of the blanket than under it. It made sense to her, so she'd gone with it.

Justice had been white with exhaustion and pain by the time she got him up the slope. Covering the short distance, their progress made in laborious inches, had been a nightmare that left them both shaking. Before that, with his help, she'd gotten him into clean clothes. She'd made trips up and down the slope, dragging the trash bags of clothing and other supplies, but at last everything was done and night had fallen.

She was shaking with cold again, but she managed to reach out and drag one of the full trash bags closer until it covered most of the opening into the shelter. They lay in the total darkness for a few seconds, the only sound the harsh gasp of her breathing; then he turned on her battery-operated book light. The small light threw harsh shadows on his strong-boned face as he struggled closer to her, his expression revealing nothing of what the movement must have cost him.

Silently he eased her into his arms again so they were lying as close together as they could get, and he arranged the piles of clothing over both of them. Then he turned the light off, to save the battery, and they lay there together until her breathing was less labored and their shivering had almost ceased.

"When you feel like it," he said, his voice deep and soothing in the utter blackness surrounding them, "we'll finish off that Snickers and drink the rest of the water. I think we both could use a couple of aspirin, too."

"Uh huh." That was all she could manage

by way of an answer. She was so tired that every cell in her body ached. Yes, she was hungry, but if getting food required moving then she could do without eating. The pieces of foam were as cushiony to her battered body as any bed she'd ever slept in, and there was something deeply comforting about lying so close to him that she could feel his breath stirring in her hair, feel his chest moving as he breathed. His scent and warmth enveloped her. Resting her aching head on his shoulder, she slept.

Cam knew the instant she went to sleep; the tension flowed from her muscles, her breathing evened and deepened, and she lay bonelessly against him. He rested his lips against her cold forehead for a moment, then turned his head a little so his cheek was against her's and he could share what little warmth he had. If they lived through the night it would be because of her dogged determination — that and the mind-boggling amount of clothing she'd packed.

He'd watched her as much as possible, though moving his head made his headache almost blindingly severe. When she was in his field of vision he'd watched her stagger around, then crawl around, and it infuriated him that he couldn't help her, that he had to lie there like a useless piece of shit while she half killed herself trying to take care of the both of them. She had pushed herself way past the point where most people would have sat down and said, "I can't do any more," and in taking care of him she had seriously neglected her own health.

He suspected she was dehydrated, because if she'd stopped for any nature calls during the day, he hadn't noticed, and since regaining consciousness he'd paid very close attention to her, listening to her movements even when he couldn't see her. She had allowed herself only a few sips of water, but at the same time she'd pushed herself physically all day long.

On the other hand, he'd tried to replenish the fluid volume he'd lost. He had drank steadily, if not a lot at any one time, from the mouthwash bottle as the snow inside it melted, replenishing the snow from what he could reach. At one point he'd painfully rolled on his side and taken a leak — careful to aim away from the area where he was getting the snow — and Bailey had been so focused on accomplishing all her tasks that she hadn't even noticed.

She was so exhausted he'd let her sleep for a while before waking her to eat and drink. Holding her wasn't exactly a hardship. Even with all the layers of clothing between them he could feel the firmness of her body, the resilience of her breasts. She kept herself trim, almost too slender for his tastes, but her muscle tone said she did it by exercise and not by starving herself.

Good muscle mass would help keep her warm tonight, too, but even then she'd have a tougher time dealing with the cold than he would. That was another reason why he was letting her sleep now, while she could. As the temperature kept dropping she'd get colder; they both would, even with all these clothes around and over them. Their shared body heat might be enough to keep them fairly comfortable, but he suspected that around dawn the temperature would be around zero, with a windchill about thirty below. That was damn cold by anyone's standard. The shelter did the job of protecting them from the wind, but it wasn't airtight. Guess he'd have to suck it up and cuddle with her all night long.

What a hardship.

He wasn't above taking advantage of the forced intimacy of the situation, at least as far as he was able to take advantage of anything. Nothing overt, though; for now it was enough that they'd spend the night in each other's arms — literally. Even if they were rescued first thing in the morning, which he didn't think could possibly happen, tonight would always be a bond between them. They would have slept together, used each other's heat to stay alive, talked through the long hours of darkness. There wouldn't be any going back to her former frostiness. He didn't think she'd try, but if she did he wouldn't let her get away with it.

Cam didn't pursue many women; he'd never really had to. Most pilots didn't, unless they were bum-fuck ugly. Growing up in Texas, he'd played high school football, and that was pretty much guaranteed to make you popular with the girls. From there he'd gone straight into the Air Force Academy — cool uniforms, all the military machismo — so no problems there. Then he'd gone to flight school, got his wings, started moving up in rank. By then he'd been married, to the daughter of a colonel, so he'd deflected all the female attention that came his way. Later, after he was out of the military and divorced, nothing much had changed. Now he was a pilot *and* a business owner, and while he wasn't a hound dog like Bret, when he wanted sex it was seldom difficult to find.

Bailey, though, had all the signs of being difficult. She hadn't been embarrassed by his hard-on, but neither had she shown the least bit of interest. Because she'd been married he had to assume she wasn't a lesbian, so she was either totally, completely uninterested in him, or it was those damn walls she'd built around herself. Either way, he was anticipating a challenge. He almost smiled in predatory satisfaction.

When he judged she'd slept about an hour, he turned on the little book light so she'd be able to see who he was and wouldn't be startled, then gently shook her awake. "Bailey. It's time to eat."

She surfaced a little, only to sink again as soon as he stopped shaking her. He shook her harder. "Come on, honey, you need to drink some water even if you don't want to eat."

Her eyes opened, blinking slowly, and she glanced around for a moment as if she didn't know where she was. Then she focused on him, and beneath the mound of clothing that covered them her free hand clenched on his waist. "Justice?"

"Cam. Now that we're sleeping together, I think you should call me by my first name."

A sleepy little smile touched her mouth. "Don't get pushy. You can't rush these things."

"I won't tell." He studied her face as best he could in the small light. There was no way to tell for certain, but he thought she was still pale. Her right cheekbone was a little swollen, and a bruise darkened the skin under her eye. She'd been battered, too, but she'd kept going. "You have a black eye," he said, drawing his hand from under the covers to gently touch her cheekbone.

"So what? Both of your eyes are black."

"Won't be the first time."

She yawned. "I'm so tired," she said drowsily. "Why did you wake me up?"

"You need water; you're dehydrated. And you need to eat something, if you can."

"You're the one who lost so much blood. You need the water more than I do."

"I've been drinking some all day, as the snow melted. Come on, don't argue. Drink." He hauled the mouthwash bottle out from its resting place against his hip. He watched as she dutifully swallowed a couple of times, but she was so exhausted he could tell even that was an effort. The bottle tilted in her hand, threatening the precious liquid cargo, and he hurriedly took it from her and recapped it.

"That's good," he said in encouragement. "What about the rest of that Snickers bar? Feel up to splitting it with me?"

"I just want to sleep," she said fretfully. "My head hurts."

"I know, honey. Remember those two aspirin we were each going to take? You need
something in your stomach so the aspirin
won't upset it. Bite." He held the candy bar
to her lips and she took a small bite. He
watched as she chewed and swallowed, before taking some of the candy himself. Then
he made her take another bite. One last bite
for himself, and the candy bar was gone.

Next he had to open the first-aid kit, which
she'd put in the shelter with them, and that
necessitated lifting himself up on his elbow.
Every muscle in his body protested the
movement, but his head went into outright
revolt. He paused a moment, fighting nausea, until the hammering pain settled from
excruciating down to mere agony.

When he could open his eyes, which were
watering from the pain, he saw that she'd
closed her eyes again. "Bailey, wake up. Aspirin."

Once again she made the effort to open her
eyes. Carefully he fumbled through the kit
until he found the two doses of aspirin,
sealed in their individual plastic squares.
Using his teeth, he tore open both squares,
swallowing two of the tablets before giving
the other two to Bailey. They each had another sip of water, to wash down the aspirin,
then he stowed the bottle under the covers

again so the water wouldn't freeze during the night.

Turning off the book light and plunging them once again into darkness, he settled her by touch, turning her so they were face-to-face, their legs tangled together. Remembering how she'd covered their heads earlier, he pulled one of the garments over their heads. There was still an opening for air, he could feel the frigid gap as clearly as if it were solid ice, but the air they were breathing was marginally warmer.

"Good night," she murmured, the words slurred, as she nestled closer and pressed her face against his shoulder.

"Good night," he said. He kissed her forehead, draped his arm over her hip, and settled himself to catch what sleep he could.

14

The cold woke her. Bailey surfaced from a fretful sleep, shivering. She ached all over, and felt generally miserable. Complete darkness surrounded her and she almost panicked, would have panicked, if not for the unmistakable sensation of being held tightly in someone's arms. On a subconscious level she recognized the scent, the feel of him, and knew there was no cause for alarm.

Or maybe there was, since his left hand was tucked inside the elastic waistbands of both her sweatpants *and* her underwear, resting on her bare butt.

Just as her hands were tucked under his shirt, she realized, seeking the warmth of his skin.

Icy air seeped through the heavy layers of clothing that covered them. Chills raced over her spine. Was there a gap in the covers? She reached behind her back with a questing hand, to see if she'd dislodged some of the garments.

"Are you awake?" Cam asked in a low tone, so if she wasn't the question wouldn't disturb her. She could feel the faint vibration the sound made in his chest, almost like a deep masculine purr. It made her want to nestle even closer, if that was physically possible.

"I'm cold," she replied in a murmur. "And would you move your hand, please?"

"Which hand? This one?" His fingers wiggled against the cleft of her bottom, disturbingly close to, well, disturbingly *close.*

"Justice!" she said in sharp warning, narrowing her eyes at him even though the thick darkness made the action useless.

"I have brain damage, remember? I'm not responsible for my actions — or for the actions of my hand, which acted of its own volition and without my knowledge."

She made a derisive little sound, but she was fighting a smile. Lying with him like this in the darkness was seductive, she realized. They were doing it to survive, but the reason behind the action in no way weakened the sense of intimacy the circumstances had forged between them. Her innate caution began sounding an alarm. If she weren't careful, she could find herself drifting into exactly the kind of impulsive relationship she'd seen cause so much trouble in so many lives, her own parents' among them. With such firsthand experience of the havoc bad personal choices could make on whole families, she'd always been ultra-careful not to let her emotions rule her head.

Bailey didn't do impulsive, not in her financial life and certainly not in her personal one. She didn't *know* Cam Justice; she'd been acquainted with him for a few years, but she didn't know him — and their acquaintance hadn't been cordial. She doubted he'd changed much in the past twelve hours or so, and she knew she hadn't. To go from barely tolerating each other to sleeping together — in the literal sense, of course — in such a short length of time was mind-boggling enough by itself, without letting the situation cause her to make stupid decisions.

So instead of laughing, she said, "Move it or lose it."

"Isn't that supposed to be *use* it or lose it?" He sounded amused but he moved his hand, pulling it out of the back of her pants and tucking his fingers, instead, just under her shirt. She didn't quibble about that; after all, she was still warming her hands on him.

And she liked touching him. The thought set off another alarm, but not recognizing the fact when it was staring her in the face seemed even more dangerous. What was there not to like? He was tall and lean, his body hard with muscle. He wasn't handsome, but the rugged masculinity of his features appealed to her. She flashed to the sudden image of seeing that face above her in bed, of those strong arms braced on each side of her as her legs twined around his hips —

She jerked her thoughts away from the fantasy. *Don't go there.* She didn't believe in acting on sexual attraction, because if ever there was a situation when hormones took over decision-making from the brain, that was it. The stronger the attraction, the more control she exerted. In fact, she made it a point to avoid men to whom she was strongly attracted. She'd never had a passionate affair, never been in love, and didn't intend to start now. Love and passion should come clearly marked with signs that read: Caution: May Cause Stupidity.

Her back and legs were aching so much she couldn't get comfortable. She shifted around, searching for a better position. After yesterday, she was probably covered with bruises, and it wasn't surprising that she felt sore after being in a plane crash. She shivered as another chill swept over her. "What time is it?" she asked. When daylight came, she'd be able to move around, and the temperature would start rising.

He moved his left hand again, lifting it and pressing a button on the side of his watch so the face was briefly illuminated. "Almost four-fifteen. We slept about four hours. How are you feeling?"

He was asking *her* that? He was the one with a huge gash in his head. He was the one who'd almost bled to death, who had gone into hypothermia. He was concussed, and could barely move under his own steam; she doubted he could walk ten yards unaided. Maybe such a disconnect from reality was a defect in the male chromosome.

"I have a headache, I ache in every muscle, and I'm cold," she said succinctly. "Other than that, I'm good. How about you?"

Instead of answering he touched her face, his fingers cool on her skin. "I think you have a fever. You say you're cold, but your skin feels hot to me. In fact, I'd probably be cold if you weren't giving off so much heat."

"I don't have a fever," she said, irrationally insulted by the suggestion. "I'd have to be sick to have a fever, and I'm not sick. *Sick* sick, anyway. I have altitude sickness, and according to that handy-dandy first-aid booklet altitude sickness doesn't cause fevers. It causes headache and dizziness, which I have. Had. I'm not dizzy now, but, hey, I'm not standing up either."

She couldn't be sick. She had things to do. She was on *vacation*. As soon as they were rescued from this stupid mountain, she was going white-water rafting with Logan and Peaches, and she refused to let a stupid bug derail her plans.

"Like I said, I think you have a fever." Ignoring her rejection of the idea, he went on, "Have you been exposed to anything lately, that you know of?"

"No, and if I do have a bug, you'll get it, too, because we've been drinking from the same bottle, so you'd better hope I don't." Irritated, she turned onto her right side so she no longer faced him. When she did, pain shot through her right arm. What the —?

"Crap," she muttered, then, more loudly, "Crap!"

"Crap, what? Is something wrong?" He clicked on the book light and the bright little LED bulbs almost blinded her for a second.

"You lucked out. I don't have a bug. I had a piece of metal stuck in my arm this morning . . . yesterday morning. I pulled it out and forgot about it. Now my arm's hurting. I guess it's infected," she said glumly. Okay, so she had a fever. Damn it.

"So you took care of me and didn't take care of yourself." There was a grim note in his voice. "Which arm?"

"The right one."

"Let's see."

"It can wait until daylight. We can't even sit up in here, so —"

He began unbuttoning the outermost shirt she wore. Seeing he wasn't going to listen to reason, she pushed his hands away and resumed the task herself. "All right, all right. I don't see what difference a few hours will make, but if putting some antibiotic salve and a Band-Aid on my arm will make you feel better —"

"God, you're grouchy. Are you always like this when you first wake up?"

"No, I'm always like this when I have a fever," she snapped as she struggled out of the first shirt and went to work on the second. "Damn it. Crap! I don't have time to get sick." She pulled off the second shirt.

"Just curious," he commented, watching the proceedings with interest. "How many shirts do you have on?"

"Three or four. I was cold, and I gave *you* my nice, warm down vest."

"Which I deeply appreciated."

"You're full of it, Justice," she muttered. "You were barely conscious and didn't know what was going on."

When she was down to the last shirt, she paused. She didn't have on a bra, and she wasn't about to strip off to the waist for him to enjoy the view. Feeling very put upon, she struggled to roll over onto her stomach. Considering the many layers covering them, the idea was much easier than the execution. Finally, feeling like a fish flopping around on a creek bank, she managed to get onto her stomach and pull her aching arm out of the shirtsleeve. "There," she mumbled into the space blanket.

"Hell, Bailey, you didn't even clean it up!" Annoyance was plain in his voice.

"No, I was preoccupied with other things, like keeping you from bleeding to death, then keeping us from freezing to death," she said sarcastically, just as annoyed as he. "Next time, I'll get my priorities straight."

"Where did you stash those wipes?"

With her left hand she fumbled around the shelter, located the pack, and flipped it over her back. "Here you go."

The wipe was cold, but it felt good on her arm. She winced as he swabbed at the puncture wound and pain stabbed the muscle. "Ouch!"

"No shit. Does it feel as if something's sticking you?"

"Yes, but —"

"That's because there is. You pulled out the biggest piece, I guess, but left this one in. It looks sort of like a needle . . . hold on . . . got it."

She set her teeth against the burning ache. He was pinching hard on her triceps muscle now, making the wound bleed, and swabbing the blood up with his free hand. This wasn't fun, but he'd kept quiet while she sewed up his head, so she could keep quiet while he tended her arm.

"The skin is hot and a little swollen," he said. "So, yeah, I'd say this is what's causing your fever. I don't see any red streaks, though." She felt the coolness of salve, then pressure as he slapped a couple of adhesive bandages over the wound — or wounds. She didn't know if there was one puncture site, or two. "Let's hope this is enough to keep the infection under control."

She fought her way back into the shirt, keeping her back turned to him as she buttoned it up. She thought about taking ibuprophen, to hold the fever down so she'd feel more comfortable, but decided against it. The fever wasn't a serious one; it was just high enough to make her ache, but the heat was one of her body's weapons against the infection. She could stand a little discomfort while her immune system and the invading bacteria waged war.

"Drink the rest of the water," he instructed, pulling out the mouthwash bottle. "No arguments. With a fever, you'll get seriously dehydrated if you don't drink."

She didn't argue, instead drinking the water without comment. Dawn was just a couple of hours away; they'd melt more snow then. For now, she wanted to rest, and maybe start feeling a little warmer.

She curled on her side, tucking her feet closer to her body. Justice began piling more clothes on top of her, until the mound was so heavy she could barely move. Then he put his arm around her waist and pulled her as close against him as she could possibly be, her back to his chest, her butt to his crotch, his thighs cradling hers.

Spooning was . . . nice, she thought. And surprisingly warm. She could endure this for a couple of hours . . . just until sunrise.

But it was a damn good thing he was injured, and a damn good thing they'd probably be rescued tomorrow, because otherwise her resistance would need some serious reinforcing.

15

Seth Wingate wasn't an early riser, but that wasn't a problem the next morning because he hadn't gone to bed at all. If he'd followed his normal routine he'd have been in one of Seattle's hottest nightspots around ten-thirty or eleven the night before, then moved on to another one around midnight. He'd pick up a babe somewhere, maybe smoke a little dope, screw her in some semiprivate place if he felt like it, drink a lot, and make it home before dawn to fall asleep on the sofa if he didn't actually make it to the bed. That was if he'd followed his normal routine — but he didn't.

Instead of hitting the clubs he had stayed home. News of the missing plane was an item on all the local stations. A couple of reporters, both print and TV, called and left messages. Tamzin called twice, left messages both times, but he hadn't returned her calls either. He didn't want to talk to the stupid bitch; there was no way of knowing what monumentally dumb thing she'd say next. The messages she left on his answering machine were bad enough: "Call me when you get home. How soon can you get our money released? By the way — *thank you.* I don't know how you did it, but you're brilliant!"

She also sent text messages to his cell phone, which annoyed him even more. Finally he turned off both phones. He'd have to dump the answering machine, get a new one; this one was digital, so even though he could erase her messages, he wasn't certain some forensic computer geek couldn't get erased messages from it somehow. Better to be safe than sorry.

That was a new outlook for him, because "safe" had never been part of his vocabulary.

Neither had "sober," but he added it that night. He badly needed a drink, or some dope — something — but he didn't dare have even one drink to take the edge off. If the authorities, whoever the "authorities" were in this case, came knocking with any questions about his stepmother and the plane crash, he needed all of his wits about him. He had let his temper, and the booze, goad him into doing something stupid. Now he had to walk a very fine line, or his ass would be in deep shit.

Seth paced through the hours of the night. He walked through his large, expensive condo, staring at everything in it as though it belonged to a stranger. He roamed like a ghost searching for its soul, in and out of rooms, fighting the urge to have a drink and at the same time facing the darkness of his own depths.

When morning came, he felt thin and insubstantial, as if he were indeed a ghost. He'd never felt less capable of accomplishing anything than he did that morning, but at the same time the need had never been more urgent. He sensed a point of no return yawning at his feet. If he didn't act now, he didn't know if he would ever again have the opportunity, or the will to do anything about it.

When the sky finally lightened, illuminating the beautiful snow-covered peak of Mount Rainier to the southeast, he knew what he had to do.

First he went into the kitchen to see what he could scare up for breakfast. He seldom ate at the condo, so he didn't have much available. He found some moldy sliced cheese, which had never been opened, in the refrigerator; he threw it away. There was no bread for toast. He did have some coffee, so he brewed a pot. There was half a box of stale saltines in the cabinet, and an apple that hadn't quite gone to rot wilting away in a bowl. The apple and the saltines at least filled the empty spot in his queasy stomach, and even settled it. The coffee made him feel less bleary — not completely alert and awake, but less bleary, and that would have to be good enough.

He showered and shaved, and dressed in the most conservative of his three suits. He had a shitload of casual clothing, club-hopping clothing, sailboat clothing, but he'd spent most of his life avoiding the type of situation where he would need a stuffy business suit, so his selection was limited. His father, on the other hand, had probably owned fifty suits. He wondered what Bailey the Bitch had done with them. Dumped them in the trash, probably.

He looked at himself in the mirror again, just as he'd done the day before. There were shadows under his eyes and his expression was . . . strange. That was the only way he could describe it. He didn't look like himself to his own eyes.

Then he got in his car and did something he'd sworn he would never do: he drove to Wingate Group headquarters, with all the other lemmings.

He was rather surprised, and annoyed, to find that he couldn't get past the security checkpoint because he didn't have an employee badge. This was an *office building,* for fuck's sake, not the White House, or even a post office. When his father had still been alive, Seth had been able to come and go as he wished, though mostly he hadn't wished at all. He didn't think he'd been here in . . . five, six years, maybe longer. He certainly didn't recognize either of the security guards.

He looked around as he waited for one of the guards to call W. Grant Siebold, the CEO. When Seth had been growing up, Siebold had been "Uncle Grant" to him, but that had changed. He hadn't seen or heard from Grant since his father's funeral, and then the son of a bitch had practically been stuck up Bailey's ass, he'd stayed so close to her, so Seth hadn't bothered speaking. With a kind of grim amusement, Seth thought to himself that Grant's attitude would probably undergo a sea change now that Bailey was no longer in the picture, or controlling all those millions of dollars.

Finally he was given the go-ahead, a temporary pass that clipped to the breast pocket of his jacket, and directions on how to get to Mr. Siebold's office — as if he needed directions, considering the office had once been his father's.

The layout of the office had changed, though; the elevator opened into a spacious foyer, which widened into a waiting area with several comfortable chairs, lush greenery, a tropical fish tank built into the wall, and a lot of reading material. Evidently people were expected to wait a long time. Guarding this was a strictly professional woman who looked to be in her mid to late forties, whose desk was beside a set of carved double doors. According to the nameplate on her desk, her name was Valerie Madison. He'd never seen her before. The last time he'd seen Grant's secretary, she'd been a gray-haired, glasses-wearing fifty-something who'd always given him candy. He guessed she was either retired or dead by now.

"Please have a seat," Valerie Madison said, lifting the phone. "I'll let Mr. Siebold's assistant know you're here."

Oh, so *she* wasn't Grant's secretary? Now the secretary — excuse me, *assistant* — had a secretary?

Seth didn't sit. He watched the bubbles slowly rise in the fish tank, watched the fish swim aimlessly around. They weren't accomplishing anything, weren't going anywhere, but they endlessly performed their circuits of the tank as if this was their express purpose in life. They were too stupid to even be unhappy.

Behind him, the assistant's secretary's phone gave a discreet little beep. He heard the murmur of her voice, too low for him to make out the words. She replaced the phone, stood, and opened the door. Silently he nodded to her, passed through the doors, and found himself in another outer office. This one was smaller, more comfortable, more like a very tasteful living room than an office. Soft music, some kind of New Age shit, sort of oozed from all four corners of the room. He'd go fucking nuts if he had to listen to that crap all day long.

The woman sitting at an antique French writing desk, on which perched a curved pedestal supporting a flat-screen Mac, was both a little older and a little rounder than the version outside, but just as businesslike. Her salt-and-pepper hair was wound into a sort of figure eight at the nape of her neck, and her vivid blue eyes were calm and noncommittal. "Please have a seat," she said. "Mr. Siebold will see you as soon as he's finished with his present call."

He looked for her nameplate, which was an engraved brass bar. *Dinah Brown.* The name was as no-nonsense as its possessor. He said, "I've been trying to think of Grant's previous secretary's name."

"That would be Eleanor Glades."

"Mrs. Glades!" he said, snapping his fingers. "That's right. She used to give me candy. When did she retire?"

"She didn't," said Dinah Brown. "She died of a massive heart attack, twelve years ago."

Twelve years — and he hadn't known it. Why would he have? But shouldn't his father have mentioned it, even if his mother hadn't? The Siebolds had been their close friends, and losing his secretary would have shaken Grant.

But maybe they had mentioned it, and he simply hadn't listened. He hadn't listened to his parents a lot. He had, in fact, raised not listening to an art form.

"You may go in now," she said, rising and opening the door for him. "Mr. Siebold, Mr. Wingate to see you."

Seth went into the office that had been his father's — at least he was pretty sure it was the same office. Well, it was in the same location. Everything else had changed too much for him to say it was the *same*. His father had preferred clean lines, uncluttered surroundings, function before style. His office furniture had been leather. Grant Siebold's office was decorated in more of the comfortable, stylish but inviting decor that characterized the outer office. The furniture was upholstered. At least the New Age music wasn't piped in here, too.

"Seth." Grant Siebold rose from behind his desk; he was as trim as ever, lean almost to the point of thinness. He'd gone a little bald, and a lot gray. His gaze was shrewd and penetrating. "Have you had any news of Bailey?"

He was a little taken aback that the older man asked, and even more surprised to detect a note of genuine concern in his voice. For some reason, Seth had assumed that his own dislike of Bailey was universal among his father's old friends and associates, for his mother's sake if not for the way Bailey had screwed her way into control of a massive fortune. He knew that, since his father died, socializing with her had screeched to a halt, a circumstance that had given him great pleasure.

"Nothing," he said briefly.

"Terrible thing. I was awake most of the night, hoping to hear something," Grant said, indicating one of the chairs with a wave of his hand. "Have a seat. Coffee?"

"Yes, thanks." Seth thought another shot of caffeine couldn't hurt. He sat down. "Black." Grant hadn't offered to shake hands, an omission that could only be deliberate. In the business world, shaking hands was as automatic as breathing. Seth doubted the gesture hadn't been made because Grant considered him an old friend, almost like a son; no, the subtle message was that Grant wasn't happy to see him and didn't want to extend a hypocritical welcome.

He waited until the cup of coffee was in his hand and Grant had reseated himself before getting down to business. "Now that Bailey's dead —"

"Is she?" asked Grant, his eyebrows rising. "I thought you hadn't heard anything."

"I haven't. It stands to reason, though. The plane disappeared, and they haven't shown up anywhere. If there was mechanical trouble and the pilot was able to land the plane at some podunk airstrip, or on a road, in a field — we'd have heard. They'd have radioed in. They haven't been heard from, so that means the plane crashed, and they're dead."

"A court wouldn't see it that way," Grant said in a cool tone. "Until Bailey's death is confirmed, or a reasonable length of time has lapsed and she's declared dead, she's still officially in charge of your trust fund."

Seth could see it in Grant's face: he thought that was why Seth was here, to find out how soon he could take control of his own money, part of which was tied to stock in the Wingate Group. Grant was also one of the trustees of the fund, but only in an advisory capacity; all final decisions had been Bailey's.

"She can't be, if she isn't here," Seth said, struggling to keep the temper from his voice.

"Provisions were made for automatic dispersal, so you don't have to worry. You'll still get your allowance."

Allowance? The word burned through his mind. He was thirty-five years old, and he was relegated to the same level as a ten-year-old. The indignity had never occurred to him before; he'd seen the trust fund as his rightful inheritance, not an *allowance.*

"I want an audit," he heard himself say. "I want to know how much the bitch siphoned off."

"Absolutely none," Grant barked, his sharp gaze narrowing as his temper rose. "In fact, the fund has had a very healthy growth, thanks to her. Why do you think your father chose her?"

"Because she screwed him into blind stupidity!" Seth shot back.

"On the contrary, the whole idea was his from the very beginning! He had to talk her into it, into marriage, the whole —" Grant broke off, shaking his head. "Never mind. If Jim didn't tell you what his plan was, I certainly won't, because he knew you better than I ever will. All I'll say is this: Bailey has taken as much care with your money as she has with her own, and that's saying something. She's one of the most careful investors I've ever seen, and there hasn't been a dime taken from the fund other than the monthly disbursements to you and Tamzin."

Seth's attention sharpened and he skipped over everything Grant had said about the money. "Plan? What plan?"

"Like I said, it's not my place to tell you. Now, if that's all —"

"It isn't." Seth stared down at the coffee in his hand, furious that he'd let himself be sidetracked. He hadn't come here to talk about Bailey, or ask about his money. He hesitated for a moment, trying to think of the best way to approach the subject, but nothing occurred other than just saying it. The necessity galled, but it was now or never.

"I need a job. I'd like to start learning the business . . . if there's an opening." He hated having to ask; this was his father's company, he should automatically have a place here, but he himself had deliberately distanced himself from it and there was nothing automatic about it now.

Grant didn't immediately respond. He

leaned back in his chair, that shark gaze giving nothing away. After a moment he asked, "What kind of job?"

Seth started to say "Vice president sounds good," but he bit back the words. He was acutely aware that he was the supplicant here, that he hadn't built up a supply of goodwill from which he could draw. "Anything," he finally replied.

"In that case, you can start tomorrow in the mail room."

Seth went cold. Mail room? He hadn't expected a corner office, but he *had* expected an office . . . or at least a cubicle. Hell, in that case, why not make him a janitor? Then he gave a wintry smile as the answer occurred to him. "I suppose the cleaning is done by a professional service, huh?"

"Exactly. If you're serious about working here, you'll take the job seriously, no matter what it is. If you blow it off, if you get here late — or don't bother showing up at all — then I'll know you're just fucking around as usual. My time is valuable. I don't see any point in wasting any of it on you until you've proven it *won't* be wasted."

"I understand." Seth hated saying that, hated being in the position of begging, but he'd put himself there; he had no one else to blame. "Thank you." He put the coffee cup on a table and stood; as Grant had pointed out, his time was valuable.

"One thing," Grant said.

Seth paused, waiting.

"What brought this on?"

He gave another wintry smile, this one underlaid with bitterness. "I looked in the mirror."

16

Bailey pushed the trash bag of clothing away from the shelter's opening and began crawling out into the gray morning light. She paused with one hand in the snow, staring at the whiteness around her. "Crap."

"What's wrong?" Justice asked from behind her.

"It snowed some more," she growled. "The plane's covered." Not completely, but near enough. The snow cover made spotting them from the air even more difficult, even if the mountains weren't wreathed in misty clouds, which they were. Visibility was no more than fifty yards, max. This latest development was almost like adding insult to injury. Why couldn't they have a heat wave, a nice warm chinook to melt some of the snow and make waiting for rescue just a tad easier? She was cold, and she wanted to be warm. Her head still ached; her entire body ached. She still had a fever. All she wanted was to be

rescued off this damn mountain, and now —
more snow. Great.

She'd fallen into a fitful doze just before
dawn. Now the sun was well up, not that she
could see it through the clouds, and she had
an urgent nature call. So did Justice, and she
was torn between the necessity of helping
him and the feeling she couldn't wait that
long. Her own urgency won out. "I'll be
right back!" she called, hurrying — as much
as she was capable of hurrying — deeper
into the trees. When she emerged it was to
find he'd managed by himself; he was leaning against a tree, his back to her.

She stopped where she was, to give him a
moment of privacy. That little bit of exertion
had completely exhausted her and she
closed her eyes. The realization of how sick
she was swept through her — not deathly
sick, but enough so that she felt frail, and
that was unsettling. Between the fever, the
cold, the altitude, and the lack of food and
water, she wasn't capable of doing a lot
today. It was a damn good thing she didn't
need to do a lot. They could eat another
candy bar, melt some more snow to drink,
and rest in the shelter while they waited for
a rescue team to locate them.

Justice was better than he'd been yesterday.
He'd managed to take a few steps under his

own steam, but he still looked terrible, with that huge bandage covering the top half of his head, two black eyes that were almost swollen shut, and all the other scrapes and bruises he'd sustained. His physical capability didn't run to much more than lying in the shelter either.

She was a little indignant at the injustice of *her* having the fever when *he* was the one with the nasty cut on his head, a concussion, and the recipient of some inexperienced field doctoring, while all she had was a small puncture wound. Where was the logic in that? In retrospect, though, she should have poured some of that mouthwash on her arm, too.

"You can open your eyes now," Justice said, and slowly she did so.

He was leaning against the tree for support, his posture telling her that even that much effort had wrung him out. White vapor formed in front of his face with every breath he puffed out, and he was visibly shivering. His only shoes were the black lace-ups, and they did nothing to keep out snow. His pants were his suit trousers. He didn't even have a T-shirt to layer under his white dress shirt. He had wrapped a couple of her shirts around his shoulders and neck for extra warmth, but there wasn't much more that he could do to protect himself from the elements. Seeing him merely reminded her that she was the one who'd have to take care of their needs.

Slowly, cautiously, she made her way on rubbery legs down the slope to him and pulled his arm around her shoulder while she put her arm around his waist and grasped his belt to hold him in case he began toppling over. "Let's get you back in the shelter. How's the head?"

"It hurts. How's yours?"

"About the same. Are you seeing double, feeling nauseated?"

"No, nothing like that." Using her for support on one side, and bracing his other hand against trees as he came to them, he labored to take each step. Sometimes he wavered and she had to grab him, hold him until he could get his legs steady again, but overall the process wasn't nearly as exhausting or time-consuming as it had been the day before.

He stopped once, lifted his head to survey the mountains around them. She could tell he was listening for something, but she heard nothing other than what she'd heard from the beginning: the wind whistling through the silent mountains. "Do you hear anything?"

"Nothing."

She caught the grim note in his voice. "We should hear helicopters or something by now, shouldn't we?"

"I hoped we would, but not necessarily. The weather could have delayed them. We know it snowed up here, so there was some sort of weather system moving through. A more realistic guess would be around noon, at the earliest." He shivered, his entire body tensing against the cold, then he said prosaically, "There's no sense in standing out here freezing our asses off when there's nothing we can do."

Bailey agreed wholeheartedly with that and helped him the few remaining feet to the shelter. As he half crawled, half dragged himself inside, she said, "Give me the bottle and I'll fill it with snow again. Are you ready for breakfast?"

"What are we having?" Swollen and blackened as they were, his gray eyes still glinted with humor as he held the mouthwash bottle out to her.

"The same thing we had for dinner: a candy bar. I actually have three more, so we can each have a whole one if you want."

He paused, the humor fading from his expression. "We'd better ration them," he finally said. "Just in case."

Just in case they weren't rescued today, he

meant. The idea was almost overwhelming. Another night on the mountain, in the dark and the cold? The darkness hadn't been absolute, but they'd used her little book light sparingly. Not knowing how long it would take a rescue team to reach them was unnerving. What if no one came tomorrow either?

Silently she took the bottle and moved to a clean patch of snow. She wore a pair of socks on her hands now, which made scraping snow into the bottle with the poker card a little clumsy, but no way did she want to let herself get as cold as she had the day before.

The task was a small one, a minuscule one compared to the herculean labors she'd faced the day before, but it was almost more than she could handle. Wearily she crawled back into the shelter, welcoming the protection from the wind. The air inside the shelter definitely felt warmer than that outside, whether just from the absence of the wind or from their body heat it really was making a difference. She didn't care what made it feel warmer, just that it did.

Light crept through tiny crevices; the interior was dim, but not dark. There was no need to turn on the book light in order to find where she'd put the candy bars. She was starving, but when she began chewing the first bite off her half of the bar, her appetite suddenly fled and the candy began growing in her mouth. She fought back the nausea and managed to swallow it, but folded the paper around the remainder of the candy and put it back in the plastic zip bag.

"Aren't you hungry?" he asked, frowning at her.

"I was, until I started eating. I'll take another bite in a little while." Her mouth felt grungy, so she rooted around until she found the pack of disposable foam toothbrushes. She took two from the pack, stuck one in her mouth, and extended one to him. "Here."

"What is this?" he asked, frowning at the pink circle of cut foam as if it were alive.

"A disposable toothbrush. It doesn't need water. This shelter's too small for morning breath on top of yesterday's and last night's breath, so take it and brush."

His mouth quirked in a smile as he took the small stick and began swabbing the foam around in his mouth. Bailey was pleasantly surprised by the minty taste, and by how much cleaner her mouth felt when she finished. Now if she could just have a nice, hot shower . . .

Dream on, she told herself as she relaxed her aching body on the cushions and dragged a pile of clothing over herself. The clothes would cover them better if the garments were straightened out and layered, but she was too tired and felt too sick to deal with it just now. Justice stretched out behind her, then he pulled her close and rearranged the pieces of clothing so nothing was between them except what they wore.

How odd it was, she thought, that in just one night they'd already established a sort of routine. They already knew, and automatically sought, the positions where they fit best together and were most comfortable. He was a good six inches taller than she, maybe more, so with her back to him they spooned together almost perfectly. His arm draped over her waist, and his hand slipped up under her shirt for warmth, so his hand was resting on her stomach. It was odd, she thought, how fast the situation had forged a sense of familiarity, even intimacy, with him, but she supposed that was a survival mechanism. Together they had a better chance of making it off this mountain alive than they would have alone.

"We could play cards, I guess," she said, thinking of the hours ahead of them.

"Or we could just lie here," he countered.

"Sounds good." Just lying there was honestly all she felt like doing. After another moment of silence, she felt herself drifting to sleep.

Cam didn't think Bailey's fever was any higher than it had been before, but she was obviously sick. When she woke, he would check her arm to see if red streaks had begun radiating out from the wound. He hoped the antibiotic salve and her fever were doing the job, though, because if sepsis had begun then their situation had gone from serious to critical. In the meantime, sleep was the best thing for her — for both of them. They would burn fewer calories, and need less food and water.

He had really thought the ELT would have led a helicopter to them by now, but the weather was a complicating factor. A helicopter couldn't land in this terrain, of course, but it could pinpoint their location for the rescue team, as well as drop much-needed provisions. Thanks to Bailey's ton of clothing they weren't doing too badly keeping warm, but a camp stove would have been nice, as well as some bottles of water and energy bars.

Thinking of energy bars reminded him of the trail mix bars he'd put in his coat pocket yesterday morning. He didn't know where the coat was now, but he'd definitely like to have it, and the trail mix bars could be a godsend. The problem was, neither of them was capable of searching for his coat, and even if they found it the bars might have fallen out. Of course, if they were rescued today, then he didn't care about either the coat or the trail mix bars.

He figured he was basically okay, physically. He was weak from blood loss, the concussion made his head hurt like a son of a bitch, but he evidently didn't have any injuries to either his brain or anything internal. If he had, he expected he wouldn't have lived through the night. He didn't have any fever — or if he did, it was so slight he couldn't tell. A day or so of rest, some food and water, and he'd be good to go.

He was worried about Bailey, though. Altitude sickness wasn't something to be taken lightly, and neither was an infected wound. The hell of it was, she was having problems with both because she'd concentrated on taking care of him instead of herself.

So, because there was nothing else he could do, he held her as she slept. He listened to her breathe, and he stayed alert for any rise in her fever. He also listened for the beat of helicopter blades, and he prayed they came soon.

17

Bret had stayed in the office all night, occasionally putting his head down on his desk for a brief nap. Karen had gone home to change clothes and pick up some food; she came back wearing jeans and a T-shirt and carrying Chinese takeout. When she came back she was also accompanied by her leather-wearing, tattooed, pierced, and bearded boyfriend, whose name, it turned out, was Larry.

Larry was evidently there to take care of Karen, because he brought her coffee when she wanted it, massaged her neck and shoulders, held her when she cried. Karen, who was usually the toughest of the tough, was shattered by the possibility of Cam's death.

The small airport usually shut down at midnight, but the news that Cam's plane had disappeared kept some people around. It simply seemed impossible to go home as if things were normal, to do anything routine, until they found out for certain what had happened. The head mechanic, Dennis, paced around with a drawn look, wondering if there had been something he'd overlooked during routine maintenance.

The situation was thoroughly discussed over the Chinese takeout. Everyone seemed to think something must have gone mechanically wrong; there had been a weather system that would have produced some rough air, but nothing drastic enough to cause the plane to go down. Cam didn't make mistakes in the air; he didn't misread his altimeter or forget how high a mountain was. He didn't hotdog. He was thorough and calm. So either something had happened that had caused him to lose consciousness, or something had gone mechanically wrong with the plane.

A small plane crash warranted a search-and-rescue operation, but not a wholesale investigation by the NTSB the way the crash of an airliner would. The search wouldn't even be based out of Seattle, so Bret had no idea what everyone was doing hanging around the terminal, unless, like him, their nerves wouldn't let them sleep, so they figured they might as well be here.

He knew the routine. The first step was to find the plane. Until the wreckage was located, no one knew what they were facing. No search teams were sent out blind, because the area to be covered was too vast. But waiting was agonizing — waiting to hear, waiting to know for certain.

Around nine that morning, when they were all running on fumes they were so exhausted, Karen fielded a telephone call. Whoever the caller was, her features sort of crumpled before she swallowed and regained control of herself. "It's for you," she said to Bret, her voice subdued. "It's Mrs. Wingate's brother."

Bret winced, and went into his office to take the call. "This is Bret Larsen."

"I'm Logan Tillman, Bailey Wingate's brother. What the hell is going on?" roared the voice in his ear. "We can't find out anything here, and when I called Bailey's house to see if anyone there had any news, her stepdaughter answered and all but laughed at me, said my sister got what was coming to her. What did she mean by that? Do you suspect the plane was tampered with, that this was deliberate?"

The questions came too fast and furious for Bret to answer. He said, "Whoa. Whoa! No one has even mentioned the possibility that the plane could have been tampered with. I don't know what Tamzin meant, but it wasn't that." Out of the corner of his eye Bret saw Karen standing by his office door, not even trying to hide the fact that she was listening. Neither was Dennis, or the two other people currently in the office checking to see if there had been any news.

"She all but came out and said it." Logan Tillman was furious; his voice blasted over the phone line. "Something about only fools crossed her brother."

Bret pinched the bridge of his nose. "Tamzin isn't the, ah, tightest lug nut on the wheel. She says whatever pops into her head, whether it's based on reality or not. At this point we don't suspect foul play, or sabotage, or anything else. Ah, where are you now?"

"Denver, where we were supposed to meet Bailey."

"Have you checked into a hotel?"

"No, we've been here at the airport all night, hoping —" Logan's voice broke on the word.

"Yeah, we've been here all night, too. Listen, check into a hotel, get some rest. Wearing yourself out won't accomplish anything. Yeah, I know, I should take my own advice. Give me your cell number, and I'll call you myself the minute we hear anything. I'll give you mine, too. Call me at any time." He rattled off his cell number, then jotted down

Logan's. "Look, don't give up hope. Cam, that's my partner, has come through some tight situations before. He's the best."

When he hung up, Bret propped his head in his hands. God, he was exhausted. If only there was something he could do, anything, that would keep him occupied. Waiting was a bitch, yet that was all he could do, all any of them could do.

"It's a possibility," Karen said from the door.

Bret raised his head. "What is?"

"That the plane was tampered with. You know Seth Wingate called day before yesterday asking about Mrs. Wingate's flight, when she was leaving. He's never done that before." Her jaw was set, and her eyes radiated fire.

"Be careful what you say," Bret warned. "There isn't a shred of proof that anything was done to the plane. If it really had been tampered with, do you think Tamzin would be *telling* people about it?"

"Like you said, boss, she isn't the tightest lug nut, now is she? She could have been under the influence of any number of substances, legal or illegal, when she said it. That doesn't mean it isn't the truth."

Boss. The word hung in the air like a flaming sword. That was a title she'd reserved for

Cam, the better to skewer Bret in their long-running joust. Bret's hands clenched, and he turned to stare blindly out the window.

They had dozed off and on all day, emerging from the shelter only when necessary, to get more snow to melt or to take care of their physical needs. Every time Bailey woke it seemed as if Justice was making her drink water, though she insisted he drink his share, too. At some point he also insisted that they swap places in the shelter, that she take the side against the wall, while he was in front of the lopsided opening. She didn't see what difference it made, but she crawled in first and let him take the other side.

She realized the difference it made when he was the one to crawl out to get more snow.

"I should be doing that," she protested when he returned. "Swap sides with me again."

"No," he said calmly. "I'm okay, just weak. You should stay quiet, let your body adjust to the altitude."

She started to ask why, when they were going to be rescued, but hesitated because they still hadn't heard those helicopter blades they'd been listening for. The hours were getting short again, and she was beginning to accept that they faced another night on the mountain. The realization made her want to cry, but that was pointless, and she couldn't afford the moisture loss.

"You're concussed," she pointed out to Justice. "*You* should stay as quiet as possible, too."

"I'm not jogging around, believe me. And I don't have a fever."

Bailey groused about that a little, because being the one with the fever still seemed like a gross injustice to her, but she was still really tired and in a short time she was asleep again.

Late in the afternoon Cam said, "I need to check your arm while it's still daylight."

She gave him a narrow-eyed glare, because if daylight were involved, that meant being out of the shelter. "You want me to pull my shirts off *out there?*"

"Yep. The bandage needs changing. You can take a bunch of this stuff with you, keep it wrapped around you so everything except your arm is covered."

He crawled out, taking the first-aid kit with him. Bailey struggled halfway out of her three shirts while she was still inside the shelter, pulling her right arm from the sleeves. She tried to look over her shoulder at her triceps to see if there were any red streaks, but in the dimness it was impossible to tell. Draping a bunch of other clothes around her so she didn't flash her breasts at him, she crawled out, too.

There was nowhere to sit without getting their pants wet, so she stood with her back to him while he bared her arm and peeled off the bandage. "It doesn't look any worse," he said, to her relief. "It's still red around the puncture site, but the redness isn't spreading." He put more antibiotic on the wound, slapped another bandage over it, and she eased her arm back into her shirtsleeve, did up the buttons.

"While we're out here, I should probably check your head," she said.

He touched the thick bandage on his head. "Is there enough gauze to redo this?"

There was, but only one more time. What if they weren't rescued tomorrow? The thought sent a chill down her spine, or maybe that was a chill from the fever. Either way, the idea of a *third* night on the mountain was horrendous.

Nevertheless, his bandage needed changing. "I don't have to use as much this time," she finally said. "I'll put a pad over the cut, and wrap the Ace bandage around your head to make sure no trash or debris gets into the stitches."

There was still no place to sit, and he was so much taller than she that even unwrapping the Ace bandage was awkward. Finally he pulled one of the trash bags over and carefully knelt on it, while she still stood. "Is that better?"

"Much." Carefully she removed the rest of the bandage, hoping the antibiotic salve she'd put on the stitches would prevent the gauze from sticking. It had, for the most part. There were a few places where she had to tug on the gauze to pull it free, but nothing drastic. At least, he didn't scream or curse, for which she was grateful.

Her repair job looked almost as bad as the cut had, she thought, biting her lip. Dried blood crusted around the holes where the stitches were, and in a thin line along the cut, making her wonder if she hadn't pulled the edges together tightly enough. Then she realized that some of the swelling had gone down, which meant the stitches weren't as tight as they should be. "It's going to leave a hell of a scar," she warned. "You may need plastic surgery."

The look he gave her was mildly incredulous. "For a scar?"

"I'm not a doctor, remember? This isn't exactly a neat job." She felt embarrassed, as if she'd failed at some test, though she didn't know what else she could have done. Left the cut open until the swelling went down? That didn't seem like a viable alternative. Not only would the cut have been more likely to get infected, but wouldn't leaving it open make the scar worse?

"Does it bother you? The scar," he asked.

"Hey, it isn't on *my* head. If it doesn't bother you, then don't worry about it."

He grinned as she used an alcohol wipe to clean off the dried blood. "You aren't oozing with sympathy, are you?"

"I'm not an oozer. Sorry."

"What I meant was, does it bother you to look at it?"

"I won't be looking at it, because I'm going to cover it with a bandage. But scars in general don't bother me, if that's what you're asking." Picking up the tube of antibiotic salve, she squirted a line of it over the stitches, from one end to the other. Covering the wound took two sterile gauze pads; she used strips of tape to hold them in place, then rewound the Ace bandage around his head. "There. You aren't as good as new, but you're better than you were yesterday."

"Thanks to you," he said as he climbed to his feet. She reached out to help him, holding him until she was certain he was steady.

He looped one strong arm around her, tilted her chin up, and kissed her.

18

Bailey froze in dismay, caught in his surprisingly powerful grip. She hated having to deal with sexual issues. They'd been getting along so well; why did he have to ruin things by making a pass? He was stronger than she'd expected, given his physical condition, which meant she might have to put some muscle into pushing him away, but she didn't want to maybe cause him to fall and make his concussion worse —

But the kiss was light and brief, his lips cold against hers, his head lifting before she could put thought into action. "Thank you," he said again, and released her.

She stood there in the cold, flummoxed. Okay, now she was officially confused. Was that a pass, or not? If he'd intended it to be, then it was the most *non*sexual pass she'd ever experienced, which kind of defeated the purpose. If the kiss had been intended as a "thank-you," then just saying the words would have sufficed.

She was the first to admit she wasn't the best at catching sexual signals, and it seemed to her that relationships were hair-raising enough without one or both of the people involved operating on mistaken assumptions. In her book, it was better to ask and be certain, even if that wasn't how these situations were usually handled. She shook off her mild shock and resumed helping him to the shelter, wedging her shoulder under his left arm and putting both arms around his waist. "Was that a pass?" she demanded, frowning up at him.

He paused, his expression mild as he glanced down. "Why do you ask?"

"Because I couldn't tell. If it was a pass, then I want you to know up front that sex isn't in the cards. If it wasn't, then never mind."

He actually laughed, his arm tightening around her shoulders in a brief hug. "Trust me, when I make a pass at you, you'll know it. That was just a thank-you."

"*Saying* 'thank you' would have been enough."

"So would saying 'you're welcome,'" he said drily.

Color burned in her pale face. "You're welcome. I'm sorry. I was being pissy, and

I didn't mean to be."

"It's okay." They had covered the four yards or so to the shelter. He dropped his arm from around her and eased to one side, indicating for her to enter the shelter first. She did, realizing for the first time how much easier getting in and out was when no one else was inside. "Wait, let —" she began, but he was already crawling in behind her. She drew her legs up to give him as much maneuvering space as possible. He got turned around, his long legs making things difficult for him, then he stretched out on his stomach and pulled the trash bag closer to plug the entrance.

They settled in, straightening and arranging the heap of clothing so they were better able to cover themselves. Bailey sighed as she relaxed her aching body, lying on her side facing him. After doing nothing but lying around and dozing for most of the day she should be bored and restless, but instead she was still so tired she felt as if heavy weights were attached to her legs and arms. She also felt incredibly grungy; being dirty and sick was somehow much worse than being clean and sick.

Depression settled on her like a wet rug. "Why didn't they come today?" she asked, her tone desolate.

Cam rested his head on the piece of foam that served him as a pillow. They were lying face-to-face, close together in the dimming light as the sun sank lower, bringing another icy night closer and closer. Her gaze roved over his battered face. She could still see the way his lashes curled, and the day's worth of whiskers that adorned his jaw, but soon he would be only a darker shadow in the gloom of the shelter, before the darkness became complete.

"I don't know," he finally said. "The ELT should have brought a helicopter right to us."

"Maybe it's damaged," she suggested, her heart sinking as the possibility registered with her. If no one knew where they were —

"ELTs can take a lot of abuse, especially with the plane as relatively intact as it is."

"Intact?" she echoed incredulously. "Have you looked at it lately? The left wing is gone! Half the cabin is gone!"

One corner of his mouth curled in faint amusement. "But we're both alive and in one piece, and *most* of the aircraft is still there. I've seen crashes where all that was left was a few burned pieces of metal."

"Like if we'd crashed into a rock face?" For a moment she flashed back to those sickening moments before impact, when she'd

229

stared at the craggy rocks looming ever closer and knowing that she was about to die.

"Like that. That's why I wanted to get us down to the tree line. We were going down, no way to stop it, but the trees made the difference between living and dying."

"They cushioned the impact." She shuddered a little, remembering the incredible force with which they'd hit, the sensation of being body-slammed by a giant. She couldn't imagine what the crash would have been like without the trees, but she did know they wouldn't have lived through it.

"Exactly. The trees right on the edge of the tree line are pretty spindly, and wouldn't have done much to help, but I didn't want to descend so far that they were too sturdy. I needed small to medium trees, I guess: strong enough to slow us down, absorb the impact, but limber enough to give."

"Good idea. It worked."

"I guess it did. We're alive."

She wanted to tell him how impressed she'd been with him then, watching him coax every bit of lift he could from the air currents, fighting gravity, using his skill and strength to keep them in the air as long as he had, but though her throat worked the words wouldn't form. To her horror she felt tears forming and she clenched her teeth, willing the tears not to fall. She wasn't soggy by nature, despite those annoying times when she woke to find tears on her cheeks. She didn't know what *that* was all about. She did know that she refused to let herself turn into a weakling, sobbing because she'd been upset and scared. Finally she managed to say in a reasonably even tone, "You saved our lives."

Even in the dimness his sharp eyes didn't miss much. His expression softened as he touched her hair, smoothing a strand away from her face. "And then you saved mine. I'd have gone into shock and died if you hadn't stopped the bleeding. I guess we're even."

She had a strange but potent urge to turn her face into his hand and kiss his palm. What on earth was wrong with her? First tears, and now this? Maybe the fever was getting worse. Maybe she was suffering from post-traumatic stress. A plane crash was pretty damn stressful; she was entitled to a few ragged nerves.

"Have you had wilderness survival training, or emergency response, anything like that?" he asked curiously.

The change of subject gave her a chance to silently pull herself out of the emotional tailspin she seemed to be in. Still, she had to swallow a couple of times before she could speak again, and her heart was pounding as if she'd just had some sort of close call. "No, why?"

"Because you made a lot of commonsense decisions, and did all the right things with what limited resources were at hand."

"Commonsense, that's me," she said, surprised into a wry laugh. She'd experienced the havoc wrought by decisions made on the spur of the moment because one or both of her parents simply felt like it, or because they wanted something, and God forbid they stop to consider how devastating the fallout would be for their children. She never wanted to be that way. "My common sense is why Jim chose me to oversee —" She stopped, unwilling to talk about her personal life.

"All that money?" Cam finished for her, and smiled when her eyes widened in surprise. "It's common knowledge. Our secretary told me about it, but she's a scary woman, in league with the devil, and she knows everything."

Bailey gave a small hoot of laughter. "Karen? Wait until I tell her you said she's in league with the devil!"

"Hell! You know Karen?" Shock had him raising up on one elbow to stare down at her in consternation.

"Of course I know Karen. Wingate Group has used J and L for how many years? Before I married Jim, I was the one who called her to make arrangements for flights."

"I should have known," he muttered. "Hell. Shit. If you tell her that, she'll make my life miserable until I either die or crawl over hot coals to apologize." He eased down onto his back and stared upward. "Promise me you won't tell her."

"Don't tell me you're afraid of your secretary." She snickered, delighted to uncover this facet of Captain Tight-ass Justice. She could see the smile that threatened to break out, and loved that he recognized and privately enjoyed the benefits of an alpha female secretary.

"She owns us," he said with exaggerated gloom. "She knows where everything is, how everything works, and everything's that going on. She handles everything. All Bret and I do is show up, sign what she tells us to sign, and fly the planes."

"You could fire her," she suggested, just to provoke him.

He snorted. "Get real. We raise 'em smarter than that in Texas. I might have to do more than sign a few papers if she wasn't there."

"You're from Texas?"

"Don't tell me I've lost the accent." He eased onto his side again, curling his arm under his head.

"No, but I've read that pilots sort of naturally adopt a drawl, so you could have been from anywhere."

"The Yeager syndrome," he said. "I didn't have to adopt a drawl. I was born with it, though Yeager was from West Virginia and I'm a born-and-bred, died-in-the-wool Texas boy and the accents are totally different."

"If you say so." She let doubt drip from every word.

"Yankee. You have to be born to the music of the tongue to hear the variations."

She had to laugh, especially when the slightly teasing note in his voice invited her to. She wanted to tell him that "music of the tongue" sounded like something from the Kama Sutra, but bit the comment back just in time. If she didn't intend to let him venture into sexual territory, then she shouldn't lead an expedition there herself.

"Where are you from?" he asked.

"Kansas, originally, but I've lived in Ohio, California, Oregon, Maryland, and Iowa."

"As a kid, or since you've been grown?"

"Mostly as a kid. Once I was out of college, I picked a place and stayed there." Roots were nice. Stability was nice.

"My folks didn't move around. They still live in Killeen."

"Where's that?"

"Didn't you learn any geography in all those schools you went to? It's about halfway between Dallas and San Antonio."

"Sorry," she said, rolling her eyes. "There wasn't a lot of emphasis on Texas geography in the schools I went to."

"The level of ignorance today is shocking. How can a school not teach about Texas?"

"Beats me. So you grew up in Killeen?"

"Yep. My parents still live in the same house I grew up in. I have one brother and two sisters, and we all went to the same school, a lot of the time had the same teachers. I moved around plenty when I was in the air force, though. Seeing new places was fun, but the moving itself was a pain in the ass. Why did you move around so much?"

"Divorce ping-pong," she said. "Played with kids, instead of balls."

"That's a bitch. You have brothers and sisters?"

"Of an infinite variety."

"They come in something other than male and female?"

She chuckled, enjoying the banter. "One brother and one sister, two half brothers I never see, three half sisters I never see, and a whole raft of stepbrothers and stepsisters whose names I have to think about, and most of whom I wouldn't recognize if we collided head-on." She thought she'd recognize the guy with red hair and a cleft chin, but she never could remember his name. He was her mother's second husband's son, one of them, with his second wife — her mother had been his third. Thinking about it all made Bailey's headache worse.

"Are you close to your brother and sister?"

She noticed he didn't ask about her parents, but then he was a smart guy so he probably figured that would be a pointless question. "My brother, Logan. He and his wife, Peaches, were the ones I was going rafting with. My sister, not so much. She has her own issues."

On a peripheral level she noticed how comfortable she was now, not physically, but mentally. Rescue would reach them tomorrow, and this whole nightmare would be over. She wouldn't recommend being in a plane crash, not fun on any level, but she thought she'd gained a friend from the experience. She felt a small ping of astonishment that she would ever consider Captain Sourpuss Tight-ass Justice a friend, but she'd discovered he wasn't a sourpuss, and the only thing tight about his ass was the way it looked, which was pretty damn yummy.

"You're going to sleep," he commented. "I can tell by the way you're breathing."

She hummed an agreement in her throat. He adjusted his position, pulling her closer, and she settled into his arms, against his warmth, as if she had always slept there.

19

On the third morning, the day dawned sunny and bright. When Cam crawled out of the shelter, he discovered that he was considerably stronger than he had been the day before, plus his headache had lessened. The swelling of his eyelids seemed to have lessened, too. He didn't feel like jumping hurdles or running marathons, but he walked unaided, albeit slowly, and without having to hold on to anything.

Bailey was feeling better, too; her fever had broken during the night, drenching her with sweat. That hadn't been a good thing, not in below-freezing weather. She had made him roll onto his side facing away from her, and she had pulled off her damp clothes and put on dry ones. Considering the very limited space in the shelter, he wished he could have seen the contortions, but he hadn't cheated by taking a peek. After she'd turned into a statue when he kissed her, he didn't want to spook her again. In the same spirit, he'd made doubly sure he hadn't prodded her with an erection even though he'd awakened several times with a real urge. The time was coming, though . . .

But first they had to get off this damn mountain.

Their food situation was becoming critical. There were two candy bars left, and they were becoming weak from lack of food. The fact that they'd both slept most of the past thirty-six hours had helped because they hadn't burned many calories, but if they weren't rescued today . . .

He hadn't revealed to Bailey how disturbed he was that they hadn't been rescued yesterday. A satellite should have picked up the signal from their ELT, and even though the mountain had had cloud cover all day, a rescue team could have been dropped off at a lower, more accessible location, and made it up to them.

The problem was that an ELT was battery-powered, and would transmit for only twenty-four to forty-eight hours. They'd passed the twenty-four-hour mark yesterday morning, and were fast coming up on the forty-eight; if the signal hadn't been picked up by then, it wasn't going to be picked up at all. When a rescue team hadn't reached them yesterday, he'd started to worry that maybe the ELT's batteries had been weak and had petered out before a search had even been started.

He looked up as Bailey made her way through the trees back to the shelter, stopped in front of it, and gave him a determined look. "You have to stay out here a while," she said, and her tone of voice didn't give him any options. "I can't stand it any longer. I *stink*. I don't care how cold it is, I have to wipe myself off and put on clean clothes. And after I finish, *you* have to clean up."

"You put on clean clothes last night," he pointed out, just to devil her. "And I don't have any clean clothes."

"That's your fault," she shot back. "I don't know what made you think you needed only one change of clothes for an overnight trip."

"Maybe the fact that one is all I ever carry."

"Yeah, well, you have to plan for emergencies. What if you'd spilled coffee down your clean shirt at breakfast? You'd be stuck."

He wanted to laugh, but he didn't. Maybe it was the way she stood so ramrod straight, or the mulish set of her jaw, that made him think better of it. But it was funny, listening to her lecture him about clothes. Maybe if she were still wearing the sophisticated pants and jacket she'd worn when she boarded the plane the lecture wouldn't have seemed so out of place, but her appearance now made bag ladies look fashionable.

She wore so many clothes she had no shape, and the flannel shirt tied over her head was the crowning touch. No, maybe that would be the socks on her hands. Then again he had her shirts and pants wrapped around him, because he obviously couldn't wear them. If she looked better than he did, that was really bad. And if he could have gotten her socks on over his hands, he'd be wearing a pair of them, too.

"You win," he said, smiling. "I should have packed more. I'm going to poke around the plane while you're cleaning up, so take your time."

Immediately her green eyes shadowed with worry. "Are you sure you're strong enough —"

"I'm sure," he cut in. "I feel a lot better today." Okay, "a lot" was stretching it, but he'd had all he could take of lying around, and he wanted to check out some things.

She chewed her lower lip. "Call if you start feeling dizzy or anything," she finally said, and dropped down to crawl inside the shelter.

Cam turned and surveyed the wreckage, studying it with the eye of a pilot. He looked at the trajectory, marked by broken trees and debris. He saw where the left wing had dipped and caught a jagged outcropping of rock; that was probably where he'd lost the wing. The plane had then skewed violently to the right, and almost out of the trees into the rocky slope, which would have been a disaster.

What had saved their asses was that the fuel hadn't ignited. The impact of crashes were survivable a lot of times, but the resulting fire wasn't. Even with the engine dead the electrical wiring still could have sparked a fire. Maybe Bailey could have made it out alive, but he certainly wouldn't have.

The fuselage wasn't resting on the ground, but was sort of propped on the broken right wing, and impaled on a tree. The limb sticking through the fuselage was what had anchored the plane, kept it from flipping upside down. As long as the limb held, the plane would stay there. He hoped to hell it didn't break while he was in the cockpit; wouldn't that be a bitch?

He hauled himself up onto what had been the copilot's seat, before Bailey scavenged the foam pads and leather upholstery, and was now little more than a frame. The first thing he checked was the ELT. "Fuck," he said softly, as soon as he flipped the switch. The indicator light was off — the battery was dead. The big question was: Had a satellite picked up the signal before the battery died, or had the battery been dead from the beginning? The ELTs were inspected once a year, as per code. The battery could have been dead for months, because the reality was that, other than the yearly inspection, no one checked the damn things.

If the satellite had located the beacon, he was fairly certain Search and Rescue would have gotten to them sometime the day before. They hadn't, and now he didn't think they would, at least not in time. What troubled him most was that he hadn't heard any Civil Air Patrol planes flying their search patterns, or a helicopter. He'd radioed their location, and though they hadn't actually gone down there they were close enough that they'd have been able to hear a helicopter searching that sector.

He knew a search had been organized. A plane didn't go missing for two days with no one bothering to look for it. So where the hell were they searching?

He wondered if his radio transmission had gone out. What if CAP had no real idea where to look for them? Mathematically the target area could be mapped out using the amount of fuel and maximum flying distance, but that was a hell of a lot of territory. Logically, he had to assume he and Bailey would have to get themselves off the mountain, something that was much easier said than done.

The cockpit display was shattered and the radio busted, neither of which was a surprise. He poked around, looking for anything of use that Bailey might have overlooked, but she'd been thorough. Just about all that was left in the cabin that was usable were the seat belts; he pulled the shoulder straps as far out as possible before cutting them. The lap belts weren't all that long, but they were usable. They were strong, and could be made into webbing to help them carry stuff. It wasn't as if they could pack Bailey's suitcases again and roll them down the mountain, but maybe he could use the seat belt webbing and turn one of the cases into a sort of backpack, just for carrying the most essential items. If his roll-aboard case was large enough, it would be the ideal size.

The flashlight that he always put in the cockpit with him was gone. He was sure it was around somewhere, but likely covered by the new snowfall they'd had, and God only knew how far it had been flung on impact. They needed it, if they were going to walk out of here, but the odds of finding it weren't good.

Likewise, he needed his suit jacket, and the trail mix bars in the pocket — the bars more than the coat. The coat would be nice, but he'd be able to get by the way he was doing now; they really, really needed the bars for energy, though.

Now that he knew the ordeal they faced, he looked at the wreckage with different eyes. Sharp pieces of metal or glass could be made into a crude knife, just in case his pocketknife was lost, or a blade broken. It never hurt to have backup. Maybe he could make some snowshoes, too, using some of the material Bailey had used to construct their shelter. The theory was simple enough. The question was whether or not the terrain was too rough, because snowshoes were clumsy.

The farther they descended the more plentiful food would be. He was a Texas boy; he'd grown up setting traps for rabbits and squirrels. He'd be able to find food for them then, but they needed food now.

He made his way to the other side of the plane. The slope was much steeper there, with stretches of almost sheer rock that would have made it impossible for him to navigate if he hadn't been able to hold to the trees. He followed the path upward that the plane had made coming down, using his upper body strength to pull himself up when there was no footing to be found.

Snow crunched under his shoes, came up over the sides, and worked its way inside, wetting his socks and freezing his feet. He couldn't trek out of here wearing dress shoes, but damn if he knew what he'd do. He could ignore the cold for now; hell, maybe Bailey would warm his feet against her breasts again. If that didn't make cold feet worthwhile, he didn't know what would.

Debris was scattered all up the glide slope: chunks of twisted metal, torn wiring, broken limbs. If the wiring was in pieces long enough to be useful, he picked it up, wound it into coils, and stuck it in his pocket. He found a bent wing strut, then the twisted and crumpled door from the pilot's side. Looking at the damage, he could only think that he'd got off easy with a concussion and a gash on his head. Off to the side he could make out a round shape that had to be one of the tires, covered with snow.

He reached a tree that looked as if it had been struck by lightning, with the bark blown off and limbs broken, except the gash in the wood was new. The damage was about twenty, twenty-five feet up the tree. He looked around and saw small pieces of debris but nothing large enough to have been the wing.

He climbed higher, curiosity driving him, but found nothing. Finally the cold got to him, forced him to turn back. He was feeling a little breathless and shaky, too, which wasn't unexpected considering how much blood he'd lost. The only good thing about being too hurt to move was that the time spent had let him adjust to the altitude.

He paused a moment to orient himself. He was above and to the left of the crash site, with their little shelter lying just uphill and to the right of the site. Bailey had yet to reemerge, so she was still inside with those premoistened wipes of hers, doing away with b.o. and the sticky residue of fever-sweat. He grinned, wondering if she would come rushing out without all her clothes if he yelled for help. She might, but then she'd kill him, so he refrained. He'd see her naked, but all in good time.

His gaze swept past the shelter, up the mountain, looking for the summit — and saw the wing, about forty yards away.

"I'll be damned," he said. He'd been looking on the left side of the wreckage for the wing; he must have assumed that because it was the left wing, it would have landed on the left side of the site, because he couldn't remember actually giving the location any thought beyond locating where it had struck the tree. Instead, when it was torn off, the wing had flipped up and over, coming down on the right side. It was, in fact, almost directly behind the shelter, but farther back than they had ventured.

Cautiously he worked his way over to it. By the time he reached it he was seriously tired, but breathing fairly easy.

Unimaginable forces were at work in a crash. Metal was twisted and bent as if it were made of flimsy cloth, rivets popped, nuts and bolts sheared as cleanly as if they had been cut. The wing had been bent in two by the force with which it struck the tree, the metal tearing open along the stress line. He could see the framework, the yards and yards of electrical wiring hanging from where the wing had attached to the plane, the cables, the ruptured fuel tank.

Something that looked like a deflated balloon, hanging out of the ruptured tank, caught his attention.

He stood there, staring at it, the back of his neck prickling with the sudden awareness of danger. Fury swept over him, a rage so powerful his vision misted over with a red haze.

There hadn't been a mechanical malfunction. The plane had been sabotaged.

20

Cam wasn't in sight when Bailey crawled out of the shelter. She was as clean as she could get without having a real bath and she felt a little shaky, but immensely better. She still had a headache, but it wasn't nearly as severe as it'd been for the past two days. With the fever finally broken, the only places she ached were where she was bruised. The dizziness and nausea weren't completely gone, and she definitely felt weak from the combination of fever and lack of food. Overall, though, she could feel a vast improvement in her physical condition.

"Cam?" she called. There was no answer, and a tingle of worry trickled down her spine. He was too weak to go traipsing off on his own. What if he'd fallen? Alarmed, she followed his footprints to the plane, then saw where he'd gone around it. He wasn't anywhere in sight. "Cam!" she called again, louder this time. "Cam!"

"I'm up here."

His voice came from farther up the slope. She turned and caught a glimpse of him through the trees, working his way down.

"What are you doing up there?"

"Looking for the wing."

What difference did it make where the wing was? It wasn't as if he could reattach it to the plane and fly them out of here. Maybe it was a pilot thing, wanting to know where all the parts were. What concerned her was that he'd gone so far from the camp, alone, in his weakened condition — and wearing dress shoes. His legs would be soaked to the knees, and his feet would be icy.

Annoyed, she started up the steep slope to meet him — partly to give him assistance if he needed it, but partly so she could get started blasting him for his carelessness. Her annoyance grew with every step, because each one of them was difficult; she had to hold on to trees, practically crawl over rocks, and once she stepped into a hidden hole and one leg sank thigh-deep into snow. She yelped in shock, then said, "Damn it!"

"What happened?" Cam asked sharply. He was working his way around a rocky outcropping and was currently out of sight.

"I stepped in a hole," she called back, scowling in his direction even though he couldn't see her expression. She pulled herself out of the hole and brushed the snow from her pants. Some of it had gotten down into her hiking boot; she could feel the iciness spreading on her leg. She pulled the sock off her right hand and began digging under the top of the boot, removing the remaining snow before she got even more wet.

Cam stepped around the rock; he was using the trees as handholds, just as she was. "Did you twist your ankle?"

"No, I just got snow in my boot," she said, disgruntled. She straightened and pulled the sock back on her hand as she glanced up at him. What she saw made her stiffen, as if bracing for a blow.

She had seen his face cold and expressionless, she had seen the way his mouth quirked when he was amused, she'd seen him grin, seen the wicked sparkle in his eyes when he was making some sarcastic comment. This expression, however, revealed another person entirely. His mouth was a grim line, his gray eyes narrowed and lit with a cold fury that sent a chill down her back. His face was white with anger, making his eyes look all the more vivid and piercing. If she had ever seen anyone with a killing expression, she was seeing one now.

"What's wrong? What happened?" She

stood motionless, her eyes wide as she watched him approach.

He reached her and took her elbow in his hand, turning her around and drawing her with him. "Someone tried to kill us," he said, the words terse. "Rather, I think someone tried to kill *you*. I was collateral damage."

Bailey stumbled, shocked speechless for a moment. "What?" she asked incredulously, her voice climbing into a squeak. Her heartbeat leaped into a gallop.

His strong hand held her as she recovered her balance, his fingers tightening on her elbow. "The fuel tank was sabotaged to make it register more fuel than it actually held."

Her thoughts split in two directions. Part of her mind concentrated on the fuel tank, trying to understand how, while the rest of her brain was preoccupied with his bald statement that someone had tried to kill her. "*Me?* How? Why do —" She clamped her lips shut on the incoherent babble and took a deep breath. "Start over. What makes you think the fuel tank was sabotaged, and why do you think I'm the target?"

"When the wing was torn off, the fuel tank ruptured." He paused. "You did know the fuel tanks are in the wings, right?'

"I've never given it any thought," she said

honestly. "I don't care where they are, so long as they hold fuel." They reached the shelter and stopped, both of them a little breathless from exertion.

Cam turned her to face him, holding both her elbows now. His grim mouth curved into a brief, wintry smile as he looked down at her. "There was a clear plastic bag in the tank. Extremely low tech. You fill the bag with air, close it up, and it takes up volume in the tank. You can trick the valve to show the tank is full when in reality most of the space in the tank is taken up by the bag. And because it's clear, you can't see it when there's fuel in the tank."

"But . . . but — *why?*" Muted anguish filled her tone. This whole experience had been a nightmare, but she'd coped. She'd handled the terror of crashing; she'd handled being solely responsible for their survival that first day. She'd handled freezing cold, miserable wind, lack of food, being sick and feverish, even being dirty; she didn't know if she could cope with the idea that someone had deliberately tried to kill them. "Why do you think I'm the one —" Her throat clogged.

"Because Seth Wingate called J and L the day before we left, asking about your flight," he said bluntly. "He's never done that before."

The words hit her like a body blow. "Seth —" For all their hostility, she'd never thought he'd physically harm her. She'd never been afraid of him, even though she knew he had a hot temper. She even understood his and Tamzin's hostility toward her, because she was certain if she'd been in their shoes she'd have felt the same way. That didn't mean she'd liked it, or them, but she'd understood it. To know that someone hated her enough to try to kill her made her sick to her stomach. She wasn't an angel, but neither was she a low-life scum who deserved killing.

"No," she said numbly, shaking her head. It wasn't that she didn't believe him, it was that the whole scenario was more than she could grasp. "Oh, no . . ." In her memory she heard the echo of Seth's snarled *You bitch, I'll kill you* the last time she'd talked to him, when she had let him provoke her into taunting him with a possible reduction of his trust fund disbursement. She'd never before responded to any of his jibes and accusations, instead acting as if he hadn't said anything at all. If that had tipped him over the edge . . . this was all her fault.

She grasped for any flaw in Cam's theory, any hole in his logic. "But . . . but you have more than one plane. . . . How would he know which one?"

"If you know anything about planes, you could figure out which one we'd use for your flight to Denver. The Lear — nope, it's the biggest plane, the one we use for cross-country. The Skyhawk doesn't have the necessary altitude to cross the mountains, so it was either the Skylane or the Mirage. I would have used the Mirage, but it was in for repairs — and now that makes me wonder if the Mirage wasn't deliberately damaged, forcing us to use the Skylane."

"But why? What difference would it make?"

"Maybe he's more familiar with the Cessnas. I do know he's asked Bret about flying lessons before, and Bret steered him to an instructor. Flying isn't the same as sabotage, but it shows he was interested. And hell, the information isn't hard to get. I don't know how he worked it, if he damaged the Mirage himself, or if he talked to Dennis and found out the Mirage was in for repairs. The only way we'll find out for certain is to ask Dennis — or go straight to the cops and let them do the asking, which is my preference."

"When we're rescued —" she began, but he shook his head, interrupting her.

"Bailey . . . no one's coming for us. No one knows where we are."

"The ELT. You said the ELT —"

"It's dead. The battery's dead. Or the ELT was tampered with, too. Either way, it isn't working. I'm not even sure my radio was working, there at the end. I know it was at the beginning, but thinking back, I can't remember exactly when I last heard radio traffic."

"But how can that be timed?" she demanded. "How do you make a radio stop working at a certain time? How could anyone know where we'd be when we ran out of fuel?"

"Our location would be simple math. A weather report would give the winds, I'd be flying at normal power, the Skylane has a known range. Our *exact* location couldn't be pinned down, but someone smart could figure out how big the plastic bag should be to displace *X* gallons of fuel, and make sure we had enough to reach the mountains." He lifted his head and looked around him, at the silent, majestic, unbelievably rugged landscape. "I'd say getting to the mountains would be critical to the plan — somewhere remote, where the plane wreckage likely wouldn't be found. Hell's Canyon is pretty damn remote. The hiking trails don't even open for another month, so there isn't anyone in these mountains to maybe spot the plane coming down and give searchers an idea where to look."

"How do you know I'm the target?" she asked miserably, because she was dying inside. "How do you know it isn't you?"

"Because Bret was supposed to take the flight," he pointed out. "He was going to take it even though he was sick. Karen called me at home at the last minute to take his place, because he was too stubborn to admit he shouldn't be flying. Face the facts, Bailey," he finished with an undertone of impatience.

"So you —" Her throat closed on the words, nausea rising in her throat. She swallowed, tried to get control of her voice. "So you're the —"

"I'm the unlucky bastard who got to die with you, yeah."

She flinched at the words, the hated tears burning her eyes. She wouldn't cry, she *would not*.

"Hell," he said roughly, cupping her chin in his cold hand and tipping it up. "I meant that he would look at it that way, not that *I* do."

Bailey managed a tight little smile that didn't waver too much, though hurt had congealed in her like a giant ball. She handled it the way she always had, by locking it away. "You have to look at it that way; it's certainly how I would. You had the bad luck to fill in for a friend, and you almost died because of it."

"There's another angle."

"Oh, really? I don't think so."

She was completely unprepared for the way his expression changed, morphing from the cold, set anger of the past several minutes to something that was almost more alarming. His gaze grew heated, the curve of his mouth that of a predator closing in on his prey. He adjusted his grip on her chin so that his thumb probed at her bottom lip, pulled it open a little. "If I hadn't almost died," he drawled, "I might never have found out that cold-ass bitch act you put on is just that: an act. But you're unmasked now, sweetheart, and there's no going back."

21

Bailey snorted, glad for the momentary distraction, which she suspected was why he'd changed the conversation. "For that matter, I thought you were a stick-up-your-ass sourpuss." She knew the subject of someone trying to kill her wasn't finished, but she needed some time to absorb the details, time for her emotions to settle.

"You did, huh?" He tweaked her lower lip, then released her. "We'll discuss that later. God knows we'll have plenty of time, because we won't walk out of here in a day — or even two days."

She glanced around the site; strange how familiar it had become, how safe she felt here in comparison to how she felt about striking out on their own. For one thing — the shelter. They couldn't take it with them, and the thought of building another one *every day* was daunting. On the other hand, there was no food here. If no one was coming for them, they had to save themselves, and that meant getting off this frozen mountainside before they became so weak they couldn't.

"All right," she said, bracing her shoulders. "Let's get packed up."

His lips quirked a little in that way he had. "Not so fast. I don't think I could make it very far today, and we could probably both use another day to get acclimated to the altitude."

"If we wait another day, we'll be out of food before we even start," she pointed out.

"Maybe not. If we could find my suit jacket, I put a couple of trail mix bars in the pocket. I haven't mentioned it before because neither of us was capable of looking for the coat, plus I expected we'd be rescued and wouldn't need it."

A couple of bars would double their food supply, and could well make the difference between living and dying. He also needed a coat, any coat, before they started out. Thinking of clothing sent her thoughts down another path. "You can't walk out of here with those shoes."

He shrugged. "I have to. They're all I have."

"Maybe not. We have the leather I cut from the seats, plus plenty of wiring to use as laces. How hard can it be to make some moccasin-type coverings for your shoes?"

"Probably harder than you think," he said drily. "But it's a great idea. We'll take today to get ready. We need to drink as much as possible, to get ourselves hydrated before we start out. If we could melt the snow faster, we could drink more."

"A fire would be nice," she agreed with just a hint of sarcasm. The only heat source they had was their body heat, which *did* melt the snow they packed into the mouthwash bottle, just not very fast. "Too bad neither of us packed a box of matches."

His head came up and his gaze sharpened. He turned and stared at the plane. His entire posture shouted that he'd just remembered something.

"What?" Bailey demanded impatiently, when he didn't say anything. "*What?* Don't tell me you have a box of matches hidden somewhere in that plane, or I swear I'll take all my clothes away from you."

He paused, said thoughtfully, "That just might be the most peculiar threat anyone's ever made to me," then headed to the plane.

Bailey hurried after him, crunching through the snow. "If you don't tell me —!"

"There's nothing to tell you yet. I don't know if this will work."

"*What* will?" she yelled at his back.

"The battery. I might be able to start a fire with the battery, if it hasn't discharged too much, and if the weather isn't too cold. For all I know, the battery might be dead. Or damaged." He began pulling away the limbs that blocked him from the wreckage.

Bailey grabbed a limb and started tugging, too. The propellers hadn't been turning when they crashed so the trees had suffered less damage than they would have otherwise, but that meant fewer of the limbs were broken, which in turn meant they weren't easy to move out of the way. Where was a hatchet when she needed one? "You can start a fire with a battery?" she asked, panting, as the limb sprang back into place. She gritted her teeth and attacked again.

"Sure. It produces electricity, and electricity equals heat. That's simplistic, but if there's enough juice left in the battery" — he twisted a limb until it snapped, then tossed it aside — "I can connect a strand of this wiring to each of the terminals, then to a piece of wiring that I've stripped the insulation from. With luck and enough juice, that'll heat the uninsulated wire enough that it'll ignite a piece of paper, or some kindling if we can find any wood that's dry."

"We have paper," she said instantly. "I

brought a little notebook, plus a few paper-backs and magazines."

He paused and slid a glance at her. "Why? One book I could understand, but you were going white-water rafting. I've been rafting, so I know how tiring it is. You'd have been too beat to do much reading. And what was the notebook for?"

"Sometimes I have a hard time sleeping."

"You could've fooled me." He grunted as he grasped another limb and pulled. "You've conked out both nights."

"And these are such *ordinary* circum-stances, aren't they?" she said sweetly. "I've been absolutely *bored* to sleep."

He chuckled. "Considering how much we both slept yesterday, the wonder is we slept at all last night."

"The benefits of being sick and concussed, I guess."

When they'd moved enough debris that he could get to the battery, he huffed a big sigh of relief. "It looks okay. I was really afraid it wouldn't be, given how much damage there is back here."

"Can you get it out?"

He gave a brief shake of his head as he surveyed the bent and twisted metal that partially covered the battery. "No way, not without some metal cutters. But if I can get my hand in here without slicing my fingers off —"

"Let me do it," she said quickly, moving to his side. "My hands are smaller than yours."

"And not as strong," he pointed out, leaning his shoulder past a tree and reaching as far as he could with his right hand. As he did she noticed that his fingernails were blue with cold, and she winced. She knew from experience just how miserable and painful bare hands felt in this cold and wind.

"You need to warm your hands before you get frostbite," she said.

He made one of those male grunting sounds that could have meant anything from "I agree" to "Stop nagging," and other than that paid absolutely no attention to her. She couldn't force him to warm his hands, so she crossed her arms and shut up. There was no point in wasting her breath talking to him. The sooner he either failed or succeeded, the sooner he'd stop to take care of himself.

She stood it for about three seconds. "A plain case of testosterone poisoning, if I've ever seen one," she commented.

His head was partially turned away, but she saw his cheek crease as he grinned. "Are you talking to me?"

"No, I'm talking to this tree, with about the same result."

"I'm okay. If I can get a fire started, I'll get warm then."

Some imp of Satan whispered to her and she said, "Well, if you're *sure*."

"I'm sure."

"Because I thought I might warm your hands the same way I warmed your feet, but since you're okay — never mind."

Her words hung in the frozen air. Part of her wondered if she'd lost her mind, but she couldn't unsay them, so she tried her best to look casual.

He went very still, then slowly backed out, straightened, and turned to face her. "Maybe I spoke too soon. My hands really hurt."

"Then you'd better hurry with that fire," she said cheerfully, and made a shooing motion with her hands. "Chop-chop!"

He gave her an "I'm going to get you" look, then reached back into the plane's innards. The angle at which it was resting made reaching anything awkward, and the trees were in the way. Finally he said, "Okay. Now let's cut some wire. We need to have everything ready before I try this, because if there is any juice there may not be much, and one try may be all we get."

"What do we need to do?"

"First, we fix a place as sheltered from the

wind as we can manage, and make a fire ring with rocks. Then we find some dry wood to use as kindling. Probably some of the smaller pieces you stuck into the shelter to fill in gaps will have dried a little by now. I doubt we'll find anything any drier. If you'll do that, I'll start scraping some inside bark from these trees."

The wind was a problem; it swirled through the mountains, meaning there really wasn't a sheltered area. Finally, frustrated, she opened up her suitcases and stood them on end, lining them up and making a rough hook shape in front of their shelter. It was an imperfect solution, at best, because the suitcases couldn't be so close to the fire that *they* caught on fire, so they afforded only partial protection from the swirling wind.

She cleared snow out of the enclosed area, then Cam used the screwdriver from the tool kit to drive into the frozen earth, over and over, breaking it up. He used the claw of the hammer to dig out the loosened dirt. The fire pit was only a few inches deep when he hit rock, but it would have to do.

There was a plethora of loose rocks for lining the bed of the pit. Cam gathered them while Bailey looked for dry wood. As he'd predicted, the driest that she found came from their shelter. Every time she pulled a stick from its place, she blocked the space that was left with a new branch she broke from a tree. They still had to sleep in that shelter one more night, so she wanted it as snug as possible.

Using his knife, Cam peeled a section of outer bark from one of the trees, then scraped the inner bark until he had a double handful of what looked like the makings of a bird's nest. Carefully he laid out the fire with the scraped bark and some rolled-up pieces of paper torn from her notebook, the kindling on top of that, then some bigger pieces of wood on top of the kindling. "It's green wood so it isn't going to burn all that hot, but the good news is it won't burn fast, either," he said. If they could get it to burn at all, she thought, but left that unsaid.

If the battery worked, they had to have some means of getting the flame from the plane to the waiting fire pit. The wind was unceasing, which meant he couldn't just roll up a sheet of paper, catch it on fire, and walk it over to the pit. Bailey emptied all their first-aid supplies from the olive drab metal box and gave it to him. Using the handy screwdriver again, he punched holes in one end of the box, lined the bottom with some of the dirt from where he'd dug the fire pit, then stripped some of the needles from one of the evergreen trees and put them on top of the dirt. He rolled up another sheet of paper, then cut off a strip of gauze and loosely stuffed that inside the roll of paper.

Bailey watched silently. They had stopped talking during the past half hour, because the preparations were simply too important. Having a fire was too important. She felt almost giddy at the thought.

All that was left was the wire. He completely stripped the insulation from a short piece, then bared both ends of two much longer pieces. Then he quickly connected one end of each of the longer pieces to the short piece, twisting the bright copper wires together.

They approached the plane side by side. She held the box, he had the wiring.

"If this works, when the paper ignites, close the lid and take the box to the fire," he instructed. "I'll have to unhook the wires from the battery so we don't waste any of the power; we might have to do this again. Rolling the paper up will slow down the burn, you'll have plenty of time to get it to the fire. Go ahead and start the fire."

She nodded. Her heart was pounding so hard she felt almost sick. *Please work,* she prayed silently. They needed this so much.

She stood beside him, holding one of the

insulated wires positioned so the uninsulated wire was touching the tip of the roll of paper. Cam had to actually wedge himself between one of the trees and the wreckage, a foot or so off the ground, so he could reach the battery with both hands and connect the long wires, one to the positive terminal and one to the negative. When he was finished he remained in position, his sharp eyes trained on the first-aid box in Bailey's hands.

She tried not to shake as she held the naked wire to the paper. "How long will it take?"

"Give it a few minutes."

She felt as if they gave it an hour. Time crawled as they stared in an agony of anticipation at the paper, waiting to see a wisp of smoke, a scorch mark, praying for something to happen.

"Please, please, please," she chanted under her breath. Nothing was happening. She closed her eyes because she couldn't bear to watch any longer. Maybe if she didn't watch the paper would start smoking. It was a childish hope, a silly thought, as if her watching would prevent it from happening.

"Bailey!" Cam's voice was sharp.

Startled, she opened her eyes. The first thing she saw was the thin, delicate twirl of smoke, as transparent as a mirage. It snaked upward almost hesitantly, to be snatched by the wind. Gingerly she shifted her position just a little, bringing the box closer to the protection of her body.

A brown scorch mark began growing on the paper, spread to the piece of gauze tucked inside. A bright, tiny flame began licking at the gauze. The edges of the paper caught, began to curl.

"Go," said Cam, and she carefully closed the lid so it was almost shut, then wheeled and hurried to the fire pit. Kneeling beside the squat pyramid of kindling, paper, and wood, she gingerly opened the box, trying as best she could to shield the fragile flame. The roll of paper was half consumed.

Carefully she eased the roll out of the box, inserting the burning end into the nest of scraped bark and paper in the center of the stack.

With a spark, the lovely little flame whooshed brighter and higher, leaping to engage the paper, and then the bark. As she watched, the small sticks of kindling began to smoke, then glow as the flame caught.

She began laughing, so beside herself with delight she thought she might cry, too. She turned to see Cam striding toward her, a wide grin on his face. With a whoop of joy, she jumped up and ran to him, throwing herself into his arms. He caught her, lifting her off the ground and giving her a little whirl.

"It worked!" she half shrieked, clutching those broad shoulders and wrapping her legs around his hips for support.

He didn't say anything. His hands gripped her butt, pulled her tightly against him. A rock hard erection pushed urgently into the softness and heat between her legs. Startled, she looked up, her laughter dying in mid-note. She saw his vivid gray eyes, glittering with heat and hunger, and then he kissed her.

22

His lips were cold, but there was heat in the kiss, a compelling hunger and expertise that drew an immediate response from her. The usual alarm sounded deep in her brain, but somehow it was less urgent, and for the first time in a long, long time, maybe forever, she ignored it. Instead she coiled her arms around his neck and kissed him back, parting her lips at the insistence of his and allowing the smaller penetration of his tongue to entice her to play.

A confusing mixture of guilt and pleasure filled her. She hadn't meant to precipitate this, hadn't meant to go down this road, yet now that she was on it she wanted to stay.

She should take her legs from around his hips, she knew, and withdraw to a less blatantly sexual footing, but she didn't. Feeling the strength of his response was exciting, and the beckoning pleasure of what awaited her, if she just relaxed and let go, was a siren song of temptation. Even beyond that, and underlying it, was the simple pleasure of being held, the very human need for physical contact. She had been starved for so very long and suddenly she couldn't deny herself any longer.

She had slept in his arms, and he in hers, for two nights now, and though their physical closeness had been a necessity to share their body heat and stay alive, knowing that didn't lessen the elemental trust and sense of connection formed during those long, dark hours. She'd never had that before, never wanted it. The best way to safeguard her emotions was to keep people at a distance, to rely only on herself; she'd learned that in lessons both early and hard.

Yet here he was, close and strong and warm, and she didn't want to let him go.

He was the one who broke off the kiss, lifting his mouth and looking down at her with a heavy-lidded gaze. The bruises under his eyes and the scrapes on his face should have diminished the potency of that look, but somehow didn't. Hot intent burned there, promised more. His hands still gripped her bottom, still moved her against his swollen penis in a slow rhythm that made her heart pound and her breath come in gasps. Then the corners of his mouth kicked up in a rueful smile. "I hate to break this up," he drawled, "but I'm about to fall down."

She stared blankly at him for a second, then realization dawned. "Oh, damn it! I forgot! I'm sorry —" As she spoke she hastily unwrapped her legs from his waist and slid to the ground, her face turning hot from sheer mortification. How could she have forgotten how weakened he was? Just yesterday he'd barely been able to move around under his own steam!

He staggered a little and she quickly jammed her shoulder under his arm, grasping him around the waist to steady him. "I can't believe I forgot," she mumbled as she helped him toward the fire.

"Personally, I'm glad you did. I enjoyed the hell out of it, but what little blood's left in me went south and I got light-headed for a minute." He winked at her as she helped him sit down in front of the fire. The only thing to sit on was the trash bag of clothes they used to close the entrance to the shelter, but they were using her clothes for everything else, so why not a seat?

"God, that feels good," he groaned, holding his hands out to the flame, and with a start Bailey looked around.

She'd forgotten about the fire, too. How could she? Excitement over the fire was what had sent her running to him in the first place. But as soon as he'd kissed her, *zap,* everything else in her mind had vaporized. What if the flame had started flickering out, what if she'd needed to adjust the position of the suitcases to block the wind? This fire was precious; she should have been watching it, tending it, not jumping into Cam Justice's arms and riding him like a rodeo bronc.

"I am *such* a numskull!" she muttered, watching the smoke spiral upward before being dissipated by the wind. The greener limbs had begun to sullenly burn and the smoke was heavy, far heavier than it would have been with a really good campfire, but miraculous for all that. "I should have been watching the fire."

"But we wouldn't have had as much fun," he pointed out. "Stop beating yourself up. You aren't responsible for the world."

"Maybe not, but if this fire had gone out, neither of us would have been a happy camper." Standing as close as she dared, she cautiously held her hands out. She could feel the heat of the fire on her face and it felt so good she almost moaned. People took things for granted, like heat, and food, and water. She didn't think she would ever again travel without a pack of waterproof matches in her luggage, as well as a few other necessities she could think of, like a satellite phone. And long, insulated underwear. And a few dozen packages of field rations.

"We'd have lived. We've lived without one for two days. This just makes us a little more comfortable."

Physically, maybe, but it was a huge boost to her morale, which had suffered some major blows already today, and it was just midmorning.

"Although," he continued reflectively, "I wish I'd remembered about the battery before now."

"Why? Neither of us was capable of doing anything about it," she pointed out. "You were too injured to move, and I was too sick."

"If I'd known what the payoff was for starting a fire, I'd have dragged my naked body through the snow to get to that battery."

Bailey burst out laughing. The ridiculousness of that image was just too much to resist — not the naked part, because she thought he'd be damn fine to look at, judging from the parts she'd already seen, but anyone being willing to drag themselves naked through snow for a kiss.

He reached out and hooked his fingers in her waistband, dragged her backward. "Sit down," he instructed. "We need to have a talk."

There was an iron note of command in his voice. Bailey lifted her eyebrows at him. "Is that tone of voice supposed to make me click my heels and salute?"

"It worked on the men under my command."

"Of which I'm not one," she pointed out.

"Thank God. If you were, there are regulations against some plans I have involving you. Do you want to hear about them or not? If you do, sit down."

He pulled on her waistband again. More than a little stunned, she found herself sitting beside him on the stuffed trash bag. The contents were a little uneven and she listed to one side; he put his arm around her shoulders to hold her upright.

"I'm being honorable here," he said, slanting a glittering look at her, "and giving you fair warning. But this is probably the only time, so don't get used to it."

She started to ask, Fair warning about what? but was afraid she knew the answer. Maybe "afraid" was the wrong word. Alarmed, yes. Annoyed. Terrified. And most of all, excited.

"When I thought we would be rescued, I tried my damnedest not to do anything to scare you off," he said as casually as if they were discussing the stock market. "I knew you'd be back on your own territory, able to call the shots and avoid me if I made my move too soon. But now, I know rescue isn't coming, and I have you to myself for days, maybe as long as a couple of weeks. It's only fair to tell you I plan to have you naked in a day or so, once we're at a warmer altitude and we're stronger, feeling better."

Bailey opened her mouth to say something, anything, then closed it because no words came to mind. Her mind was oddly blank. She should be . . . what? All her usual responses to a come-on seemed to have taken a vacation, because she couldn't think of a single one. She tried again to say something, only to once more close her mouth. She should shut him down cold, the way she usually did when people tried to push past her defenses, and it flummoxed her that she couldn't.

"Is there a reason you're imitating a guppy?" he asked with a little smile, tilting his head to the side.

Afraid she wouldn't be able to say anything coherent, she shook her head.

"Any questions?"

A million of them flooded her brain, most of them wordless, all of them things she couldn't say. She shook her head again.

"In that case, we need to get to work. We have a lot of preparations to make."

He started to stand, but this time it was Bailey who did the waistband-grabbing.

"I left the pack of aloe wipes, and your clean change of underwear in there," she said, indicating the shelter. She was glad her voice was working again, though what she was saying seemed completely inane. "You need to get cleaned up, or you're sleeping outside tonight."

Five minutes later, she could still hear him chuckling inside the shelter.

Getting her mind back on practical matters was an effort, but she was galvanized by the realization of how much needed to be done before they began trying to get themselves off the mountain.

One of the first things, as Cam had said, was to rehydrate themselves, and that meant melting as much snow as possible, as fast as possible. The rocks he'd placed around the fire absorbed heat, but didn't seem so hot that the plastic mouthwash bottle would melt, so she packed the bottle with snow and put it on the outside of the ring, against the rocks.

The second thing, as far as she was concerned, was Cam himself. He was woefully unprepared for this weather. *She* had plenty of clothes, not a single item of which would fit him. On the other hand, she had plenty of them, and if one might not fit him, maybe two together would. His shoes were the big problem, but she had the leather from the seats. She needed to make a sort of overshoe that would provide insulation, keep the snow out of his shoes, and give him traction — a tall order, because she wasn't a cobbler. She couldn't cut and sew the leather into the proper shape. Neither could she waste the leather by cutting it in a way that wouldn't work at all.

She got the notebook and pen to try drawing a diagram of how she needed the leather to fold, so she could work out the cuts beforehand. She clicked the pen and drew the point across the paper, but the paper remained blank. The ink in the pen was frozen. Frustrated, she laid it against the warming rocks, too. Some of the snow in the mouthwash bottle had already melted, she saw. No doubt about it, fire was a marvelous thing.

The plane had been sabotaged, and Cam's logic about who had been behind it was hard to refute. Seth had tried to kill her, and hadn't cared at all that he would have killed Cam, too. That was difficult to accept, difficult to comprehend. The last two days had been a nightmare of pain and freezing cold and sickness, of pushing herself far past her endurance. But sitting there watching the fire, she felt her spirits rise. No wonder primitive people danced around a fire; they were probably hysterical with joy to have heat and light. She leaned forward, stretched her hands out, and felt the heat on her palms. She would never, ever take heat for granted again.

She felt better. The swelling and redness in her arm had receded. Cam was better. No one was coming to rescue them, so they would rescue themselves. For the first time, she felt confident in her own mind that they would survive, because now they had fire.

And when they got back to Seattle, there was going to be hell to pay.

23

The J&L office was like a morgue. Sheer physical necessity had forced both Bret and Karen to go home for sleep on the second night, but as Karen said as she left, "It feels as if we're abandoning him."

The Civil Air Patrol search grids had turned up nothing. Bret had requested all the Skylane's service records and he and Dennis, the head mechanic, had gone over and over them, looking for any unresolved problem that could have become catastrophic. There was nothing; the Skylane had been reliable, in for the normal maintenance and small things like the pilot's window defroster.

The man in charge of the search, a stocky gray-haired man named Charles MaGuire, was dedicated but pessimistic. He was a veteran of these searches, and he knew they almost never turned out well. If there were survivors, you knew it almost immediately.

Otherwise, if the crash was in a remote site, the bodies, or what was left of them, would eventually be recovered . . . most of the time.

"The transponder signal was lost . . . here," he said, pointing to a point east of Walla Walla. "In the area of the Umatilla National Forest. We've concentrated the search grid there. But FSS picked up a garbled Mayday transmission about fifteen minutes after that. A lot of static, only a few words came through. We don't know if it's the same plane, but we don't have anything else corresponding with a Mayday message. Obviously we don't know the rate of speed or altitude, but we have to assume that the plane was in trouble from the time the transponder was lost."

"Cam would have radioed then, he wouldn't have waited fifteen minutes," Bret pointed out.

"Maybe he tried. Obviously there were problems with the radio, too. I don't know of any electrical problem that would take out both the radio and the transponder, but an accident of some kind . . . they were hit by something, maybe."

"If the plane was capable of staying in the air that long, Cam would have landed it," Bret said positively. "You're talking about a guy who never panics, who was practically born with wings."

"If something hit the aircraft, he could have been injured," MaGuire said. "The passenger, Mrs. Wingate . . . was she the type who would panic and be useless, or would she have grabbed the wheel and kept the plane from nosediving?"

"She'd have grabbed the wheel," Karen said immediately. As usual, she was right there, listening to every word. "And the radio. It doesn't take a genius to figure out the radio. But she was in the backseat; she'd have had to lean over the seats and reach around Cam to get the wheel."

"Anything could have happened up there. If they lost the windshield, you're talking about a tremendous wind force, but you can't drop your speed enough to make any real difference, or you crash. She probably wouldn't have known how to reduce power, anyway." MaGuire shrugged. "The point is, something was very wrong with the aircraft. We can think of scenarios, but we simply don't know what happened, only that something did. If we take the point at which the transponder signal was lost, estimate the distance they could have flown in the length of time before the Mayday transmission was received, then that stretches the search area all the way to Hell's Canyon. That's a damn big area, and some of the roughest terrain in the country. My guys are in the air every day-light minute, but this is going to take time."

Bret was a member of the Civil Air Patrol, but he was excluded from the search for several reasons, the most compelling being that J&L Executive Air Limo hadn't closed its doors when Cam's plane disappeared. There was still a business to run, and people who depended on that business for their living. He hadn't flown the day before because he hadn't had any sleep, but today he had to take a charter. Karen refused to let the business grind to a halt, even though her eyes were swollen from crying and every so often she would bolt to the bathroom for another crying jag. Bret would make the flight she'd scheduled, or answer to her.

"There's also the possibility the plane was tampered with," Karen told MaGuire, giving Bret a defiant look. She was sticking to her theory, regardless of what he said. He wearily pinched the bridge of his nose.

MaGuire looked startled. "What makes you say that?"

"Mrs. Wingate's stepson called the day be-fore the flight, asking about it. He's never done that before. They aren't friendly, and that's an understatement. She controls all the money, and he wants it."

Scratching his cheek, MaGuire darted a glance at Bret. "That's interesting, but in itself doesn't mean anything. Would the stepson have had access to the aircraft, and would he have known how to sabotage a plane so it wasn't detectable beforehand?"

"He has some knowledge of planes," Bret said. "He's taken a few flying lessons, I think. But whether or not he'd know enough —" He shrugged.

"He could have hired someone," Karen interrupted irritably. "I didn't say he had to do it himself."

"True," MaGuire admitted. "What about access?"

Bret scrubbed his hand over his face. "This is a small airfield. It mostly serves private planes, and our charter service. There's a fence around the field and security cameras, but nothing like what there would be at a commercial airport."

MaGuire walked to the window and looked out, his hands stuffed in his pockets. "You don't want to think there's foul play involved, and I have to say, in all the years I've been doing this, I've never seen anything that made me think a plane had been deliberately sabotaged. Until someone presents some evidence that tampering took place, I don't see any point in worrying about it. On the other hand, it's always good to think about security. Is someone here twenty-four hours a day?"

Bret shot a look at Karen. She'd narrowed her eyes and looked belligerent, but she didn't say anything. He guessed that if MaGuire worked here, his personal mail would disappear for the next millennium. "Sometimes, but it depends. The mechanics may work late, or we may have a late flight scheduled. A private plane may come or go. I'd say there's no predictable pattern."

"Not knowing when someone might show up would make it difficult to plan something like that. In the absence of, say, a hole cut in the fence or a break-in here in the terminal, I don't think that's an avenue of investigation that we should pursue. We'd be better off directing our available resources to locating the crash site."

That was the correct response from a man who'd had to make hard decisions before, but Karen didn't like having her theory shot down. She'd accepted that Cam was dead, but she hadn't yet accepted that there was no one she could blame for it. "Stick your heads in the sand then," she snapped, and stalked out of Bret's office.

Bret sighed and dropped heavily into his chair. "I'm sorry," he muttered. "She's having a hard time accepting this. We both are, I guess. I pulled all the Skylane's service records and repair write-ups, and the mechanic and I have gone over them looking for something, anything, that could indicate what went wrong. It's hard, not knowing what happened."

"I'm sorry," said MaGuire. "I wish I could do more. These situations, where we know they're gone but we can't find them, are the toughest we deal with. People need to know. One way or another, they need to know."

"Yeah," Bret said heavily. As if compelled, he picked up the Skylane's file and opened it again, leafing through each copy of the maintenance reports, the fueling slips, the myriad pieces of paper required on each of their aircraft. Karen had everything on computer, backed up at an online data bank, but in the early days they'd lost all their records because of a catastrophic computer crash and filing their tax reports had been a nightmare. Since then they'd also kept a paper file, regardless of how redundant and archaic. Bret and Dennis had even compared each report with the computer file, to see if anything had been left out or entered incorrectly, something they hadn't breathed a word of to Karen because she'd have taken their heads off for even suggesting she'd made an error.

MaGuire watched him with sympathy, knowing how difficult it was to accept that sometimes shit did just happen, with no rhyme or reason.

Suddenly Bret stiffened, and flipped back to the beginning of the file. MaGuire frowned, reading his body language, and went to stand beside him. "Don't tell me you found something."

"I don't know," said Bret. "Maybe I read it wrong. It was the fueling report for that morning." He leafed through the file again, pulling out the paper that was third from the top and staring at it. "That's wrong!" he said forcefully. "That's just fucking wrong!"

"What is?"

"This is! Look at the number of gallons pumped. There's no way."

MaGuire looked at the fuel report. "Thirty-nine gallons."

"Yeah. The Skylane's usable capacity is eighty-seven gallons. This doesn't make sense. The fueling order was to fill the tanks. With a full load, he'd have had to refuel in Salt Lake City, so there's no way he'd take off with less than half what he needed to get there. Even if he had, when he saw the reading he'd have radioed in and refueled at Walla Walla, not flown right past it."

"Yeah." MaGuire frowned at the report, thinking hard. Karen had come to the doorway and stood there, watching and listening, every cell of her body broadcasting her alertness. "We need to get in touch with the fuel company, find out what their records show. Maybe this is an error."

Fueling was handled by a licensed contractor. A phone call elicited the information that their records indicated thirty-nine gallons had been pumped into the Skylane at 6:02 the morning of the flight, and the reports from that day had matched the pump's total. More phone calls, and soon they were talking to the truck's operator, who said flatly, "I filled the tanks, just the way the order reads. I checked the valve, and I visually verified. I even thought it was unusual that so much fuel had been left in the tanks, but thought a charter might have been canceled after the plane was already fueled."

A plane, especially a charter or commercial plane, didn't carry unnecessary fuel. Fuel was heavy, and the more a plane carried, the more power was needed to get it where it was going. Usually the refueling order was for enough to get the plane to its destination, with a little extra in case it had to be rerouted or circumstances called for a delay in landing. "Little" was a relative term, of course, but Mike, who had flown the Sky-lane to Eugene the day before, would never have taken on over half a tank more than what was needed. To be certain, Bret pulled the fuel records from the day Mike had flown the plane. There was no way he could have flown to Eugene and back, and had that much fuel left.

"So what does this mean?" Karen fiercely demanded. "Cam thought he had enough fuel to get to Salt Lake City, but didn't? Somebody tampered with his fuel gauge?" Her fists were clenched, her knuckles white.

MaGuire's face looked as if it had grown additional lines and wrinkles. "It means there's a possibility the fuel tanks looked full when they weren't."

Bret closed his eyes. He looked sick. "The simplest way is to put a clear plastic airbag in the tank," he told Karen. "Fill it with air, no one can see it, and the tank won't hold as much fuel as it should. It isn't complicated."

"I told you!" she said, trembling with pent-up fury. "He must have had something in mind or he wouldn't have called that day!"

"I think we should see if there are any se-curity tapes," MaGuire said briskly.

24

Seth had filled out the required paperwork for becoming an employee of the Wingate Group, met his supervisor, was shown where to report, and given an employee badge. Grant Siebold had greased the way for him, he learned; he didn't have to piss in a cup for a drug test the way every other new employee did. He assumed the "omission" would be discovered at a later date, after any drugs he'd smoked or swallowed would have had time to clear out of his system. He got the message, loud and clear: if he ignored this obvious warning and continued with his old ways, when his urine tested positive for drugs he'd be kicked out on his ass.

He'd have to do some online checking, see how long marijuana showed up in the system. Thank God, smoking a little weed was as deep as he'd waded in the drug pool; his preferred anesthesia was alcohol. But even that was off the table now.

Then he went shopping. He'd seen the dress code, even in the mail room: dark pants, white shirt, tie. The shoes could be lace-ups or loafers, but nothing resembling an athletic shoe. Black socks.

He had always despised the corporate drones and their boring dress code, but now he applied himself with a vengeance to looking just like them. A trip to Nordstrom's, where he resisted the more stylish choices, accomplished that. On the way home he listened to his voice mail messages. Most of them were from people he'd partied with, wanting to know where he'd been last night. He didn't return any of the calls. Tamzin's he deleted without bothering to listen to them.

He remembered that he didn't have any food at home, so he detoured to a grocery store. Again, what he bought was out of his norm, because he didn't even go down the wine or beer aisles. Oatmeal. Cereal. Fruit. Orange juice. Milk. Coffee. His stomach turned flips at the thought of putting any of that in his mouth, but he knew he'd have to eat. Crackers and canned soup rounded out his planned menus.

Life as he'd known it was over. If he were to survive, he couldn't afford any more wrong choices or irresponsible behavior. Bleakness filled him like a rainy day, stretching in an endless parade of weeks, months, years, that all looked exactly the same and promised not one minute of sunshine. So be it. He'd earned the grayness.

After he got home and had put the perishables in the refrigerator, he stripped off his clothes and lay down on the bed, hoping he could nap. The sleepless night he'd spent had left him exhausted, but he couldn't go to sleep. Memories marched through his head like army ants.

He must have dozed eventually, because the ringing of the phone jarred him into a sitting position. Grabbing the phone, he focused blearily on the Caller ID. His pulse gave a leap when he recognized the number. He punched the talk button and said, "Bailey?" in a cautious, incredulous tone.

"Bailey!" Tamzin gave a tittering laugh. "Good God, wash your mouth out with soap!"

Fuck. Seth sat up and swung his legs over the side of the bed. "Tamzin. What are you doing at Bailey's house?"

"This isn't *Bailey's* house," she said viciously. "It was our mother's house, and now it's mine. You don't need anything this big; I have a family and you don't."

"How did you get in?"

"You don't think she changed the alarm

code, do you? It's still the same as it was when Dad was alive. And of course I have a key."

There was no "of course" to it; Seth figured she'd light-fingered the key one day while she was visiting, probably even before their father died.

"Get your ass out of there," he said flatly. "Legally Bailey is still alive, and you can't touch anything."

"What do you mean, legally she's still alive? A death certificate hasn't been issued yet?"

"Don't you ever watch the news?" he snapped. "The crash site hasn't been found yet. There's no body. No body, no evidence of a crash, so no death certificate."

"What's taking so damn long, then? How long can it take to find an *airplane?* It isn't as if it could have crashed in some farmer's cornfield and he wouldn't *notice.*"

The wave of dislike that swept over him was so strong that he had to bite the inside of his cheek to hold back what he wanted to say to her. He couldn't let his temper get the best of him. He could never again say whatever popped into his head, without thought for the consequences. Instead he said, "If she isn't dead, and she finds out you've made yourself at home in what she thinks of as her house, she'll cut your fund disbursement down to twenty dollars a month. Trust me on this."

There was a pause, then Tamzin asked in a radically altered tone, "You mean there's really a possibility she could come back?"

"I mean it's better not to take the chance. The house isn't going anywhere. If it takes us six months to have her declared dead, it'll still be there."

"But I've already told people . . . well, they just misunderstood is all. Oh, you'll get a kick out of this. Her stupid brother called — you know, the one who came to Dad's funeral. She was supposed to meet him in Denver. I let him know just what a bitch she was and how glad we are that she's gone."

Oh, fuck. "What, exactly, did you say?"

"I let him have it with both barrels. I couldn't stand him, the way he wanted to be so friendly when our father had just died. I told him only a fool crossed you, and she'd got just what she deserved."

The satisfaction in her voice was jarring, and like a lightning bolt Seth realized that his sister hated him. Maybe she thought that if he was in prison she'd have sole control of all the money. Or that she could arrange for his murder, and then all the money would be hers, free and clear. Maybe she'd resented him all his life, because their father had made it plain he wanted Seth to succeed him at the Wingate Group. Whatever her reasoning, he suddenly knew beyond a doubt that no one had ever hated him as much as his sister did.

"Just so you know," he said slowly, "I have a will."

"So? It isn't as if you have any other brothers or sisters." Meaning she expected to get his money whether he had a will or not.

"If anything happens to me, I've left it all to charity. You don't get a fucking penny." He disconnected the call and sat there for a moment, shivering. Then he called his lawyer, and turned his statement into fact.

On the first day of his employment, he was there half an hour early. He hadn't been able to sleep much, and he was afraid there might be a traffic tie-up that delayed him. He was unaccountably nervous. How difficult could sorting and delivering mail be? The toughest part would be enduring the curious stares, because he was almost twice the age of the youngest mail-room employee. At least no one would know him on sight, except for a few of the highest-ranked executives, and he doubted he'd see any of them. If he did take mail and packages to their offices, their assistants would take it, not the executives themselves. He was glad of that degree of separation.

The other mail-room employees began filing in, most of them carrying the requisite Starbucks cups. Seth was swimming against the tide there, because he wasn't the coffee-house type. Coffee was okay, but he liked it ordinary and unflavored, and it didn't break his heart if there wasn't any available. Maybe he should cultivate the taste, he thought, to fit in. Or buy one cup of the stuff, dump the coffee, keep the cup, and pour his ordinary brew into it. He wondered how long one of the cups would last before disintegrating.

The other clerks eyed him, unsure what to make of him. Maybe they thought he worked upstairs. What the hell; they were young and he wasn't, so he made the first move. "My name's Seth," he said. "I'm starting work here today."

They exchanged glances. One of the young women, a tall, skinny girl with the cold eyes of a mongoose, said, "Here? In the mail room?"

"That's right."

More glances. "Did you just get out of prison or something?"

Just trying to keep my ass out of one. "No," he replied casually. "I was in a coma for fifteen years, and finally woke up."

"No shit?" one of the guys said, looking startled. "What happened?"

"I huffed a can of nonstick spray."

"Bullshit," the mongoose said. "You'd have to have severe brain damage to be in a coma that long."

Mean, but smarter than these other kids. "Who says I don't?" he finally said, and turned away.

The mail-room supervisor was a short, dumpy, gray-haired woman with the unlikely name of Candy Zurchin and all the fashion sense of a babushka. Her wardrobe seemed to run to navy blazers, gray skirts, and lace-up black shoes, and she ran the mail room with a no-nonsense efficiency that put Catholic schools to shame. Certainly she had the number of all the youngsters under her command, including the mongoose, who said "Yes, ma'am" whenever Candy told her to do something — and said it without sarcasm, which was the remarkable thing.

Seth reined in his ego, his pride, and his temper, and did whatever she told him to do, quietly and without complaining. The work didn't require a lot of brain cells, but when he looked at the job objectively he could see where this was good training, because while it was hugely boring it also required an attention to detail and discipline.

The inclination to slack off was almost over-whelming; some of the clerks gave the job less than their all. He knew that if he were an upper-echelon executive, though, he'd pay close attention to Candy Zurchin's rec-ommendations and comments.

Two days ago, he wouldn't have paid any attention to her at all.

The job was simple: sort and deliver all the incoming mail and packages, pick up all the outgoing stuff, apply the proper postage or shipping labels, pack the stuff that needed packing, and get it all out of there that day. Over and over. It seldom varied, and it never ended. He was astonished by the sheer vol-ume of snail mail. Hadn't these people ever heard of e-mail? But e-mail seemed limited to intradepartment and employee-to-employee communications; letters to outside contacts and important stuff like contracts still went to paper.

Maybe Siebold had given Candy instruc-tions not to let him hide in the basement, be-cause that very first day, she sent him out with a cart piled high with letters, insulated envelopes, and packages. "The way to learn is by doing," she said briskly. "The offices are clearly marked. If you can't find some-one, ask."

The floors he was delivering to were, of

course, the upper ones. If being recognized humiliated him into quitting, Grant Siebold wanted it to happen sooner rather than later.

Seth learned a lot of things. He learned that the mail-room clerks were largely invisible. He learned that one assistant had a perfect manicure because she paid a lot of attention to it. He learned who played computer games. He learned who was liked and who wasn't, something that was easily picked up from the assistants' attitudes. One vice president was drinking on the job; Seth smelled the faint but unmistakable odor as soon as he entered the office, pushing his cart. He also smelled the air freshener that had been sprayed to kill the smell. The assistant caught him sniffing the air and gave him a cold-fish stare that said, "You know nothing, you see nothing, you smell nothing." He nodded and continued on his way.

He learned that he had delusions of grandeur, because not one person recognized him.

25

Late that afternoon, Cam took his new leather overshoes for a test drive — or rather, a test walk. They were crude, laced up part of the way with the laces from his own shoes and electrical wiring the rest of the way, and the holes had been punched into the leather with his knife. But they were supple, they covered his dress shoes and came almost as high as his calf, and Bailey had made them large enough that pieces of cloth — she'd sacrificed a shirt — could be stuffed around his feet for insulation. Plus, without his shoes laced up, he'd been able to wrap part of the cloth around his feet before putting the shoes on. Altogether his feet had a lot more protection now, and, thanks to the fire, were actually warm.

The day had been extremely busy, but oddly not too arduous. They had sat side by side on the stuffed trash bag in front of the fire, she working on his overshoes, he making a rudimentary sled for hauling what precious supplies they had, as well as some rough snowshoes for them. As the snow in the mouthwash bottle melted, they drank it. Because the melt rate was much faster now that they had a fire, for the first time since the crash they were able to drink enough that thirst wasn't a constant factor.

She was oddly content, sitting beside him in mostly silent companionship while they worked. It wasn't that she didn't worry, because how could she not? They faced a long and dangerous ordeal, one they might not survive. The mountains were treacherous and incredibly rugged, unforgiving of mistakes. Even if they did make it out, there was still the fact that someone had deliberately tried to kill them, and all the arrows pointed to Seth.

Proving he was behind it could be difficult. For one thing, all the evidence was here, scattered across the mountainside. Even if the wreckage could be found again, any forensic evidence might well have been destroyed by the elements. On the other hand, cold might preserve evidence; she simply didn't know. She had to face the very real possibility that, even though she and Cam knew someone had tried to kill them, they might never be able to prove who did it.

How could she carry on as before, knowing that? How could she deal with Seth? She couldn't. She would have to renege on her agreement with Jim, and even under the circumstances she didn't like doing that.

But all of that was in the future, assuming she had one. All she was assured of, she realized, was right now. The concept was both liberating and comforting. She wasn't on tenterhooks, waiting for a rescue that she now knew wouldn't be coming. They had a plan, and they were putting that plan into action, relying on themselves and their own ingenuity, their personal determination and fortitude. She was good with that.

Once she had his overshoes made, she began working on the problem of his clothing. Taking two of her flannel shirts — and thank God she'd brought plenty in preparation for two weeks of rafting — she buttoned them together, making one big, ungainly garment out of two. It was an awkward arrangement, but otherwise there was no way anything she had would fit over his chest and shoulders. The sleeves were too short, and the two unused ones dangled down his back, but it was a layer of warmth he hadn't had before and wasn't constantly having to be repositioned. He put it on immediately. The two shirts didn't match so the look was odd, but neither of them cared. What mattered was warmth.

She would wear the down vest, they decided. For one thing, it fit her. He would wear her brand-new rain poncho, which wasn't much insulation but would at least block the wind. She had a couple of other ideas for additional layers, if she could work out the details.

Keeping his legs warm was a problem. While she could put on a couple of pairs of sweatpants, all he had was his suit pants. Even though the sweatpants had an elastic waist, he couldn't get in them. He was too tall, and she was lean from all the workouts she did.

Finally she had an idea. "I think I can make something like chaps," she told him.

He looked up from the snowshoe he was making from tree branches and wiring, his brows arched in fake astonishment. "Don't tell me you packed a cowhide, too."

"Smart-ass. Just for that, you can freeze."

He leaned over and bumped her shoulder with his. "I apologize. What's popped out of the Idea Factory this time?"

"I have four microfiber towels."

He thought about it, and nodded. "Okay, I can actually see taking towels along for a two-week camping trip. Makes sense."

"Thank you, Mr. Skeptical," she said drily, then explained. "If I cut small slits all along the edges — not cutting the edge itself, but about an inch back — then I could weave a strip of cloth through the slits to make a kind of belt and tie that end around your waist, then lace the edges together the same way down your legs, and presto, you have chaps."

"For someone who can't sew, you're a handy wench to have around."

She had to laugh. "I think it's ironic. I've always hated anything to do with a needle and thread, and now I'm not only having to make stuff, I literally had to sew up your head. That's just *wrong.*"

He looked at the snowshoe in his hands and chuckled. "Tell me about it. I've always hated snow, hated being cold — and now look."

"If you hate snow, how do you know how to make snowshoes?"

"The principle is simple — distribute the weight over a wide surface — so all you have to do is make a general grid design that you can strap on your feet."

She watched him painstakingly construct the shoe from the smaller, more flexible evergreen branches, his big hands nimble and sure, as if he'd done this a thousand times. Again she was aware of that strong

307

sense of contentment, the feeling that she was right where she belonged — not stuck on this mountain, but here in the moment.

The struggle to survive, as exhausting and harrowing as it had been, had been external. Inside, she'd felt oddly free of stress, because her choices were simple: do what needed to be done, or die. Make a shelter. Stay as warm as possible. Melt snow to drink. That was it. There was nothing complicated about survival, whereas life was nothing *but* complications.

At the same time, man, she couldn't wait for this to be over. She wanted a hot shower. She wanted a flush toilet. She wanted a *supermarket*.

"Know what I'd love to eat, right now?" she said in a tone rich with longing.

He made a choking sound, then howled with laughter. Bailey's mind was wandering down the produce aisle, so far removed from sex that she stared blankly at him for a moment before realizing what she'd said. Her face began to heat. "Not *that.*" She swatted him. "Shut up. I was thinking of a big pot of corn and potato chowder, steaming hot, with bacon crumbles and shredded cheese on top." Her mouth began to water as she all but tasted the dish.

He wiped the tears from his eyes with his

thumb and said, "Me, I'm more of a meat eater." The glittering look he gave her told her that he wasn't thinking of prime rib, and her face got hotter.

She pushed at him, trying to force him off the trash bag. "Leave! Get away from me, you dirty-minded *man*."

"Guilty as charged," he drawled, not budging an inch. "On all counts."

"I mean it! Leave. Go try out your booties."

He was still chuckling as he got up and walked off. Bailey watched him stride toward the plane, her gaze unconsciously lingering on his ass and long legs before she realized what she was doing and jerked her eyes forward. Though the fire didn't really need it, to occupy herself she added another piece of wood.

He was seducing her, she realized, truly seducing her, using words and laughter and their forced reliance on each other. She couldn't walk away from him, she couldn't wall him out, because their survival depended on their closeness, their cooperation.

Maybe she should just let him do it, her innate caution whispered, let him have sex. The seduction process would stop then; there wouldn't be a point to it any longer. If she gave him sex, he'd stop this assault on her heart because he'd think he had already won it. Her emotions would still be safe.

She had never fallen in love, never wanted to. Now, for the first time in her life, she was afraid that the danger of doing so existed, afraid that Cam Justice could get close enough to really do some damage to her when he moved on. She was trapped by their circumstances, and the realization was terrifying. She couldn't get away from him, and she couldn't freeze him out. If he had been any other man she could have, but he saw through her. She didn't know how, but he did. Somehow she'd revealed too much and there was no going back.

She hated feeling vulnerable. She hated the suspicion that in just a couple of days she'd come to care for him more than she'd ever let herself care about another human being, except perhaps her brother, and that was entirely different.

The urge to track Cam with her gaze was maddening, like an itch. Unwillingly she gave in, watched him crouch down to inspect the right wing. Not much of his hair was visible, because of the bandage still wrapped around his head, but at least his head was covered against the cold. He looked like a hobo, with his hodgepodge of clothing — most of which he had tied on or wrapped around him, rather than actually wearing it, but he still carried himself as if he wore a military uniform because he didn't give a damn if he looked like a hobo. He didn't give a damn if he had to wear a woman's clothes, though admittedly her selection of sweatpants and flannel shirts wasn't exactly feminine. She suspected he wouldn't have cared if everything she'd brought was adorned with ruffles. What did a ruffle matter, when matched against that kind of self-confidence?

Suddenly he reached up under the plane, then got on his knees and began working himself beneath the wing. Alarmed, she got to her feet. Was he crazy? No, the plane hadn't moved an inch in all this time, but that didn't mean it *couldn't,* especially with him moving around under it, bumping it, tugging on it.

"What are you *doing?*" she called, hurrying toward him, intending to physically drag him out if he didn't come out of his own volition.

He backed out, dragging something black with him, a grin on his bruised face.

"Found my jacket," he said triumphantly.

The plane was black. The jacket was black. Crushed into the snow, blending against the background of crumpled black metal and dark shadows, the fabric had gone unnoticed. It was great that now he had a coat, at least, but all she cared about was —

"Are the bars still in the pocket?" she asked urgently.

He patted the pocket, still grinning. "Yep."

"Do we eat them now, or in the morning?" She was so hungry she thought she could wolf down half a cow.

"In the morning, for energy. We can split another candy bar tonight. Sugar saps your energy, but all we're going to be doing tonight is sleeping anyway."

She sighed. He was right, and she knew it; she hated it, but she agreed. The bars were probably frozen, anyway; better to let them thaw overnight.

He beat the snow from the coat, and Bailey took it from him. It would need to dry before he could wear it, but at least they had a fire so they *could* dry it. He must have been thinking along the same lines, because he looked up at the sky. "I'd better gather more firewood while we still have some light left. Is there anything else you need to do?"

"Work on those towel chaps for you, I guess. They won't take long, maybe half an hour. By the way, how are the overshoes?"

"They're great. Snow didn't get down in my shoes, and I actually have better traction now." He wrapped his hand around the back of her neck and drew her to him for a quick kiss, a kiss that somehow lingered. Then he pulled away and gingerly rested his forehead on hers. "Let's get everything finished, so we can go to bed."

26

Bailey was worried that when Cam said "bed" he had more on his mind than "sleep," but he was not only a better strategist than that, he was realistic about his own physical condition. They each ate half a Snickers, drank water, brushed their teeth, and settled down in the shelter. The fire flickered in its pit, sending tiny pinpricks of light through the shelter's stick walls, so for the first time they weren't in complete darkness. The amount of heat wafting inside couldn't have been much, but it was either enough to make a difference or the mental lift the fire afforded made them think they were more comfortable.

The faint warmth wasn't enough, however, to make sharing their body heat unnecessary. Even as she curled into his arms, she was achingly aware that every time she did so she was deepening the connection she felt to him. There was nothing else she could do, no way off this road and no way to avoid the emotional cliff looming in front of her. Even though she knew the drive would end in a crash, all she could do was enjoy the ride.

Despite being physically more comfortable, sleep was elusive. She dozed, but woke every time he left the shelter to replenish the fire. Once she woke with a start when he shook her, saying, "Bailey. Bailey. Wake up. It's okay, honey. Wake up."

"Wha—?" she asked groggily, struggling up on her elbow and peering at him in the faint light. "What's wrong?"

"You tell me. You were crying."

"I was?" She swiped her hand over her wet cheeks, said "Damn it," and flopped back down beside him. "Nothing's wrong," she muttered, embarrassed. "I do that sometimes."

"Cry in your sleep? What are you dreaming about?"

"Nothing, as far as I know." She hitched one shoulder in a shrug she hoped was negligent. "It just happens." And it was stupid. She hated crying anyway, but when there was no reason for the tears they were particularly annoying. They made her look weak, something she couldn't bear. She turned on her side away from him and cradled her head on her arm. "Go back to sleep, everything's okay."

His warm hand slid over her hip, settled into place on her stomach. "How long have you been doing this?"

She wanted to tell him all of her life, so he'd think it was nothing unusual and forget about it, but her mouth blurted the truth before her brain could catch up. "About a year."

"Since your husband died." The hand on her stomach was suddenly tense.

She sighed. "A month or so after that."

"So you loved him."

She heard the sudden flat tone of his voice, the faint incredulousness, and abruptly she was sick to death of living with all the misconceptions and assumptions. "No. I respected Jim, I was fond of him, but I didn't love him any more than he loved me. It was a business deal, pure and simple — and it was his idea, not mine." If she sounded defensive, well, she was — defensive and sick of the whole thing. At the same time, she felt relief at finally talking about it to someone. Other than herself, only Grant Siebold knew the whole story, and she seldom saw him now that Jim was dead.

"What kind of business deal?"

She couldn't read anything from his tone now, but she didn't care. If he thought the worse of her for going along with Jim's scheme, and profiting from it, then better she should find out now.

"Jim had a . . . Machiavellian streak. He was really good at reading people, he was really good at making smart business decisions, so I guess he got in the habit of manipulating people. Don't get me wrong, he wasn't unscrupulous. He had a strong moral code."

"I always liked him. He was friendly, down-to-earth." Still that noncommittal tone.

"I enjoyed working for him. He didn't cheat on Lena, didn't look at his female employees as his private playground, so I didn't have to be on guard with him. He was friendly, interested, he gave me investment advice that I sometimes took and sometimes didn't. He said I was too cautious. I told him I didn't take chances with my retirement. He laughed at me, but he was interested in some of my investment choices." She took a long breath, let it out. "Then Lena died."

"And he got lonely."

"That's not what happened," she said irritably. "The thing is, Jim and Lena had made out their wills years before, when Seth and Tamzin were little. Like most couples, they made each other their total beneficiaries, leaving it to the surviving spouse to figure out what to leave to the kids. Even though Jim went on to make a huge fortune, he had a blind spot when it came to his will and they had never updated it. When Lena died, he realized he had to change the will, but when he looked at his kids he didn't like what he saw."

"Neither did anyone else," Cam said drily. "Still don't."

"We're in total agreement there." Especially since Seth was the only person on their suspect list. "Anyway, he was in the process of setting up their trust funds when he found out he had advanced cancer. He'd always hoped Seth would wake up, settle down, and start taking an interest in the company, but when he found out he was dying he knew he couldn't afford to give Seth any more time. So he hatched this plan."

"Let me guess."

"Oh, please do."

He made an amused sound in his throat at her sarcastic tone. "You're a tough cookie, you know that? That's probably why he picked you. Okay, here goes: he wanted to hire you to oversee their trust funds, but knowing you'd have to deal with Seth and Tamzin for the rest of your life, you charged so much that the only way he could afford you was to marry you."

She went from being annoyed to laughing, because, oh, if she'd only known! "I wish I'd been that smart. But you're sort of on the right track. Remember, Jim was a manipulator. He was always juggling this and dangling that, pulling on a thread over here, tossing a bone over there. He couldn't help it; that was his basic personality. He didn't have any hope for Tamzin, but he never gave up on Seth. He thought that if he married me and gave me control of their trust funds, Seth would be so humiliated and outraged that he'd see the light and turn his life around."

"Yeah, that worked out real well. If Seth's seen a light, it was the one above the bar in his favorite nightclub."

"Yeah," she agreed, and sighed. "If Seth started acting like a mature adult, then I was supposed to turn over control of the trust funds to him — *but* Seth couldn't know about that part of the arrangement. Jim said Seth was smart enough he could fake whatever he had to fake long enough to get control, then revert back to his old self. Jim was sure this would work. So far, it hasn't."

"He didn't have to marry you," Cam pointed out. "He could have handled all of this simply by the way he set up the funds."

"Marrying me was part of the stick he used

to beat Seth into shape, though. If I was just a trustee of the fund, in the background, Seth might be pissed about it but he wouldn't be humiliated. It was everything about me: I'm younger than Seth; I supposedly took advantage of an older, dying man; I moved into their mother's place. Having people know that Jim gave control of their money to *me* was supposed to be the kicker."

He said, "Well, that answers one question."

"And that question is . . . ?"

"Why he married you."

Wasn't that what this entire conversation was about? What else was there? "What's the other question?"

"Why *you* married *him*."

Bailey thought she'd answered that. She frowned over her shoulder at him, though he likely couldn't tell in the tiny amount of light coming from the fire. "I told you. It was part of the deal."

"But why did you agree to it? Marriage is an extreme step."

Not in her family, it wasn't. Her parents had looked at marriage as a legal convenience, to be dissolved whenever they got a whim to move on. She didn't go into all that, though. Instead she said tiredly, "I've never been in love. So I thought — why not? He was dying. I would do that for him, and in

320

exchange he'd make sure I was financially secure."

"So he did leave you some money."

"No, he didn't." The relief had faded, and she was getting very sick of this conversation. "I have privileges, such as living in the house, my expenses taken care of, and I'm paid a very nice salary for managing the funds, but I didn't inherit anything. All of the privileges stop if I remarry, but the salary continues as long as I do the job."

"Got it. I won't even ask what you consider a 'very nice' salary."

"That's good, because it's none of your business," she said acerbically.

He snuggled her closer and rested his chin on her shoulder. "I'm curious about something, though. You've truly never been in love? Ever?"

The change in subject made her uncomfortable and she shifted restlessly. "Have *you?*"

"Sure. Several times."

It was the "several" that made her wince. If it were truly love, wouldn't it be only once? Real love shouldn't fade. Real love expanded, made room for children and pets and a host of friends and relatives. It didn't come with an expiration date, and after that date you moved on to someone else.

"When I was six, I fell madly in love with my first grade teacher. Her name was Miss Samms," he said reminiscently, and she could hear the smile in his voice. "She was fresh out of college, she had these big blue eyes, and she smelled better than anything I'd ever smelled in my whole life. She was also engaged, to some bastard who wasn't nearly good enough for her, and I was so jealous I wanted to beat him up."

"I gather you were smart enough not to try," Bailey said, relaxing. She couldn't take a six-year-old's crush on his teacher seriously.

"Barely. I didn't want to upset Miss Samms by killing her boyfriend."

She snickered and he punished her with a pinch. "Don't laugh. I was as serious as a heart attack. When I grew up, I was going to ask Miss Samms to marry me."

"So what happened to this grand love?"

"I started second grade. I was older, more mature."

"Um hmm. Mature."

"I chose a more appropriate love interest the next time. Her name was Heather, she was in my class, and one day she pulled up her skirt and showed me her panties."

She barely managed to restrain another snicker. "My goodness. Heather was fast."

"You have no idea. My heart was broken when I found her showing her panties to some other boy."

"That's a big disillusionment. I wonder how you had the strength to go on."

"Then when I was eleven . . . Katie. Ah, Katie. She could hit a fastball like you wouldn't believe. She moved away before I could get up the nerve to make a move on her — but she moved back when I was fourteen. When I was sixteen, Katie wrestled me down and took advantage of me."

"Oh, I bet! Excuse me, I mean, the nerve of some girls!"

"She was strong," he said seriously. "I was so scared of her I let her do what she wanted with me for a couple of years."

She reached back and returned the pinch he'd given her.

"Ouch! Is that any way to treat a man? I'm telling you how I was used and abused, and instead of feeling sorry for me you abuse me some more."

"Poor pitiful you. I can tell you were traumatized. That's why you named a certain body part 'Good Time Charlie.' "

"I considered 'Go Slow Joe,' but I had to go with my heart."

Bailey completely lost control of the giggles that had been building up. "Justice, you're so full of it the shelter needs shoveling out."

"You're laughing at all my trials and tribulations in the romance field? I don't know if I should tell you the rest."

"How many more are there?"

"Just one, and this one's serious. I married her."

That *was* serious, and the laughter went out of Bailey. She could tell by the change in his voice that he wasn't kidding any longer. "What happened?"

"To be honest, I don't know. I didn't cheat on her and I don't think she cheated on me. We got married while I was still in the Academy; her father was an officer, she'd grown up with the military lifestyle so she knew what to expect. Her name was — is — Laura. All the moving from base to base, the separations, she took in stride. What she couldn't handle, I guess, is civilian life. When I got out of the military, that's when things went to hell. If we'd had kids I guess we would have stuck it out, but without them, the hard fact is we didn't love each other enough to keep things together."

"Thank God you didn't have kids!" she said fervently, before catching herself. "Sorry. It's just — well . . ."

"You've been there."

"Too many times."

"I guess that's why you're afraid to let yourself care about anyone," he said, and her heart jumped violently in her chest. *She* knew why she kept people at a distance, but she'd never before revealed so much of herself to anyone. Too late, she saw that his easy humor had undermined her guard and she'd given him an enormous advantage, one that he wouldn't hesitate to use.

As if to underscore the thought, he gave a low sound of satisfaction, the sound of a predator with its prey in its grasp, and said, "I've got you now."

27

"Men!" Bailey muttered as they trudged through the snow. "Can't reason with 'em, can't shoot 'em."

"I heard that," Cam said over his shoulder. "Besides, you don't have a weapon."

"Maybe I can smother him in his sleep," she mused to herself. Her voice was muted by the cloth over the lower half of her face, but evidently not muted enough.

"I heard that, too."

"Then I assume you can hear this: You're a stubborn, mule-headed, macho *idiot,* and if you get dizzy and fall you'll probably break some bones even if the fall doesn't kill you outright, and I swear I'll leave you bleeding in the snow!" Her voice rose until she was shouting at him.

"I love you, too." He was laughing, and she wanted to kick him.

She had seldom been as furious with anyone as she was with him, but then she seldom lost her temper. You had to care about something to get angry, a fact that made her even angrier. She didn't want to care about him. He'd made what she thought was a dumb-ass decision, and she wanted to mentally shrug and let it go because he was an adult and he could bear the consequences of his dumb-ass decisions. Instead, she was fretting. And worrying about him. *And* letting her imagination run away with her, picturing all sorts of awful things that could happen to him, and there wasn't a damn thing she could do about it because he was a stubborn, mule-headed, macho idiot.

He was pulling the rough sled he'd made, loaded down with the things they'd decided they would need along the way, plus one addition he'd made that morning: the battery. Getting it out of the wreckage had taken a herculean effort, one that had left him pale and sweating — a big part of the problem was that the battery was so heavy, over eighty pounds. But he'd tested the battery, it still had juice, and he'd decided that they should take it so that if anything happened to him, she'd still be able to make a fire.

She'd yelled at him that they would have been doing without a fire anyway. He'd said no, they weren't, that when they got out of the snow and he could find dry wood, he could make a fire using friction, because he'd been a Boy Scout and knew how.

"Fine," she said. "Then you can teach me, and we won't need to drag a hundred-pound battery around! You have a *concussion*. You lost a lot of blood. You shouldn't be exerting yourself this much!"

"It doesn't weigh a hundred pounds," he'd retorted, completely ignoring the rest of her comment — as well as the fact that the battery came damn close to weighing that much.

So he'd wrestled the thing onto the sled, and the weight had made the wooden runners dig into the snow. Seeing that she couldn't dissuade him from taking the battery, she'd grabbed the traces and started pulling the sled herself, only to have him firmly move her out of the way and take over the job of sled dog.

"You can carry the backpack," he'd said maddeningly, referring to his roll-aboard suitcase that he'd rigged with straps.

She was so angry she'd considered hitting him with a snowball, but she was afraid of what damage any chance blow to the head, no matter how slight, might do to him. She also didn't want to get his clothes wet, not when she'd gone to so much effort to keep him as warm as possible. Smothering him in his sleep, though . . . that was a possibility.

The terrain was horrifyingly rugged, and unseen hazards lay under the snow. Sometimes the slope was so steep she had to hold the sled from behind to keep it from sliding past him and dragging him down the mountain. Sometimes there simply was no going down at all without ropes and mountain climbing equipment, so they had to trudge up and around until they discovered a less treacherous descent. After walking for what he said was three hours, she doubted they had managed to descend more than perhaps a hundred feet, but they had zigzagged for miles. And she was still angry.

The snowshoes were clumsy and required that she lift her knees with each step, as if she were marching in a band. Her muscles were burning from the effort. Maybe she didn't lift her foot high enough, but the tip of her right snowshoe suddenly caught on something buried in the snow and catapulted her forward.

She managed to get her hands out to break her fall, going down on her right knee and then sort of rolling to a sitting position. Her hands and knee stung, but sharp pains shot through her right ankle. Muttering curses under her breath, she held her shin and gently rotated the ankle to see if she'd sustained any structural damage.

"Are you hurt?" Cam went to one knee beside her, his gray eyes worried above the strip of red flannel that covered his own nose and mouth.

"A sprain, but I think I can walk it off," she said. Flexing the ankle hurt, but after the initial throb the pain seemed to lessen. She tried to get up, but was hampered by the snowshoes that remained securely tied to her feet. If the right one had come off when she fell, her ankle probably wouldn't have suffered at all. "Help me up."

Catching her hands, he tugged her to a standing position and held her while she gingerly put her weight on her foot. The first step was fairly painful, but the second one was less so. "I'm good," she said, releasing his hands. "No serious damage."

"You can ride on the sled if it's bothering you," he said, frowning as he studied her gait as intently as if she were a Thoroughbred.

Bailey stopped in her tracks, thunderstruck by what he'd just said. Did the man have *no* sense? "Are you crazy?" she yelped. "You can't pull me all the way down this mountain."

He glanced up, the expression in his eyes cool and determined. "I not only could, I'll do whatever I have to do to get you home."

For some reason, that simple statement rattled her. She shook her head. "You shouldn't feel that way. It isn't your fault we crashed. If anything, it's mine."

"How do you figure that?"

"Seth," she said simply. "He made me angry, I threatened to decrease the amount he gets every month, and he retaliated. It's my fault, all of it. I shouldn't have lost my temper."

He shook his head. "I don't care what you said, that doesn't justify him trying to kill two people."

"I'm not justifying his actions. I'm saying I triggered them. So you have no reason to feel responsible —"

He tugged his face mask down. "I don't feel responsible for the crash."

"— or for me," she finished doggedly.

"Things aren't that simple. Sometimes blame has nothing to do with responsibility. When you treasure something, you want to take care of it."

Treasure. The word arrowed through her, pinned her to the wall. He shouldn't be saying things like that. Men *didn't* say things like that, it was against their natures. "You can't treasure me," she said, automatically withdrawing from him, mentally if not physically. "You don't know me."

"Well, now, there we disagree. Do the math."

The last sentence left her completely at sea. "What math? Are we talking about math?"

"We are now. Let's take a break, and I'll explain it to you."

He tied the sled harness to a tree so it wouldn't start sliding down the mountain, then they sat side by side on a rock, one that had absorbed a little heat from the bright sunlight. Bailey had on so many clothes she couldn't really feel the heat, but at least a chill wasn't seeping through the layers. She pulled her own face mask down and closed her eyes for a minute, pretending the sun was warm on her face.

They drank some water, then each had a bite of the remaining trail mix bar. They'd halved one of the bars that morning, and they'd agreed to slowly eat the other one during the course of the day, figuring their energy would flag more on the first day. As they went down in altitude and oxygen became more plentiful, theoretically they'd have more energy — theoretically. She hoped they were right, because so far everything had been a real struggle.

He said, "This is the fourth day, right?"

"Right.

"Counting from eight o'clock on the first day, which was when we took off, it's now been seventy-six hours."

She nodded. The first day, the day of the crash, didn't count as a full twenty-four hours. Counting from the time they'd taken off, the first twenty-four hours had ended at eight a.m. on the second day. "I'm with you so far."

"How long does the average date last? Four hours, maybe?"

"Four or five."

"Okay, let's say five hours. Seventy-six divided by five is the equivalent of . . . fifteen dates. If you divide it by four, we're on our nineteenth date. Split the difference; we're on our seventeenth date."

"All right," she said, amused by the inventiveness of his theory, whatever it was. "Seventeen dates, huh? We're practically going steady."

"Going steady, my ass. We're on the verge of moving in together."

She gave him a quick look to see if he was joking, but he was watching her with a steady determination that rocked her down to her boots. He was serious: he wanted more than she'd ever given anyone. He wanted more than sex. He wanted a commitment — and there was nothing in the world that terrified her more.

But he . . . he said he *treasured* her. Bailey couldn't remember anyone ever, in her entire life, putting her welfare ahead of his, but that was what Cam was telling her.

"I can't —" she began, intending to give him some excuse, whatever she could think of, as a reason for not becoming involved.

"You can," he interrupted. "You're going to. We'll take things slow, ease you into the concept. I understand you're dealing with childhood baggage, and that's the kind that's hard to unpack. But sooner or later you'll trust me, and accept that someone cares about you."

She wanted to tell him that wasn't a problem. People had cared about her before. Logan cared about her. Jim had been fond of her. She had friends . . . well, she'd had some friendly acquaintances before she married Jim, but they'd distanced themselves from her so she supposed they hadn't been real friends. Even her parents had cared about her, about all their children, though ultimately not as much as they cared about themselves.

She wanted to tell him all that. The words formed in her brain, but refused to form on her tongue. She would be lying. Trust *was* a problem. Her defense against people not caring about her was that she wouldn't care first. In the don't-care category, she was already ahead of everyone she met.

Except him. She couldn't get away from him. She couldn't forget about him, couldn't *not care* about him.

And . . . he said he treasured her.

She looked into those sharp gray eyes, and felt the ground fall from beneath her. She was lost, utterly without defense against him. She burst into tears. "Oh, no," she sobbed, mortified. "I can't cry."

"You could have fooled me." He put his arms around her and held her close, rocking back and forth a little in comfort. "I think you're doing a great job."

He was overlooking the obvious. She pulled away and tried her best to suck it up, before she got into real trouble. "No, really. I'll h-have ice on my face."

"Betcha I could melt it," he said, a slow smile curving his lips.

Damn him, she was in such trouble.

28

To give themselves enough time to construct a sturdy shelter, they stopped for the day at three o'clock. They were still high in the mountains, at the mercy of icy winds, below-freezing temperatures, and possibly more snow, though the skies above were clear at the moment. Weather systems could arrive fast, and it wasn't as if they had access to the Weather Channel to keep an eye on conditions. Another factor for stopping then was that they came across a large tree that had fallen across some boulders; the tree provided a ready-made central support, which saved a lot of work. If they continued on for another hour or so, they might not find anything as suitable.

Bailey was exhausted, but to her relief the altitude sickness hadn't returned. Tomorrow, she thought, they could walk a little longer, a little farther — maybe. They were almost out of food, and when the last candy bar was gone, their energy would fast decline. They had to descend far enough to begin finding berries, nuts, edible leaves — anything — or their situation would rapidly worsen.

"I guess the first thing we do is build a fire," she said, looking forward to the warmth and psychological lift.

"Tonight, anyway," he said absently, looking out over the mountainous expanse. "After tonight, I'd rather save the juice for when we're farther down, out of all this wind."

She closed one eye, looking askance at him. That seemed like reverse logic to her. "Don't we need a fire more now?"

"For warmth, yeah, but we survived without a fire for two nights, so we know it isn't strictly necessary. I was thinking about using the fire to signal our location. We can't do it now because the wind dissipates the smoke, and I'll be damned if I've found any location that's completely sheltered, considering how it swirls."

Bailey turned and looked in the same direction where he was looking. The day was clear, the air so cold and crisp that details stood out. The massive mountains reared against the sky, white peaks outlined by pure blue. She could see the snow line, and below that rich green, which promised warmer temperatures and at least the possibility of food. "How far down do we have to go?"

He shrugged. "I don't know. I'm hoping the snow line will be far enough down. This is a federal wilderness area, so the forestry service monitors it for fires. Anything that seems to be man-made gets checked out."

So they could be rescued in a day or two, depending on how long it took them to get out of the winds. Two days ago, even yesterday, she would have been ecstatic at the possibility, but now . . . now it was too late. Two days ago she had been heart-whole. Oh, being warm and well-fed would be nice, but what if, once they were no longer bound together by necessity, Cam's interest in her waned? She didn't trust emotion anyway, and she certainly didn't trust it under emergency conditions.

She was torn, and she hated that. On the one hand, the sooner she could get some separation from him the better. On the other hand, oh dear God, she wanted this to last. She wanted to believe in a happily-ever-after, a love that lasted a lifetime. She knew people who *seemed* to love each other that long, the way Jim had loved Lena, but a niggling doubt had always kept her from buying into the concept. Maybe Jim had loved Lena, but what if Lena hadn't loved Jim? Jim had been mega-rich; maybe Lena had looked around but not seen anything better. Bailey didn't like being that cynical, but she'd seen too much to believe in the fairy-tale version of love.

Love was a crapshoot, Bailey thought, and she'd never been a gambler. She had no idea what to do, how to handle this situation. Part of her wanted to just let go and enjoy being with him as long as it lasted; after all, it was unrealistic to expect a lifetime of happiness, and probably impossible to boot. Only an idiot was *always* happy.

Was the period of happiness worth the un-happiness that followed a breakup? Most people seemed to think so, because they got on the love train time and time again. After getting tossed off they'd mope around a while, maybe act out and do something stu-pid, but eventually they were back at that station, ticket in hand, ready to board. She hadn't thought the momentary gain was worth the pain, so she'd watched the train circle around without her. Now she'd been ambushed and tossed into the baggage car, and no longer seemed to have a choice.

Cam trailed a finger down her cheek. "You've wandered off. You've been staring into space for five minutes."

Wrenched back to the here and now, her

mind was momentarily blank. "Ah . . . I was thinking about what happens when we go home." She mentally applauded herself. Good save! That was a *very* reasonable response, under the circumstances.

He looked grim. "I can't tell you. Without evidence of what he did, probably nothing, and we can't go around making charges without something to back them up or he can sue us for slander."

"He'd love that. That would give him a public forum to air all the things he'd said about me, and you can bet Tamzin would back him up." She felt sick at the thought of a lawsuit that would dredge up every ounce of muck Seth could find or fabricate. She wasn't afraid of real muck, because people who didn't take chances seldom got dirty. There were no shady dealings in her past, no affairs with married lovers, no drugs, no police record of any kind.

None of that would stop Seth, though. He could probably put on the stand fifty people who would swear they'd slept with her, or done drugs with her, or that she'd told them of a sleazy plan to marry a dying man and con him into signing over control of his fortune to her. In fact, probably the only reason he hadn't done that already was that control of the trust funds hadn't been in Jim's will, where it could be challenged. Jim had set up the funds before he died — before they married, in fact — and put her in charge, and her performance had been excellent. Seth would look like a fool challenging *that*. Moreover, the monthly disbursement was very respectable. Nothing compared to the whole of the trust fund, of course, but very respectable.

"I think we have to let him know that *we* know," Cam said. "And have told our suspicions to a third party, so if anything else suspicious happens to you, the finger will point straight to him. Unless he's gone crazy on meth or something like that, he'll understand that there's nothing he can do." He leaned over and kissed her, then briefly caught her lower lip between his teeth and gave a gentle tug. "I also suggest you move in with me, so he doesn't know exactly where to find you. You'd have to be nuts to stay in that house all alone."

Her heartbeat skittered with excitement, and her stomach clenched with dread. Bemused both by his proposition and her mixed reaction to it, she said, "There's a big gap between kissing a few times and moving in together, Justice. Moving makes sense.

Moving in with you, not so much."

"I think it makes a lot of sense," he said mildly. "But we'll talk about it later. Right now we need to get busy or we'll have to sleep in the open."

He dug a pit for the fire while she gathered rocks and wood for both the fire and constructing the shelter. The fallen tree provided most of the wood, because it had been down long enough that the wood was dry on the inside and the branches easily snapped off. They followed the same procedure as before with the battery, and within half an hour small flames were merrily licking at the firewood.

Because there were two of them working, and because Cam had a much better idea what he was doing than Bailey had had that first day, the shelter quickly came together. The angle of the tree where it lay across the large rock created, at the highest point, a space large enough that they could sit up. Cam had positioned the fire so some of the heat would radiate against the rock, and thus into the shelter. Sheltering the fire from the wind was still a problem, so he stacked limbs in a berm on the other side of the fire, building it higher until the flames stopped dancing so wildly.

The end of the job saw them both a little

sweaty and a lot dirty. The dirt factor made Bailey's nose wrinkle, but it was the sweat that was dangerous. Cam sat by the fire while she crawled into their new "home," complete with the pieces of foam she'd insisted they bring along — at least they were almost weightless — to clean up and dry off as best she could.

When she crawled out, once again bundled in layers and layers of clothing, Cam was carefully placing pinecones around the edges of the fire. "Wow," she said. "Now the campsite will smell all Christmasy. That's a touch I hadn't thought of."

"Smart-ass. After the cones are roasted, we can eat the nuts out of them. I wish I'd remembered this yesterday."

"Really? Pine nuts? They really come from pinecones?" Funny how she'd always thought pine nuts were just called that for some unknown reason. Crouching beside the fire, she poked at the cones. Who would have thought? She was ecstatic at the thought of food — warm food, at that. Nuts, any kind of nuts, would go a long way toward easing their hunger.

"They really do. Watch them and don't let them catch on fire," Cam instructed as he slid into the shelter. "I'm going to get dried off before this sweat freezes on me."

She sat down and held her hands toward the fire. After a moment she realized she was listening intently to the sounds Cam made as he undressed and briskly dried off, imagining him naked even though she knew he wasn't, any more than she had been. Had he listened to her moving around as she removed individual pieces of clothing, and imagined *her* naked? Or had he been too busy gathering up the pinecones?

Abruptly she realized that their cleaning up could almost be construed as a prelude to sex, as if they had been preparing themselves for each other. She hadn't been uncomfortable with him at all during the three nights they'd already spent together, but sex hadn't been on the table then. Now it was. And while sex in itself didn't make her uncomfortable, the prospect of sex with *him* was enough to make her nervous and self-conscious.

Maybe she was reading more into the situation than was really there. After all, he was still recovering from a fairly serious head injury. He was a smart man; he knew he shouldn't overexert himself right now.

Uh-huh, she thought wryly. That's why he'd been pulling a sled through the snow all day.

On the other hand, he *had* been pulling a

sled all day. He was probably exhausted. Sex was probably the last thing on his mind.

Sure. This was the same man who'd had a hard-on the very first day, when he'd been half-dead, and had sported one several times since then. From what she could tell, sex *was* the last thing on his mind . . . before he went to sleep, and it was the first thing on his mind when he woke up.

He'd been very low key, she realized. He hadn't been pushing her at all. The thing was, he wasn't a low-key personality. He was calm, but he was decisive and determined. He made up his mind to do something, then he did it come hell or high water. That wasn't low key.

The question was, did she want to have sex with him? *Yes!* And no. She was terrified of things going that far between them, but her objection was on a mental and emotional level. On a purely physical level, she wanted his weight on top of her and his hips wedged between her legs. She wanted to feel him inside her.

She had to decide: yes or no? If she said no, he'd stop. She trusted him absolutely on that part.

A smart woman would say no. A cautious woman would say no. Bailey had always been smart and cautious.

Until now. She glanced at the shelter's entrance, and every instinct in her whispered: *yes.*

29

Cam had another idea: he emptied out the metal first-aid kit again, and filled it with snow, then placed it on the hot coals at the edge of the fire and added a handful of pine needles. The tea was supposed to be nutritious, he said, and something hot to drink would go a long way toward their comfort.

Bailey was so on edge she could barely sit still. Half an hour ago the idea of a hot drink would have had her in raptures, but now she couldn't wrench her thoughts from the coming night. Automatically she pulled a pinecone apart as he'd shown her, searching for the small, dark nuts; not every individual leaflet of the cone had one. In the first cone she'd found maybe ten or twelve, but they were so small that didn't amount to much. The good news was, the cones were plentiful. Roasting them, then collecting the nuts, took some time, but it wasn't as if they had pressing engagements elsewhere.

Finally they had collected enough nuts for both of them to feel as if they'd actually eaten something. To her surprise, even though she ate no more than what she could cup in her palm, she was surprisingly full. They needed more roasting, so the taste wasn't all that great, but she didn't care; food was food. She wasn't at the grub-eating stage yet, but for the first time she knew what it was to be hungry enough that grubs weren't out of the question.

As the snow in the first-aid box melted, Cam added more until there was enough liquid for both of them to have about a cup. She watched the water take on a pale green tint as the pine needles steeped.

"They teach this stuff in the Scouts, huh?" she finally asked, just to break the silence. "How long were you in?"

"All the way, Cub Scouts through Eagle Scouts. It was something fun to do, and all that prior experience came in handy when I had to study escape and evasion techniques in case my plane was shot down."

"Shot down?" She stared at him. "I thought you flew a tanker."

"I did. That doesn't mean an enemy fighter wouldn't send an air-to-air missile at me if the chance came up. Think about it. You take out a tanker, there are a lot of fighters that won't be able to stay in the air. That's why a tanker isn't up there all on its lonesome."

She felt sick to her stomach at the mental image she had of a missile striking a refueling tanker. How likely was it anyone would survive that size explosion and fire?

She'd also thought flying a tanker was one of the safer jobs for a pilot to have. Now she saw it as sitting in front of a huge gas can, with morons throwing matches at it. How did military wives stand the stress? And exactly what kind of nutcase was Cam's ex-wife that she couldn't stand it when he got *out* of the military?

Unaware of where her thoughts had gone, he stuck his finger in the tea and quickly jerked it back out. "I think that's hot enough," he said. She passed him the cap from the deodorant can and he quickly dipped it into the gently steaming liquid, getting it about half full before carefully passing it back to her.

Cautiously she took a sip. It tasted the way she expected pine needles to taste: green and piney, slightly bitter. She didn't care. Beautiful, wonderful, welcome heat spread through her insides as she swallowed, and she closed her eyes in bliss. "Oh, God, that feels good," she moaned. She took another sip, then extended the cup to him. "Try it."

"I noticed you said it 'feels good,' not that it tastes good," he said as he took the cup and drank. The same expression of pleasure that she imagined she'd worn spread across his face. He wrapped his fingers around the heated plastic and sighed. "You were right on target."

He dipped again and they shared that cup, too. "Here's to the Boy Scouts," she said, lifting the cup in a little salute before passing it to him.

Feeling warmer than they had in four days, and with their hunger pains temporarily banished, they sat and watched the sun slide down the sky. Nothing about this felt unusual, she realized. She had acclimated, not just to the altitude but to him, and being alone with him. Television, shopping, doing market analysis on her computer — that all seemed to belong to another world, another life. Life had very quickly boiled down to the basics: food and shelter.

"I would say I could get used to this," she commented, "but I'd be lying."

His lips curved. "You don't think you'll ever be the outdoor type?"

"It's okay in small doses, like going rafting on vacation. But I want plenty of food, I want a tent, I want a sleeping bag. I want a way to leave when I get tired of it. This survival stuff is for the birds."

"It was fun when I was a kid, but I wasn't freezing cold, I didn't have a concussion, and no one was practicing her sewing on me — without anesthesia."

She gave him a quick look. "You weren't screaming," she pointed out.

"That doesn't mean it was anything I'd recommend."

The Ace bandage wrapped around his head was dirty, but with luck that meant it had prevented any dirt from getting to the cut. He hadn't suffered any fever at all, which meant there was no infection. All in all, she felt proud of the job she'd done taking care of him.

He reached up and touched the Ace bandage. "Think I could lose this, now?"

She shrugged. "It's been keeping your head warm."

"It's been annoying the hell out of me, too. I can tie something else around my head. By now, a smaller bandage will do."

Because she agreed, she unwrapped the bandage and removed the gauze pads that covered the wound. All the swelling was gone, and though he sported a huge bruise on his forehead and the sutured cut itself was reminiscent of Frankenstein's monster, he seemed to be healing fairly well. She pulled one of the aloe wipes from the pack and was gingerly dabbing at the cut, trying to remove some dried blood. He bore her ministrations for about a minute. "Give me that," he finally said with a growl of impatience, taking the wipe from her and vigorously scrubbing it through his hair.

"Itching, huh?"

"Like a son of a bitch." The wipe came away rust-colored by the blood that had dried in his hair. Most of it had been washed away by the mouthwash she'd poured on his head, but obviously not all. He used another wipe to make certain he'd gotten it all out, which meant that his head was very damp by the time he finished and he had to use a flannel shirt to towel dry his hair before it froze. Bailey reached for the first-aid supplies, but he shook his head. "Leave that until morning. It'll be fine tonight."

They finished the pine needle tea, and he used a stick to nudge the first-aid box off the hot coals. An idea niggled at her. She got another shirt, used it to pick up the box, and quickly wrapped the fabric around it.

"People used to heat bricks and wrap them in flannel, then put them between the sheets to get the bed warm," she said as she crawled into the shelter with her makeshift bed warmer. They had dumped all the spare clothing they used as cover in the shelter and she quickly arranged everything in the layers that worked best for keeping them warm, putting the heated bundle in the middle.

She'd been sleeping with her boots on but now she worked them off, sighing with relief as she flexed her feet and ankles, then she slipped her feet under the first-aid box. Warmth immediately began seeping through the two pairs of socks she wore.

Cam crawled in behind her. Seeing what she'd done, he laughed and began unlacing his leather overshoes, pulling his shoes off with them. His shoulder bumped hers as he sat beside her, leaning against the rock at their backs, their feet nestled together.

Her heartbeat kicked into a higher gear. Their conversation had been mundane, but beneath the calm surface she was aware of the constant sizzle of desire. When their fingers touched as they passed the cup back and forth, or when she'd touched his face as she unwrapped the Ace bandage, she had trembled with the need for more. She'd wanted to twine their fingers together; she'd wanted to lay her palm against his bristly jaw and feel the strength of the bone beneath his skin. She wanted to feel his arms closing around her, tugging her close against him the way he had during the nights.

She had spent her lifetime never feeling quite safe, and she hadn't realized it until she slept in his arms. It made no sense that she'd feel that way with him, because she'd never before been in such danger, but there it was. She *fit* with him, like two pieces of a puzzle locking together.

"We should get some sleep," he said, closely watching her every expression. "We've had a tiring day."

The sun had set and full darkness was rapidly chasing the twilight. *Soon,* she thought as she stretched out and nestled under their cover. He put on his shoes to go out and feed the fire, then returned to lie down beside her. His heavy arm draped over her waist and he pulled her to him, turning her so her face was nestled against his throat. He smelled like the aloe wipes, and wood smoke, and man.

He put his hand under all the shirts she wore, cupped her breast, rubbed the roughened side of his thumb over her nipple and brought it to tingling erection. She inhaled sharply. She'd meant to be calm, but calmness was beyond her. Her heart was pounding so hard she could barely breathe. This shouldn't matter so much. *He* shouldn't matter so much. Unfortunately, what should or should not be had no relation to what was.

He kissed her, his mouth light on hers. She was so tightly wound that for a moment she couldn't relax, couldn't respond. Just as she was beginning to sink against him, return the pressure of his mouth, he moved his lips to her temple. "Good night."

Good night?

Good night! She stiffened in disbelief. She'd worked herself into a frenzy of worry and anticipation, and he wanted to *sleep?*

"No!" she protested, outrage in her tone.

"Yes." He kissed her again, his hand still heavy on her breast. "You're tired. I'm tired. Go to sleep."

"Who died and put you in charge?" she demanded furiously. Oh, great; she'd descended to teenage taunts. This was twice in one day he'd destroyed her poise, she who never let turmoil ruffle the smooth surface of her life. She'd always been so careful not to let anyone matter this much to her, for this very reason . . .

She went very still as she gave up on her last shred of avoidance, which wasn't working anyway. She could rationalize and hedge her bets all she wanted, but she was wasting both time and effort. Could she have fallen in love with him in just four days? As he'd pointed out, the time they'd been together was now the equivalent of about nineteen or twenty dates. Logically, he was right.

This was love. This was what people talked about, this painful, giddy, sorrowful, joyful, confusing explosion of emotion that didn't respond to reason. It was like being drunk without the depressing effects that slowed thought and function. It was feeling helpless and revved up all at the same time, as if her skin were too tight for her body.

He didn't respond to her taunt, other than to kiss her forehead as if he understood the turmoil that gripped her. Well, why wouldn't he? He'd been in love before. He had experience. Maybe with enough experience she wouldn't find herself acting like a fool, either, but she hoped to hell she never felt like this again. Once was enough. If this didn't work out, she'd join a convent or maybe move to Florida where she'd be surrounded by people old enough to be her parents and she wouldn't be tempted again.

She jerked his hand away from her breast and threw it to the side. "If we aren't going to have sex, then keep your hands to yourself." Realizing she was probably in love with him just made her angrier. Also realizing that she was on the verge of a temper tantrum was humiliating. She'd be damned if she'd beg him for sex. She'd be damned if she'd let him even if *he* begged for sex. She wanted to kick him. She wanted to grab his penis and twist it. That would teach him. Instead of Good Time Charlie, he'd have to rename it Corkscrew Charlie.

She could feel him shaking, just a little, feel the ragged edge to his breathing. He was laughing, damn him, though he had the good sense to try to hide it.

Bailey turned away from him, her fury renewed by the simple fact that she couldn't even move so she wasn't touching him. They *had* to touch; they had to lie close together, had to share their warmth.

Just to show him how little he mattered, she would go to sleep. And she hoped she snored.

Temptation gnawed at her. She wanted to kill him. She wanted to mangle him. Oh, hell — it had to be love.

She'd rather have plague. At least it was curable.

Calming herself took a good half hour, a half hour during which she felt him awake and watchful, attuned to every breath she took. How dare he be concerned about her? If he was truly that concerned, he'd have given her what she wanted.

It was a testament to her willpower that she truly did go to sleep.

30

Bailey gently surfaced to the pleasure of his warm, hard hand moving from one breast to another, massaging and stroking. There was no sense of disorientation; she knew him immediately, knew who held her so securely. He lightly pulled and pinched her nipples, his hand slow and sure as he brought them to hardness. Pleasure eddied from her breasts in lazy ripples, flowing through her, beginning to call up the heat and fullness of desire.

She floated drowsily between pleasure and sleep. If she wanted more, all she had to do was push back against the erection that was prodding her. A simple invitation was all that was needed . . .

Her eyes snapped open as memory flooded back.

"Get that damn thing away from me!" she snapped, jerking away and trying to fight free of the heavy layers of clothes as well as his imprisoning arm. If he thought he could blow hot and cold and she'd jump to his tune, then his powers of perception sucked.

He fell over onto his back, laughing so hard she thought he'd choke. She thought about helping him choke. Finally she managed to roll over onto her stomach and lift herself on her elbows. She glared at him through the curtain of hair hanging in her face. He must have just replenished the fire, though she hadn't awakened when he left the shelter. The light from the fire was flickering brightly, reflecting on the rock behind him and casting enough light into the shelter that she could see him fairly well as he clutched his stomach and howled with laughter. Gimlet-eyed, she waited for him to realize she didn't see any humor in this at all.

"I can't exactly take it off and put it in my pocket when I'm not using it," he finally managed to say, wiping tears from his eyes.

"I don't care where you put it," she said flatly. "Just stop poking me with it."

"I would ask if you're in a better mood than when you went to sleep, but offhand I'd say no." He was still smiling as he settled on his side again, curling a muscled arm under his head and with the other reaching to hook his hand around her waist and drag her back into position. She went stiffly, unhappy with the situation but knowing they pretty much had to sleep in that position. The only other options were to lie face-to-face in each other's arms, which she wasn't willing to do, or for her to spoon him, which she also wasn't willing to do. His thighs slid against hers, her shoulders rested against his chest, and his body heat once more surrounded her — and the bulge in his pants nestled against her bottom, just like before.

He smoothed a tendril of hair out of her face, and irritably she jerked her head away from his touch. "I've been trying to wake you up for half an hour," he murmured.

"I don't know why. You wanted me to sleep; I was sleeping. Leave me alone."

His arm tightened around her. "I was trying to be considerate. You were so nervous you wouldn't have enjoyed it," he explained.

Her lips tightened. "How would you know? You didn't give me a chance."

"No point in *taking* the chance. You'd been getting more and more tense all afternoon. I don't know what was bothering you, but I could wait until you were either ready to talk about it or you came to terms with it yourself."

"Stop trying to be so understanding," she said grumpily. "It doesn't suit you." But she didn't elbow him when he snuggled her closer.

"So, are you ready to talk about it?"

"No."

"Have you come to terms with it, whatever it is?"

"No! Leave me alone, I told you. I want to go to sleep." She wasn't at all sleepy now, but he didn't have to know that.

He pushed her hair to the side and nuzzled the nape of her neck, his lips and breath burning on her skin. "I know this isn't easy for you, trusting someone," he murmured, the movement of his lips the softest, lightest caress. "You like being alone."

No, she didn't. She was more *comfortable* alone. There was a difference.

"It's risky, caring about someone," he continued in that soft tone, barely above a whisper. His voice soothed over her like aged, mellow whiskey. "And you don't like taking risks. You've kept people at arm's length because you know you're a softie, and the best way to protect yourself is not to let anyone get close."

A small shock reverberated through her, leaving behind a spurt of panic. "I'm not a softie." She acted calm and remote because she was a calm and remote person. She didn't cry because she wasn't a crier. She most definitely was not a softie.

"You're a softie," he repeated. "Do you think I don't remember you talking to me, after the crash, when you still thought I was a stick-up-my-ass sourpuss? Your voice was as gentle as if you were talking to a baby. You patted me."

"I did not." Had she?

"Yes, you did."

Maybe she had. "I don't remember," she grumbled. "But if I did, it was because I was grateful."

"My ass. You'd have pulled me out of the plane because you were grateful. You wouldn't have nearly killed yourself trying to take care of me. You wouldn't have given me your warmest piece of clothing when you were freezing and obviously needed it."

She sniffed. "I take my gratitude seriously."

"Uh-huh. I think you're a complete marshmallow." He repeated the charge as he slid his hand down her arm and around her waist to slide under her shirts, where it rested on her stomach. The slight roughness of his fingertips rasped against her smooth skin as he began making little circles with them. "But I like marshmallows. I like the way they taste, the way they feel." His lips moved from the back of her neck to where the curve of her shoulder began and he gently closed his teeth over the muscle there, biting down ever so slightly.

Bailey's entire body clenched. The wave of desire was so sudden and intense that her head fell back as her spine arched.

"I like biting into a marshmallow." His tongue soothed over the barely noticeable sting, then he plucked at the muscle again with his teeth while his hand swept up to her breasts and mirrored the action with her nipples.

Abruptly her heart was hammering and her breath was coming in rapid little pants as a deep throb began between her legs. She had never before been aroused so fast and so intensely, but her body was already accustomed to his touch. This was the fourth night she'd slept in his arms. He'd kissed her, touched her. Her body had been ready a long time before her mind caught up.

In one long caress he slid his hand down her stomach again, slipped his fingers beneath the elastic waistband of her sweatpants. The heat of his palm scorched the coolness of her butt as his hand moved down, then back up. When he reversed its path yet again, she felt the tug on her pants, felt them being pulled down to bare her.

She was so tense she was trembling, but it

was a tension that was far different from what she'd suffered before. Even though she was still fully clothed except for her buttocks, still covered by all their protective layers, that part of her felt excruciatingly naked, the damp folds between her legs exposed and vulnerable.

He went straight there, to the heart of her. Those lean, hard fingers delved into the folds, found her, opened her. "I like peaches, too," he whispered as he worked two fingers deep into her. "All juicy, and warm from the sun. Pull your legs up a little, sweetheart. That's good."

He played with her, the slow motion of his hand rasping over exquisitely sensitive nerve endings, bringing them achingly alive. She choked back a moan as it went on and on, driving her mad and pleasing her all at once. Then his fingers left her, left her body, left her panting and quivering, left her wanting. She lay motionless, paralyzed with anticipation, her eyes squeezed tightly shut as she heard his zipper slide down, a whisper of sound as he tore open a condom and rolled it on, then he adjusted his position a little and pressed himself to her.

Her breath hitched, caught in an agony of suspense as she waited. She lifted her arm to reach back and touch his face, slide her hand around the back of his neck.

Slowly, so slowly, he pushed . . . just a little, then he pulled back. Her flesh had barely begun giving, opening to him. She waited, and he returned, with a leisurely rocking motion that applied just enough pressure to begin entering her before he pulled back yet again.

"Cam . . ." She whispered his name, the sound floating in the darkness. The air was cold but they were snug in their shelter, cuddled together, heat burning between them in the places where their naked flesh touched. She said his name, just his name, and nothing else was needed.

He came to her again. His palm flattened on her belly, bracing her, holding her as he applied pressure and steadily held it. She felt her flesh begin to dampen, to open. The urge to push back, to hurry the process, was almost irresistible, but what he was doing was too delicious to forgo. She heard a whimper, knew it was her own, and yet she held steady.

She had never been more acutely aware of her own body, or of the hot reality of the sex act. The thick, bulbous head of his penis simply pressed, demanding entrance, and slowly her body gave to the demand until suddenly the surrender was complete and she stretched around him as the tip sank into her.

He went no deeper, but held there while she shivered and trembled, accustoming herself to the hot bulk of his intrusion. She was surprised by the intensity of the sensation, bordering on pain. It had been a long time for her and she'd expected some small discomfort, but not this feeling of shock, of being overwhelmed.

With the same slow, agonizingly gradual movement, he pulled himself out of her. Her flesh released his as reluctantly as she had accepted it; her inner muscles clenched, trying to hold him. His breath hissed out as he dragged free.

"What are you doing?" she cried in protest.

"Playing," he said, the single word rough, almost guttural. Once more his hips pressed, her flesh parted, and he lodged the head within her before pulling back. Over and over she accepted that shallow penetration until he was slipping easily in and out of her, until her body was burning and her mind was fogged so that she was aware of nothing but him, wanted nothing but him. Dimly she was aware that he was trembling, too, from the effort he was making at control, that his breath was ragged and that low, harsh sounds were tearing from his throat at every dip he made with his penis into her body. She was glad that he was also suffering. She wanted to come, she desperately needed to come, but their positions prevented that. She wanted her legs around him. If she couldn't have what she wanted, it was only fair that he couldn't, either.

She didn't know how much time passed before suddenly his "playing" was more than either of them could bear for even one minute longer. He jerked out of her and rolled her to face him, pushing violently at her sweatpants in an effort to get them off of her. She tried to help, kicking and writhing in an effort to reach them, and managed to get one leg out before he was on her, pushing his legs between hers and spreading them wide before surging into her to the hilt with one strong thrust.

Bailey hooked her legs around his, clenched his ass in her hands, and pulled him into her as hard as she could, coming on that first deep stroke, her back arched and animal cries tearing from her throat. He rode her through it, and she was just beginning to fall away from the crest, her body going limp, when he began shuddering with his own climax.

She felt almost as if they had crashed again.

She drifted, surfacing toward awareness before sinking down again. Her heart was hammering, with an odd echo that she gradually recognized as the gallop of his heartbeat. His chest was rising and falling like bellows as he gulped in air. Heat rose from their bodies in waves, and though she was half naked and somehow completely uncovered, she wasn't cold. She thought she might never be cold again.

"Holy shit," he finally said, his voice drained.

Her hand flailed limply for a moment before she managed to pat his shoulder.

With an effort he pulled himself off her and collapsed by her side, plucking at some of the garments that had been tossed aside until he was able to drag one or two of them over their bodies.

"Don't go to sleep," he warned, though he sounded as if he was halfway there, himself. "We have to get this straightened . . . get you dressed . . . I have to check the fire . . ." His voice trailed off.

After a minute he swore, and heaved himself to a sitting position. "And if I don't do it right now, I'll be asleep myself." He peeled off the condom and cleaned himself, then spent a few seconds tucking, straightening, and zipping before crawling out to see to the fire.

That was the great thing about condoms, Bailey thought drowsily: no cleanup for her. All she had to do was sleep.

A wave of frigid air washed over her and she groaned. So much for never feeling cold again. Sitting up, she managed to get her sweatpants untangled from around her leg, got them back on and pulled up, and began restoring order to the complete disarray of their covers. Cam slid back into the shelter, his broad shoulders momentarily blocking the light from the fire. He helped her get positioned, then he lay down beside her and arranged the last layer over them before collapsing on his back and pulling her close to his side.

She nestled her head on his shoulder, the fit as natural as if they'd been sleeping together for years. She felt a little dazed — no, a *lot* dazed. And relaxed. And sated. Maybe even a little sore. But most of all, she felt as if they fit together in a way that was terrifying because it was so perfect.

31

Logan Tillman, Bailey's brother, showed up at the J&L offices the morning of the fifth day. Bret knew who he was immediately, before he even introduced himself. It wasn't that he and Bailey resembled each other all that much — Logan was taller, his hair darker, his eyes bluer. But there was a similarity of expression that marked them as relatives, a certain reserve. Other than that, his face was haggard with grief, as was that of the tall, freckle-faced woman beside him.

"I'm Bailey's brother, Logan Tillman," he said, introducing himself to Karen. "This is my wife, Peaches. I — We couldn't stay in Denver any longer, with no contact, no news. We'd rather be here. Is there *anything?*"

Bret came out of his office to shake their hands. "No, nothing. I'm sorry." He was as haggard as they; he'd slept only fitfully since Cam's plane went down. Despite that, he'd begun taking flights again, because the

371

business had to go on.

Financially he was in a tailspin, something he'd never counted on when he and Cam formed their partnership. They'd done the smart thing, insured their aircraft and themselves so the business would continue if anything happened to either of them, but they hadn't reckoned on the insurance company's natural inclination to hang on to money.

Even though Cam's plane had disappeared from radar over extremely rough terrain — meaning it had crashed — because the wreckage hadn't been found and Cam's body recovered, as far as the insurance company was concerned he was still alive until either his remains were found or a court declared him dead. The cold reality was that Bret was short a plane and short a pilot, therefore less money was coming in. He was walking the floor at night, worrying himself sick about the debts that were coming due. He couldn't believe they — he — had been so shortsighted. He'd have to hire another pilot, of course, but finding someone who matched his qualifications would take time.

He realized that Karen was giving him one of her narrow-eyed looks that promised retribution if he didn't do what she wanted. He drew a weary breath. She was waiting for him to tell Bailey's brother about the fuel discrepancy.

She was right; Logan had to know. Bret didn't want to be the one to tell him, but he had no choice.

"Let's go into my office," he said heavily. "Would you like some coffee?"

Peaches shot an assessing look at her husband, as if weighing whether or not he needed a shot of caffeine. "Yes, please," she said, taking Logan's hand. He squeezed her hand in return and managed a ghost of a smile.

Bret led them into his office, got them seated in the two visitor's chairs. "How do you like your coffee?"

"Cream in one, the other black," Peaches answered. Her voice was like Tinker Bell's, light and quick. Bret had talked a lot with Bailey when he'd piloted her, and he remembered how much she'd liked her sister-in-law. Logan seemed to be the only family she kept in touch with; he was the only one she'd ever mentioned.

Their grief was so acute it lay on them like a veil of suffering. He had to get out of there. "I'll get the coffee," he said quickly, and walked out to find Karen already preparing it because of course she'd been listening. She gave him a quick, piercing look, reading his expression.

"Suck it up, boss," she said, and he gave her a wry look. So much for sympathy, but then, anyone looking for sympathy from Karen Kaminski was out of luck. He noticed that she'd been in the hair dye again; before, there had been a few striking black streaks in her red hair, but now her hair was more black than red. He wondered if this was her way of wearing mourning.

She had unearthed a small tray from somewhere and set three cups on it, some individual packs of creamer, stirrers, then poured the coffee. Silently Bret lifted the tray and carried it into his office where he placed it on his desk.

Logan leaned forward, took a cup of black coffee, and gave it to his wife. Bret watched as he added the creamer to his own coffee, and remembered that was also how Bailey had taken hers. The memory was unexpectedly sharp, unexpectedly painful. A hundred times a day he had an impulse to tell Cam something, but that wasn't surprising considering how long they'd been friends and then partners. Though his meetings with Bailey had been casual and sporadic, he'd liked her. When she unbent, she'd been funny and sarcastic and hadn't taken herself seriously.

Cam hadn't liked her at all, and the feeling had been mutual. It was ironic that they'd died together, considering.

Bret grabbed his own cup and stood with his back to them, looking out the window, as he fought to bring his expression under control.

"There's a discrepancy in the fuel records," he finally said, his tone low and flat.

There was a pause behind him, a complete absence of sound.

"What're you saying?" Logan asked carefully. "What kind of discrepancy?"

"The plane didn't have enough fuel. It took on less than half what was needed to get to Salt Lake City, where they were scheduled to refuel."

"What kind of pilot would take off without enough fuel? And why wouldn't he just land somewhere and take on more?" Logan sounded angry, and Bret knew how he felt. He turned around and faced Bailey's brother.

"To answer your first question," he said slowly, "a pilot who thought he had enough because the fuel load indicator said he did. That's also the answer to your second question."

"Why wouldn't he know? Are you saying

the fuel gauge in your plane was wrong? How could you know that, when the wreckage hasn't been found?"

Logan was sharp, Bret would give him that. He grasped immediately what Bret was talking about, asked all the right questions.

"The plane's fuel tanks were almost empty when it landed the day before. But when it was refueled that morning, it took on only thirty-nine gallons, which is less than half what just one of the wing tanks would hold."

"Then the guy doing the refueling made a mistake, but that doesn't answer why you think the fuel gauge was defective." Logan was getting angry; it was plain in the growing impatience in his tone.

"I haven't said anything about the gauge being defective," Bret said just as carefully as Logan had spoken a moment before. "I don't think it was."

"Then —"

"There are ways," he continued, still cautiously picking his words, "to make a fuel tank gauge register as full when it really isn't."

Silence fell again. Logan and Peaches looked at each other, then his brows snapped together and he said, "When we spoke on the phone, I told you what Tamzin had said and you blew it off. Are you saying now that sabotage *is* likely?"

"I don't know. Until the crash site is found, everything's conjecture." Tiredly he rubbed his forehead. "But nothing else makes sense. Cam was the most careful pilot I've ever met. He checked and he double-checked; he didn't take anything for granted when it came to flying. There's no way he *wouldn't* have noticed a fuel gauge that showed the tanks were almost empty."

"How hard would that be, to tamper with a gauge?"

"It isn't hard at all," Bret admitted. "And it isn't the gauge that's tampered with, it's the fuel tanks themselves. They're made to look full when they aren't."

"You've told the authorities about this?" Logan barked. "And about what Tamzin said?"

Bret nodded. "Without evidence, without finding the wreckage, there's nothing that can be done."

"Surely to God there are security tapes. This is an airport, for crying out loud!"

"A very small airport, with no commercial flights. But yes, there are security tapes."

"And?"

"And the security firm won't release them without a court order. The NTSB investigator, MaGuire, is pressing for one, but it hasn't come through yet."

"Why in hell won't they cooperate?" Pale and agitated, Logan shoved himself to his feet and paced around the room.

"Fear of a lawsuit, probably. Could just be their policy, and some people cling to policy like they can't operate without it."

"But the cops haven't picked up Seth Wingate for questioning? After what Tamzin said?"

"Did anyone else hear Tamzin say that to you?" Bret asked pointedly. "Seriously, she's not known for her stability. And Seth *is* a Wingate; he hasn't done anything with his life, but he's still a Wingate, and that name carries a lot of weight."

"Bailey had the name, too," Logan said thickly, and turned his back to hide his emotion. Tears glittering in her eyes, Peaches got up and went to him, resting her head against his back. Just that, but he calmed, turning to put his arm around her.

Bret didn't say anything, didn't explain that Bailey hadn't been the most popular person around. The social circles in which the Wingates moved had pretty much shunned her after her husband died. They'd seen her as having taken advantage of a sick, middle-aged man who had lost his wife and, fairly close on the heels of that, discovered he was himself dying. After he was gone, Bailey had remained, living in the house that by rights should have belonged to his children and controlling the vast Wingate fortune. But he wasn't going to say any of that to her grieving brother.

"So there's nothing to be done."

"Not right now. When the wreckage is found, if there's evidence of sabotage, then it's a different situation."

"*If* the wreckage is found."

"It will be," Bret said with confidence. "Eventually."

Eventually. That was the bitch. "Eventually" could mean in two days, or two years, or in the next century. Until then, it was possible someone was getting away with murder.

"I can't stand it," Logan said that night as he paced around their hotel room. He'd been doing a lot of pacing since getting the news that the plane Bailey was on had disappeared. "The fuel record itself should be enough to convince some judge that something was going on."

Peaches lay curled on the bed, her skin pale beneath her freckles. Neither of them had slept or eaten very much in the past few days. Not knowing was the worst. And yet they did know, at least, that Bailey was dead. It seemed particularly cruel to accept that, and not be able to find her body. She should have a burial, she should have the ceremony that marked the end of her life. Peaches resolutely didn't allow herself to think of what happened to bodies in the wilderness, but she knew Logan had, and it was eating at him.

The knock on their hotel door startled both of them, because they hadn't ordered room service, preferring to find somewhere cheaper to eat. After spending so much on their canceled vacation, of which they would get only a partial refund, then having to stay in a hotel or motel for the past several days, they were becoming a little worried about their money.

"It's probably Larsen," Logan said, which was logical, since Bret knew where they were staying. It was anyone's guess why he'd come up to the room instead of calling if he wanted to talk to them again.

He opened the door, and froze. Picking up on his body language, Peaches got off the bed and went to stand beside him, staring in puzzlement at the tall, dark-haired man who stood there. She didn't recognize him, but a prickle of unease let her take an educated guess.

"What the hell do you want?" Logan asked with so much hostility that she started. "How did you know where to find us?"

"To talk. And finding you was easy. I asked. You called home and told people where they could find you. All I had to do was say I'd lost your cell phone number, and that I had news about the crash."

"I don't have anything to talk to you about." He started to close the door but Seth Wingate put out his hand and blocked it. He was a powerfully built man, with a face that could have been good-looking if there had been anything in his expression other than a complete weariness of soul.

"Then just listen," he said coldly. "I didn't have anything to do with that plane crash."

"Somebody did," Logan said, his jaw setting and his eyes going flinty. "Your own sister was crowing about how dangerous it is to cross you, that Bailey got what she deserved."

"My sister," said Seth very deliberately, "is a cold-blooded bitch who may well be setting me up to take the fall."

Logan wanted to punch him in the face, but held back. Peaches was there beside him, and though he didn't mind a fight he would never willingly risk that she might get hurt. "Your sibling loyalty is really touching," he sneered.

Seth's mouth twisted in a bitter smile. "You don't know the half of it," he said. "I just wanted you to know I didn't do it." Then he turned and walked off, leaving Logan and Peaches to stand in the door of their hotel room and watch him disappear down the hall.

32

During the last of his fire-feeding excursions, Cam located the first-aid box amid the jumble of clothing, unwrapped it, and took it out to once more fill it with snow. Bailey's inventiveness in using the box as a bed warmer made him smile; she had the damnedest talent for seeing beyond an item's intended use and adapting it for her needs. If they'd been forced to stay at the crash site for much longer, he had no doubt that their stick shelter would have morphed into a mud hut, and she'd have built a windmill from the plane's metal and parts to power the battery so they could have all the fires they wanted.

After replenishing the fire, he nestled the box close to the hot coals. Having something hot to drink first thing would be great. Being able to lie in bed all day would be even better, but with their food situation the way it was they didn't have that option.

He waited while the snow in the box melted, hunkering as close to the fire as he could yet still shivering from the icy winds. After adding more snow to the box, as well as a handful of pine needles, he crawled back into the shelter for another hour of sleep before dawn, and the start of another exhausting day.

Bailey didn't wake, but she hadn't any of the times he'd gone out to stoke the fire during the night. He stretched out beside her and she came to him like a homing pigeon, draping herself over him and making herself comfortable, all without waking up. With luck, all the rest of their nights would be spent like this, but he wasn't taking anything for granted. God knew, she made heavy work for herself out of every step of a relationship. *Going with the flow* was an alien concept to her, and emotional trust was something to be avoided.

He had his own work cut out for him, either side-stepping or dismantling the land mines of her childhood. Divorce was tough on everyone, especially kids, but Bailey's personality had made the upheaval disastrous for her. She needed security on a deeper level than most, and had spent her adult life making certain she was as secure as possible. If that meant not letting herself care about anyone, so be it.

Might as well face it, he told himself cheerfully: his bachelor days were over. He'd have to go all the way with this. She wouldn't be able to tolerate just being lovers, not for any length of time, but at the same time she'd panic at the idea of a real marriage, with real commitment. He didn't know how he'd convince her to take the chance, but he'd manage, and have a lot of fun in the process.

"Here's your morning coffee," Cam said, waking her with a kiss and extending the deodorant can cap half-full of pine needle tea.

"Umm, coffee!" Sleepily she struggled to a sitting position, shifting around so she could lean against the rock, and took the cap from him. The first sip was wonderful, but not because of the taste, because of the heat — and the consideration of the gesture. No one had ever brought her anything first thing in the morning, she'd always gotten it herself. She took another sip, then offered the cap to him. "It's great — made from the finest pine needles grown in America."

He shook his head as he settled beside her. "I've already had some. That's all yours."

As hot morning drinks went, pine needle tea didn't have the kick of coffee or tea, but she wasn't complaining. All in all, she was happy to have it. In fact, she was ridiculously happy this morning, period — which was scary. She pushed the thought away for later examination and said, "So, what's on the agenda today? Shopping, a little sightseeing, then lunch?"

"I thought we'd go for a nature hike in the mountains." He put his arm around her shoulders, held her close as he pulled some of the jumbled clothing over their legs. Even with the fire burning just outside, even with the hot drink, the air was still freezing cold and their shelter was far from airtight.

"Sounds like a plan."

"We have to push hard today." He sounded somber, and she gave him a quick glance. "Maybe make a sling and lower ourselves and the sled over some vertical drops, that should gain us some time. We need to get out of this wind layer today, so we can get some smoke going."

Bailey didn't have to be told why. The pine nuts would keep them going, but they needed more food than just a handful of nuts a couple of times a day. They didn't know how many more times the battery would start a fire before it was drained of its charge, and the pinecones really needed to be heated before they would easily release the nuts, which made even that an iffy source of food. Today was do-it-or-die day — she hoped not literally, but the possibility was there, had been there from day one. They were in a precarious position.

After eating the handful of nuts, they quickly packed up their supplies, buried the fire, and headed out. She was almost glad there was no opportunity for cuddling or loverlike displays, even more lovemaking. The offering of pine needle tea surpassed any other loverly gesture he might have made, and as for more lovemaking, well, she was a little sore from all his playing, which wasn't surprising considering how long it had been since she'd had sex.

Besides, she needed time to process. Although she was very adaptive when it came to her surroundings, emotionally she was much less flexible. A day of hard physical exertion and absolutely no demands on her emotions was exactly what she needed.

Which was a good thing, because that was exactly what she got. Cam set a grueling pace, so grueling she was terrified for him. He was in the lead, so if he stepped on a seemingly solid place and it turned out to be a snowbank that caved in beneath him, he'd be gone before she could begin to react, pulling the heavy sled down on top of him.

That scenario suddenly was so real that

she yelled "Stop!" and when he did she hurried to get in front. "I'll lead," she said brusquely, setting out at the same pace he'd set.

"What the fu—? Hey!" he yelled after her, scowling as he tried to catch up.

"You're pulling the sled. I'll test the footing."

He didn't like that at all, but until he could catch her, there wasn't a hell of a lot he could do about it — and he couldn't catch up with her as long as he was pulling the sled. She settled the makeshift straps of the roll-aboard backpack more comfortably on her shoulders, and plowed ahead.

She did pick up a long, sturdy branch to use to poke into the ground ahead of her, just to make certain the ground was really there, but she didn't let it slow her down much. The possibility of being rescued either this afternoon or tomorrow pulled her along. God, she wanted off this mountain! She developed a rhythm, the poke of the stick through the snow followed by the slide of her snowshoes over the crusty top layer. The sounds were monotonous, lulling, which was in itself a danger. *Poke,* slide, slide, *poke,* slide, slide. She had to force herself to pay attention.

They slithered down slopes that the day

before they would have detoured around. Most of them she couldn't have negotiated without the sturdy stick, and at every one they had to remove their snowshoes so they could get better traction. She would go down first, and Cam would lower the sled to her, carefully playing out the rope he'd made by tying pieces of clothing together. Then she would hold the sled while he made his way down, at which point he would take over the sled again.

He didn't mention taking point, but the current system, with her testing the way, was working out so well he'd have been a fool to insist that he lead. If there was one thing Cam wasn't, she thought, it was a fool. He had an ego, but he also had a brain, and in him the brain trumped everything else. She liked that; no, she loved it. She repeated the word to herself several times. *Love, love, love.* It took some getting used to, but she didn't feel quite as panicked now as she had at first.

Just before noon, one of the straps on her right snowshoe broke. It came off in midstep and she stumbled forward, one shoe on and one off; only the fact that she dug the thick stick into the ground kept her from falling on her face. As it was she merely went down on one knee and quickly levered herself back to her feet. She tugged her face mask down and dragged in a deep breath. "I'm okay," she said as Cam pulled even with her, critically examining her for damage before he bent to pick up the snowshoe.

"I can fix it," he said after briefly looking at the torn strap. "We need a break, anyway."

They sat down on the sled and took a breather while they passed the water bottle back and forth. He removed the torn strap, replacing it with another strip of fabric cut from yet another garment. At this pace, she thought humorously, if they didn't get rescued soon, she wouldn't have any clothes left to use as a covering at night.

"We've made good time," he said, looking around him. "We're probably five hundred feet lower than we were this morning."

"Five hundred feet," she muttered. "I know we've traveled five miles, at least."

His teeth flashed in a grin. "Not quite, but that five hundred feet is significant. Can't you tell the difference in the wind?"

She lifted her head. Now that he mentioned it, she could. The trees weren't whipping about quite so much, and though the wind was cold, it lacked the icy sharpness they'd been enduring since the crash. Plus, because they hadn't been able to go straight down, but had been forced to traverse the mountain, they now seemed to be heading in a more easterly direction, away from the windward side. The temperature probably was only a degree or two warmer, but the difference in the wind velocity made things feel almost pleasant in comparison.

Her spirits had been good, but now they soared. She looked at him and grinned. "You might get to light that signal fire this afternoon after all, Tonto."

He snorted and gave her leg a light pinch, then finished threading the new strap through the snowshoe. "Good as new," he pronounced, hunkering down beside her to tie it onto her booted foot. "Ready to go?"

"Ready." She was hungry and tired, but no more hungry and tired than he was, maybe less so, because with his larger muscle mass he would burn more calories even sitting still than she would. This was their fifth day, and she reckoned she'd lost about ten pounds because of the cold and lack of food, but he'd probably lost at least fifteen. With their food completely gone now, they would begin losing strength, so they were racing against time to get to a more temperate zone. By pushing themselves so hard they were burning more calories, yes, but if the end result was getting rescued this afternoon or first thing tomorrow morning, then it was worth the effort.

When they stood, Cam flexed his shoulders and arms, working out some of the kinks before he got back into the harness. Bailey could only imagine the effort he was putting out, pulling that heavy sled over the rugged terrain. She could see the strain on his face, etched in lines of fatigue. How much longer would he be able to go on?

They set off again, using the same method as before. Even with the short break, even with all the exercise she normally did, her leg muscles were burning. But if Cam could continue, so could she.

Once Cam shouted, and she looked back to see him straining against the pull of the sled; one of the runners had slipped over the edge of a rock and the whole thing was trying to slide over. The drop wasn't that much, maybe six feet, but it was high enough that the sled would probably be damaged beyond repair. Clumsily she hurried back with the shuffling gait imposed on her by the snowshoes, squeezed past him, and got to the rear of the sled. The way the sled was made there was no place to get a good grip, so finally she just grabbed the edge of the runner that had slid off and pulled up and back with all her strength. She heard an ominous crack but didn't dare let go, bracing her legs and pulling up while Cam threw all of his power and weight into pulling forward. With the sled's center of gravity shifted to where it should be, the sled moved forward once again, and she hastily released the runner before her fingers were caught.

Her feet slid forward, and with a cry she slipped right over the edge of the rock.

She landed with a thump, hard enough to jar every bone in her body, then toppled forward on her hands and knees. "Damn it!"

"Bailey!"

Alarm was plain in Cam's deep voice and she called out, "I'm okay, nothing broken." But she'd definitely added to her already fine collection of bruises. She got to her feet and dusted the snow off her hands and knees, then looked around for the best way to get back up where he was. Unfortunately, she had to trudge back in the opposite direction for about thirty yards, then clamber up a sharp, rough grade littered with loose rocks that were hidden under the snow and made climbing treacherous. She was panting from the effort by the time she reached him.

Neither of them said anything, because there was no point in wasting their precious breath. He was okay, she was okay, the sled was okay. They pressed on.

Just before five o'clock, she skidded to a halt, staring in dismay at the half-circle shape of the cliff that yawned at her feet. The walls were vertical slabs of rock, dotted here and there with dabs of white where falling snow had found a precarious resting place. They had approached from the side of the cliff, and for quite a while the way had been becoming steeper and steeper, so much so that in some stretches she'd had to walk beside the sled and push against it to keep it moving forward. Now they couldn't go forward at all, unless they wanted the last thousand feet of their trip to be made at the speed of a free-falling body. To the right, the ground dropped away so sharply there was no way they could make it with the sled. To go around the cliff they would have to go up, a steep climb she knew she couldn't make, not now. The only other option was to go back.

"I guess this is where we make the fire," Cam said, bracing the sled against a big rock so it wouldn't go careering down the mountain. Wearily he removed the harness, then wiped the sweat from his face.

"Here?" This was bad. If they weren't rescued, there was no good place here to construct even the roughest shelter. Even the trees were relatively sparse in this area, which would make gathering firewood more arduous. She sighed; it wasn't as if they were overloaded with choices. This was the end of the trail. "Here."

He stretched his back muscles, rolled his head back and forth. Then he laughed and said, "Look."

She looked where he pointed and saw, not all that far below them, where the snow ended. There wasn't a sharp line of demarkation, but a gradual lessening of the snow and thickening of trees. Unfortunately, they couldn't get there now.

Bailey lifted her face into the wind, and realized that it wasn't much more than a breeze. Smoke from the fire might stay together enough to be noticed, if not now, maybe tomorrow. They'd build this fire big and smoky and keep it going until someone noticed and came to investigate, damn it.

Cam was already doing the prep work, scraping away snow, digging a shallow pit. Bailey let the backpack drop off her shoulders and went in search of firewood. She couldn't gather much at one time, because she had to have one hand free for balance and climbing; on a trip back, she noticed that he'd dug three fire pits. "Why are there three of them?"

"Three is a universal distress signal: three blasts of a whistle, three fires, three stacks of rocks — whatever you use, there should be three of them."

"The things I've learned on this vacation," she said drily, returning to her task. On a practical basis, three fires meant she had to gather three times as much wood. Yippee.

With wood laid in all three pits and paper and bark scrapings as tinder, Cam sparked one more fire from the battery. Carefully they built the blaze, feeding it until the wood began blazing, then using a burning stick to take flame to the other pits. Soon all three were blazing high, but there didn't seem to be a lot of smoke. She wanted hugh billows of smoke, a column of it reaching a mile high.

Cam was evidently thinking the same thing, because he added some green wood to all three fires. The smoke that was soon puffing out was more gratifying.

"Now we wait," he said, putting his arm around her and pulling her in for a slow, deep kiss. She leaned against him, too exhausted to do much more than simply loop her arms around his waist.

He dragged the trash bags of clothes off the sled and positioned them side by side. With the contents punched into just the right position, the trash bags functioned somewhat like bean bags, and they both gratefully sank onto their makeshift seats.

For several minutes they didn't speak at all, but gathered what strength they had left. When he did speak, she was surprised by the track of his thoughts.

"When we get back," he said, "don't you dare try to pull away from me."

She couldn't say the thought hadn't occurred to her several times since she'd first realized how important he was becoming to her. When she had truly panicked, however, was when she knew that it was too late to pull away. "I won't," she said simply, turning her head to smile at him. She held out her hand. He took it, folding her fingers in his, and raised her hand to hold against his cheek.

Just before sunset they were still sitting on their trash bag chairs, looking out over the mountains like two tourists, when they heard the distinctive beat of the helicopter's blades. Cam rose to his feet, waving his arms as the helicopter surged into view, swooping toward them like a moth toward three flames.

33

The helicopter hovered over them, so close that wind from the blades whipped around them and Bailey could see the sunglasses the pilot was wearing. Beside him was another man; they both seemed to be wearing some sort of uniform, so she assumed they were with the Forestry Service. There was no place for the chopper to land, but what mattered was that now someone knew where they were, and help would arrive — soon, she hoped. They hadn't built a shelter, but if need be they would sit by the fires all night to stay warm.

She was so bone-tired she didn't think she could have helped build a shelter, anyway. She didn't even stand up to wave at the helicopter, despite the excitement of imminent rescue — or fairly imminent rescue, depending on how long it took a team to reach them.

Cam was making some hand signals to the

pilot. "Tell him to go get some sleeping bags and drop them down to us," she told him. "And a couple thermoses of coffee. And a dozen doughnuts. Oh, and a two-way radio would be nice." Fatigue was making her giddy, but she didn't care.

The helicopter banked away from the mountain, returning from whence it came. She heaved a sigh as she watched it leave. Somehow this was rather anticlimactic.

Cam was laughing as he sat down beside her. "Hand signals don't run to that kind of detail."

"What did you tell him?"

"That there are two of us, and we're both ambulatory, meaning a rescue team shouldn't risk their lives trying to get to us. And that we've been here five days."

She stretched out her legs and crossed them at the ankle. This was almost like sitting on a porch somewhere, admiring the view — which was spectacular — but instead of a porch she was lounging on a steep mountainside, with a vertical cliff not far to her left. "We should probably get ready for nightfall. Gather more firewood, make a shelter, that kind of stuff."

He turned to face her, leaning forward to prop his elbows on his knees as he studied her face, reading the utter exhaustion there.

Reaching out, he took her hand. "I'll gather more wood, but I'm not up to building a shelter. It's warmer here, without the wind. We'll cuddle by the fire tonight."

"Okay. I can handle cuddling." She looked wistful. "I don't guess there was any way to tell them our names, so they can notify our families?"

Cam shook his head. "I haven't let myself think about my family," he said after a minute. "I know they're going through hell, but concentrating on staying alive seemed more important. They're probably at the search headquarters, wherever the hell that is, because there weren't any searches anywhere near us." He paused, then said roughly, "I need to see them."

She had thought about Logan and Peaches, she realized, about how they must be feeling, how worried they must be, but she honestly hadn't thought for even a moment that any of the others, even her parents, would bestir themselves out of concern for her. Her mother might shed a tear or two, use her tale of woe to drum up sympathy, but wait at the search headquarters for her daughter's body to be found? Not going to happen. Her father wouldn't even waste a tear. He'd made it plain years ago that his first three children were pretty much off his radar. Cam was lucky in his family, in knowing without hesitation that they would be there waiting for him.

"For your mother's sake," she told him, "I hope you have a chance to clean up before she sees you. You also need some clothes. And a bandage over that cut, because, trust me, she needs to know for certain you're all right before she sees it." She examined him in the brightly flickering light from the fires. His five-day beard was scruffy, and the deep bruises under his eyes were fading to an ugly purplish-yellow. All the various scrapes were scabbed over and healing. That god-awful cut across his forehead; she couldn't decide if her clumsy stitches were an improvement over how he would have looked without them, or not. She began to snicker. "You look awful."

He grinned in quick response. "You look pretty bad yourself," he said with a teasing note in his deep voice. "Like you were in a plane crash and have been living in the wild for five days. The black eye is the crowning touch, though. At least you know for certain I didn't fall in love with you because of how you look."

Bailey nearly jumped out of her skin. How could he throw things like that at her, without giving her advance warning so she could prepare herself — though how she could have prepared herself for that, she didn't know. Before she could react, he cradled her hand against his cheek once more. "If I ask you to marry me, will you run screaming down the mountain?"

Shock on top of shock. She hadn't been able to react to one before he hit her with another. The end result was that she sat there, immobilized by the impossibility of choosing which sentence to address first. Finally she managed to squeak, "I might," and left it to him to figure out which one she meant.

He kissed her palm, and she felt his lips twitch as he fought a smile. "Then I won't ask," he said gravely. "Not yet, anyway. I know you need time to get used to the idea. We should let our lives settle down, see each other under normal circumstances. There's also the problem of Seth trying to kill you, and that has to be handled before anything else. I'm thinking nine months to a year before we get married. How does that sound to you?"

For someone who wasn't asking her to marry him, he was laying a lot of groundwork, she thought. Her heart was skipping beats, but when she looked at him she wondered how she could go the rest of her life without seeing that grin, or hearing the dryness of his tone when he was making some pithy comment, or sleeping in his arms. She didn't know if she could sleep at all without him.

She cleared her throat. "Actually . . . I'm okay with the marriage part."

"It's just the love part that scares the hell out of you, huh?"

"I'm . . . doing better than I'd have thought with that, too."

"You're not panicking at the idea that I love you?"

"That part's okay, too," she said seriously. "It's the loving you in return that scares me so much."

She saw the gleam of triumph in his eyes. He didn't look down to hide it, either; he let her see everything he was feeling. "Are you saying you're afraid to love me, or you're afraid *because* you love me?"

She drew a deep breath. "I think we need to be careful and not rush into anything."

His lips twitched again. "Now, why am I not surprised you said that? And you haven't answered my other question."

There it was, the cool, relentless determination she'd seen when he was coaxing the plane to stay in the air for the precious seconds they needed to hit the tree line instead of the bare rocky summit. She could feel safe with him, she thought. He didn't give up; he didn't cut and run. He wouldn't cheat on her, and if they had children he would never leave them high and dry.

"I do love you," she admitted. The words were shaky, but she got them out, though she immediately hedged, "Or I think I do. And I'm scared. This has been an unusual situation, and we need to make sure we still feel the same after we get back to the real world, so I definitely agree with you there."

"I didn't say we needed to make sure we feel the same. I know how I feel. I said I understood why you needed time to get used to the idea."

Definitely relentless, she thought.

"That's settled then," he said with quiet satisfaction. "We're engaged."

Now that they had been spotted, they let two of the fires go out and spent the night lying close by the one remaining, talking, occasionally dozing. The space blanket and the pieces of foam kept them off the cold ground, and the usual layers of clothing kept them, if not warm, at least not freezing. After they had rested some and slept a little, he made love to her again. This time was slow, leisurely; after he entered her it was almost as if they both dozed again, but he would rouse enough every few minutes to gently move back and forth. Bailey was acutely aware that he hadn't put on a condom, and the bareness of his penis inside her was one of the most exquisite sensations she'd ever felt.

She came twice from that slow, rocking motion, and her second climax triggered his own. He gripped her hips and locked their bodies so tightly together not even a whisper could have slipped between them, and a muffled groan came from his throat as he shuddered between her legs.

After cleaning up and restoring their clothes to order, they slept some more. When dawn arrived they were awake, and waiting for the rescue team. They restored the area as much as possible, got all their makeshift gear packed up, then sat by the fire with the space blanket wrapped around them. Bailey was light-headed from hunger, and she felt strangely fragile, as if, now that the battle for survival was won, all her strength had left her. Sitting beside Cam was about the limit of her remaining capability.

They heard the helicopter just after seven, and watched it land on a more accessible patch of ground about a quarter of a mile below them. As the rescue team exited the chopper she murmured, "They'd better have food with them."

"Or what?" he teased. "You'll send them back?"

She tilted her head back and smiled up at him. He looked as hollow-eyed as she felt; yesterday had depleted them, and without food neither of them had recovered.

The ordeal was almost over. In a few hours they would be clean, warm, and fed. The real world was coming at them fast, embodied in the four-man team of helmeted mountaineers who were steadily climbing toward them, moving in a well-rehearsed symphony of ropes and pulleys and God only knew what else.

"You folks get lost?" the team leader asked when the four men reached them. He looked to be in his thirties, with the weathered look of someone who spent his life outdoors. He studied their drawn, battered faces, the long line of dark stitches across Cam's forehead, and quietly told one of his men to do a physical assessment.

"The hiking trails aren't open until next month. We didn't know anyone was missing, so it was a big surprise when they spotted your fire yesterday."

"Not lost," said Cam, getting to his feet and tucking the space blanket around Bailey. "Our plane crashed up there" — he pointed toward the summit — "six days ago."

"Six days!" The leader gave a low whistle. "I know there was a search-and-recovery mission for a small plane that went missing over near Walla Walla."

"That would probably be us," said Cam. "I'm Cameron Justice, the pilot. This is Bailey Wingate."

"Yep," said one of the other guys. "Those are the names, all right. How did you get this far?"

"On a wing and a prayer," said Cam. "Literally."

Bailey looked at the rescuer who was crouched beside her, taking her pulse and shining a light into her eyes. "I hope you have some food with you."

"Not with us, no ma'am, but we'll get you fed as soon as we get you back to headquarters."

As it turned out, he lied. After they were lowered down the side of the mountain and everyone was loaded onto the helicopter, the decision was made that they needed medical care. The pilot radioed ahead, and then they were taken to the nearest hospital, a two-story facility in a small Idaho town.

The ER nurses, bless them, expertly assessed their most urgent need and rounded up food and coffee before they were even seen by a doctor. To Bailey's surprise she couldn't eat much, just a few spoonfuls of soup, along with a couple of saltines, that the nurse brought to her. The soup was canned soup, heated in a microwave, and it tasted like ambrosia; she simply couldn't eat it all. Cam made a better showing than she did, wolfing down an entire bowl of soup and a cup of coffee.

After a quick exam, the doctor said, "Well, you're basically sound. You need to eat and sleep, in that order. You're lucky; your arm is healing well. By the way, when did you have your last tetanus shot?"

Bailey stared blankly at him. "I don't think I've ever had a tetanus shot."

He smiled. "You have now."

After getting the injection, a nurse led her to the nurse's lounge and the attached locker facility, complete with showers. Bailey stood under the hot water for so long her skin began to shrivel, but when she emerged she was squeaky clean from head to toe. The nurse gave her a set of clean green surgical scrubs to wear, and a pair of socks, over which she slipped a pair of surgical booties. She so didn't want to put on her hiking boots again; she'd been wearing those things for six days, and her feet were as tired as the rest of her.

Cam wasn't so lucky. He got stuck with an IV drip and a brain CT scan. Bailey sat with him while waiting for the IV bag to empty, which took a couple of hours. Only then was he allowed to shower and shave, his head was bandaged again, and he, too, was given a set of clean scrubs.

Then all the questioning started. They had crashed in a national recreational area, so the Forestry Service was involved. The rescue team leader had to fill out his report. The NTSB was notified. A reporter with an area newspaper heard about them on his scanner, and he showed up. The town's chief of police came by to check them out. Cam talked quietly with the two men from the Forestry Service, with the chief of police, and he talked on the phone to an NTSB investigator. Neither he nor Bailey breathed a word about sabotage to the reporter.

Things moved fast. Charles MaGuire, the NTSB investigator, was on his way. Someone loaned Cam a cell phone, and he called his parents. When he was finished, Bailey asked if she could borrow it, too, and she called Logan's cell number.

"Hello?" He answered on the first ring, giving her the impression that he'd pounced on the phone.

"Logan, it's me. Bailey."

There was a moment of dead silence, then in a shaky voice he said, "What?"

"I'm at a hospital in . . . I don't know the name of the town . . . Idaho. I'm not hurt," she said quickly. "We were rescued from the mountain early this morning."

"Bailey?"

The disbelief in his voice was so profound that she wondered if he believed her, or if he thought someone was playing a trick on him. "It's really me." She wiped away a tear as it slid from the corner of her eye. "Want me to tell you what your middle name is? Or what our first dog's name was?"

Warily he said, "Yeah. What was our first dog's name?"

"We never had a dog. Mom doesn't like animals."

"Bailey." His voice shook, and she realized he was crying. "You're really alive."

"I really am. I have some bruises, a black eye, I just ate some real food for the first time in six days, and I had to have a tetanus shot which hurt like hell, but I'm okay." She could hear Peaches in the background, her light, sweet voice asking questions so fast she was incoherent, or maybe that was because she was crying, too. "An investigator is flying down to talk to us, and then I guess we'll come home. I don't know how yet, because I don't have any money, credit cards, or ID with me, but we'll get there somehow. Where are you?"

"In Seattle. At a hotel."

"There's no sense in paying for a hotel room; stay at the house. I'll call the housekeeper and tell her to let you in."

"Ah . . . I think Tamzin is staying there."

"She's what?" Bailey felt her blood begin to boil, and sparks shoot from her eyes. Her rage was so immediate and consuming that she wouldn't have been surprised if her head had started spinning around and around.

"She was there the day after the crash. I haven't called there since to check."

"Well, check now! If she's there, have her arrested for breaking and entering! I'm serious, Logan. I want her out."

"Don't worry, I'll get her out. Bailey . . . Tamzin said something about Seth. I think he could have had something to do with the crash. He denied it, but what else would he do?"

"I know," she said.

"You do?"

"Cam figured it out."

"Cam . . . the pilot?"

"The one and only," she said, smiling at Cam the Pilot himself, who winked at her.

"I think we might get married. Listen, this

is a borrowed cell phone, so you can't call me at this number. I don't know where we'll be before we come home, but I'll get in touch with you when I know. Go eject the bitch from that house before she trashes it. Love you."

"Love you, too," he said, and she disconnected before he could ask any more questions, which he was guaranteed to do considering what she'd just told him.

"*Might* get married?" Cam drawled, his eyebrows lifted.

"He'd had enough shocks for one day," she said, going to him and nestling against him. They had spent a large part of the past five and a half days in each other's arms, asleep or awake, and something in her felt wrong if they weren't touching. She rested her head on his shoulder. "Tamzin's in my house."

"I heard."

"It really isn't my house, but I live there, and she has no business going through my things. She's probably already donated all my clothes to a church charity — if she didn't dump them in the trash."

"She definitely needs ejecting."

"She told Logan that Seth had something to do with the crash."

"Hmm. Why would she say something like that? That was stupid."

A rather obvious conclusion occurred. "Unless she *wants* Seth arrested."

Thoughtfully, Cam scratched his newly shaved jaw. "That's something to think about," he said quietly.

34

Charles MaGuire had tufted ears like a lynx, but that was where his resemblance to a cat began and ended. He was as solidly built as a fireplug, with a thick shock of gray hair and shrewd blue eyes. How he'd gotten there so fast Bailey couldn't imagine, but she guessed that when you worked for the NTSB you could take a flight to anywhere at any time.

No one had seemed to know what to do with them, and though a lot of people in the friendly little town were offering their hospitality to two strangers, in the end the chief of police, Kyle Hester, had offered to let them use his office at city hall, and that had seemed the best bet all around. Chief Hester was a no-nonsense guy in his forties, former military like Cam, so they seemed to be on the same wavelength. Cam told Bailey that he'd informed Chief Hester about the sabotage of the plane, so the chief was well aware there was more going on than just the usual hoopla over a rescue.

The chief was one of those people who got things done. Within an hour Cam and Bailey each had a new cell phone, programmed with their old numbers, delivered to them at city hall. He also had food brought in; even though they'd eaten at the hospital, he seemed to know that they wouldn't have been able to eat much at first, and they needed calories. So the food was there for them to graze on: fruit, chocolate, bowls of potato soup they could heat in the microwave in the break room, crackers and cheese spread. Bailey couldn't seem to stop eating. All she could tolerate was a couple of bites at a time, but in five minutes she'd be back for more.

The newspaper reporter had wanted to interview them, but neither Cam nor Bailey were interested in any publicity. The reason they'd crashed wasn't something either of them felt like exploiting. Chief Hester took care of that, too, shielding them from calls and preventing anyone from bothering them. Chief Hester, in short, was fast becoming one of Bailey's favorite people.

When Charles MaGuire arrived, the chief turned his office over to them. The NTSB investigator was frankly astounded they were alive, and puzzled by where they'd crashed.

On the chief's topographical wall map, Cam pointed out where they'd been rescued, and traced a line to where he estimated they had crashed. "Here's approximately where we were when we ran out of fuel," he said, and tapped another spot in the mountains.

MaGuire stared at the map. "If that's where you ran out of fuel, how the hell did you get over here?"

"Air rises on the windward side of the mountains," Cam said. "I wanted to make it down to the tree line, to use the trees as shock absorbers instead of going nose-first into a rock face. As a rule of thumb, when you're gliding, you travel twenty feet forward for each foot you lose in altitude, right?" He moved his finger along the map. "By catching the rising air currents, we made it about two or three miles in this direction, to about right here, and down to the timber line. I put it down where I judged the trees were big enough to cushion us but not so big that we might as well be crashing into rock. I had to find a patch of trees thick enough, too, because they're pretty thin where the timber first starts."

MaGuire visually measured the distance, looking bemused. "Your partner, Larsen, said if anyone could put it safely down, you could. He said you wouldn't panic."

"I was doing enough panicking for both of us," Bailey said drily.

Cam made a scoffing noise. "You didn't make a sound."

"I panic quietly. I was also praying as hard as I could."

"What happened then?" MaGuire asked. He glanced at the bandage on Cam's forehead. "You were obviously hurt."

"I was knocked out cold," Cam said, shrugging. "And bleeding like a stuck pig. The left wing and part of the fuselage was torn off, so there was no protection from the cold. Bailey dragged me out, got the bleeding stopped, got me warm, and stitched up my head." The smile he gave her was so full of pride it almost blinded her. "She saved my life then, and again when she built a shelter for us. If we hadn't been able to get out of the wind, we wouldn't have made it."

MaGuire turned to her then, looking at her with a great deal of curiosity, because he'd learned a lot about the Wingates in the past several days and he was having a tough time adjusting his mental image of Jim Wingate's trophy wife to this calm, unpretentious woman wearing surgical scrubs, no makeup, and a bruised eye. "You've had medical training?"

"No. The plane's first-aid kit had an instruction book that detailed how to set sutures, so I did it." She wrinkled her nose. "And I never want to do it again." She was glad she'd been able to do it, but she didn't want to remember the gory details.

"I'd lost a lot of blood and I was concussed, so I wasn't able to help her at all. She scavenged stuff from the plane that we could use. She used practically her entire wardrobe to cover me, keep me warm — and let me tell you, that was a lot of clothes, three big suitcases full. Thank God."

"When did you begin walking out?"

"The fourth day. Bailey's arm was injured, there was a piece of metal in it, and she didn't bother taking care of herself. The second day, neither of us was capable of doing much of anything. We slept. I was so weak I could barely move. Bailey's arm was infected, and she had a fever. The third day, we both felt better, and I could walk around some. I checked the ELT, but the battery was almost dead, so I knew if we hadn't been located by then we weren't going to be, and there was no way of telling whether or not the ELT had ever worked anyway."

"It didn't," said MaGuire. "There was no signal."

Cam stared at the map, but mentally he was back in the Skylane's cockpit, his jaw set and hard. "When the engine quit on us, all the gauges read exactly the way they were supposed to read. Nothing seemed to be wrong, but the engine stopped. On the third day I found the left wing. There was a clear plastic bag hanging out of the fuel tank. When I saw that, I knew someone deliberately brought us down."

MaGuire blew out a breath and hitched a hip onto a corner of Chief Hester's desk. "We didn't suspect anything at first, but Larsen had been going over and over the Skylane's maintenance records, fueling reports, any piece of paper that pertained to the plane. Finally he noticed that the fuel records showed the plane holding only thirty-nine gallons that morning. We checked with the guy who fueled it, and he specifically remembered checking that it was full. As of this morning we still hadn't received a court order for the airfield's security tapes, but we suspected the plane had been tampered with."

"Seth Wingate," Cam growled. "He called the office the day before the flight to verify that Bailey was going to Denver. He might have enough juice for a judge to do him a favor by delaying a court order, though I don't know what that would accomplish in the long run, unless he needed time to get his hands on the security tape and destroy it, or something."

"That's what your secretary kept insisting. He definitely behaved suspiciously, but that's also stupid behavior. Suspicions are one thing, proof is another. So far, we don't have any proof at all, just an anomaly in the fueling records."

"We've already figured that out. Unless the security tapes caught him fooling around with the plane, all the evidence is at the crash site, and retrieving it would be a bitch. The wind's brutal up there, there's no way for a chopper to do even a one-skid touch-down. The only way up is on foot."

"I didn't know Seth would even know *how* to sabotage the fuel tank that way," Bailey said. "He has a vicious temper and despises me, but I never thought he'd try to physically harm me. The last time I talked to him he threatened to kill me, but" — she bit her lip, troubled — "I didn't believe him. More fool me."

"The plastic bag in the fuel tank is low tech," Cam said. "Doesn't take a lot of skill to do that."

"That doesn't, particularly," agreed MaGuire. "The transponder and the radio, though — he knows his way around a plane a lot better than you think."

Cam slowly went stiff, his gray eyes turning wintry. "What? What about the transponder?" Bailey gave him a searching look. His voice had changed, to something dark and menacing.

MaGuire turned back to the map. "Right here," he said, pointing, "just east of Walla Walla, is where you lost your transponder signal. Fifteen minutes later, an FSS picked up a garbled distress transmission, then you dropped off the radar and were gone. If he sabotaged those, too, he was very thorough. He didn't want the crash site found — or he wanted to delay finding the site until all forensic evidence had eroded."

Cam stood very still, studying the map. "Son of a bitch," he said softly.

"An opinion everyone seems to have of him. I hate to say this, but he may get away with it." MaGuire sighed. "My biggest worry right now isn't locating the crash site, but your safety, Mrs. Wingate."

"Bailey's with me," said Cam, without looking around. "I'll take care of her."

Bailey grimaced at the caveman attitude and told MaGuire, "I intend to let Seth know that we know he tried to kill me, even though we can't prove it, but that we've also told an unspecified someone else, so if he tries again he'll be at the top of the list of suspects. I can't think of anything else we can do."

"I can," said Cam, his eyes still cold. "MaGuire, any way we can leave for Seattle right away? I want to get this handled now."

MaGuire's expression was curious, but all he said was "You sure can."

They landed in Seattle about eight that night, though Bailey had always wondered how you could call it "night" when the sun wouldn't set for over another hour. Her reserves of strength were still depleted and all she wanted to do was crawl into bed and sleep, but she wanted that bed to have Cam in it, and she hadn't been able to have more than a few words with him since he'd gone so cold and quiet when MaGuire told him all Seth had done.

In a way, that was all right. She was having some cold and quiet moments herself. For Seth to try to kill her, well, it wasn't okay, but Seth was her burden to bear and it enraged her that he'd so cavalierly counted Cam's life as of no consequence. Whether or not Cam died, too, simply hadn't mattered to him.

She was going back to a changed world. She couldn't just resume her old life as if nothing had happened. Regardless of the agreement she'd made with Jim, she couldn't deal with Seth any longer. She'd have to be stupid to risk her life and Cam's life because of an agreement she'd made with someone who was now dead. Someone else would have to manage the trust funds, perhaps one of the officers where Jim had banked. She was adamantly opposed to signing control over to Seth, because she didn't believe he should be rewarded after what he'd tried to do, but someone else could have the hassle.

They had flown back to Seattle in a plane much the same size as the poor Skylane. Without hesitation, Cam had slid into the copilot's seat, not even thinking of sitting in back with her, which had made her roll her eyes and smile because that's what you got with a pilot. Most of them lived and breathed flying, to the point where they were often oblivious to everything else. MaGuire sat in the back with her, and something in his expression told her he'd rather have been in the copilot's seat but Cam had been faster.

"He's desperate," she said, amused. "He hasn't had his hands on the controls in six days."

"But it's my charter," he said, just a tad sulky in tone. Then he shrugged and gave her a faintly sheepish smile. "I guess I should have expected it, and been faster. Most pilots I know would rather fly than eat."

She tried to be calm as they neared Seattle, but she was returning to so many changes she had trouble grasping them all, and as always change made her uneasy. She normally didn't make a major decision until she had thought about it, researched it, prepared for it. If anything in her life changed, she wanted to control the way it happened. Abruptly she had no control, and virtually everything had changed: she would be moving out of that enormous house as fast as she possibly could, and she didn't care what Seth and Tamzin did with it. She refused to deal with them any longer, which meant she had to find another job.

The biggest change, of course, was Cam. He'd moved so fast she felt like Wile E. Coyote, spinning helplessly in the dust as the Roadrunner raced past him. In less than a week, she'd gone from not liking him at all to loving him; she'd even agreed to marry him. The odd thing was, even though he was the biggest change, he was the one she felt the best about. Once she had gotten over her initial panic, she knew that being with him felt *right,* in a way nothing else ever had.

As if feeling her thoughts, he looked over his shoulder at her. He'd gotten a pair of sunglasses from somewhere, so she couldn't see his eyes, but this evidence of the link between them helped settle her nerves as nothing else could have. She wasn't alone anymore. However else her life changed, Cam would be right there with her.

The plane touched down, the pilot applying the brakes as they rolled down the runway. Bailey leaned forward to look at the terminal, where people were spilling out of the building, through the fence gate and onto the tarmac, where they stood waiting. It wasn't a large crowd, and from that distance she couldn't make out individual faces, but she knew Logan and Peaches were there and her heart lightened with pleasure.

As they taxied closer she saw them, Logan with his arm around Peaches, both of them laughing and Peaches jumping up and down a little in excitement. She knew they probably couldn't see her but she waved anyway. She could make out Bret, too, and Karen, but she didn't think she knew any of the other people. They might be Cam's friends and relatives, even though he'd talked to his parents and they'd said they wouldn't be able to get to Seattle before he did because they were traveling on a commercial airline, and they had to wait for a regularly scheduled flight. Maybe they'd been able to make other arrangements.

The pilot taxied to a stop. Cam unfastened his seat belt and got out. After a quick word with the pilot, so did MaGuire. Then Cam simply reached in and lifted Bailey out, his hands warm on her waist. "How're you holding up?" he asked as they walked toward the little crowd that was surging impatiently, waiting only until they were a safe distance from the plane before breaking ranks.

"Tired, but okay. You?"

"The same. Brace yourself!" The last was said as they were enveloped. Logan and Peaches grabbed Bailey and she was crushed by hugs from both sides. Peaches was crying, so of course Bailey teared up, too, though she fought it. Logan just held her tight, his arms around both of them, but she could feel him trembling. She caught a glimpse of Cam as he, too, was surrounded by the welcome party. She saw Karen swat him on the chest, as if in punishment for worrying her, then with a grin Cam held out his arms and she burst into tears as she rushed into them.

"You're so thin," Peaches was saying as she wiped away her tears.

"It's that new diet," Bailey said. "The Plane Crash diet. Works every time."

"Are you hungry?" Logan asked, wanting to be able to *do* something, and getting food fell into that category.

"I'm starving. I think I've eaten a ton of food today, but a few minutes after eating I'm hungry again."

"Then let's get out of here. We'll pick up something on the way to your house. I'll fill you in on what happened with Tamzin, and you can tell us about the crash. I have a million questions."

Bailey looked around for Cam again. "Not yet. Not without Cam, at any rate. I haven't even introduced you."

She could see Logan was reluctant, that he very naturally had reservations about the speed with which she and Cam had become involved, and she patted his arm. "Don't worry so much. We're actually on our . . . twenty-fifth date. Or maybe it's around the thirtieth date by now, I haven't done the math. But we know each other a lot better than you think."

"Thirtieth date? I didn't know you were dating him at all!" Peaches said in bewilderment as everyone began moving inside. "You never said a word!"

Cam was organizing things, Bailey saw, sending most of the people on their way with thanks for their welcome, saying he had a lot of work he had to catch up on. He wasn't overt about it but she knew him now, saw the calm but steely air of command that was as natural to him as breathing. Even with his bruised face and bandaged head, he wore authority like a second skin, and people were following his directions without hesitation or really even noticing.

A select few went into the J&L office, though: Bret, Karen, MaGuire. Cam held the door open, his hand extended to Bailey, so she and Logan and Peaches went inside, too. She turned immediately to Cam, introducing her family. He and Logan shook hands, with wariness on Logan's part, calmness on Cam's. Despite everything, despite all the bad stuff they still had to handle, Bailey, in that moment, was happy.

Bailey was okay, Cam saw. She'd looked so suddenly frail that morning, as if she'd pushed herself until nothing was left, that he hadn't been able to shake his concern even though food had gone a long way toward reviving her. "Is the coffee fresh?" he asked Karen. He wanted Bailey taken care of before he took care of his other pressing business.

"I just put it on." Her eyes were still shiny with tears, but she was beaming. "Do you want some?"

Karen was offering to get coffee *for* him?

Maybe he should almost die more often, Cam thought. "In a minute. If you don't mind, though, make sure Bailey gets something to eat and drink — something out of the snack machine will be fine."

Karen grinned. "Bailey?" she asked in a low voice, leaning close so no one else would hear. "It isn't Mrs. Wingate now?"

"She gave me the lion's share of what food and water we had, to keep me alive," he said. "And she did without. So, yeah, I call her Bailey now." That was true, at least for the first day. After that, he'd tried to make damn sure she was eating and drinking as much as he was.

He saw the sudden fierceness in Karen's eyes and knew she had mentally added Bailey to the list of people she cared about, which meant Bailey would eat if Karen had to sit on her and stuff food down her throat. Considering Bailey had been eating non-stop all day, he didn't think it would come to that.

He went over to Bailey, touched her arm to get her attention. "I'll be talking to Bret for a few minutes," he said.

She gave his fingers a brief squeeze, giving his face the same assessment he'd been giving hers, taking care of him. He supposed that habit would ease after a few days, but right now they were still too close to their ordeal, still in survival mode, which meant taking care of each other.

He caught Bret's eye, made a brief motion of his head. Bret's office was closer, so they went in there. Cam closed the door behind them, maybe the first time that door had been closed since they'd started the business.

He turned to his best friend, the man who'd been like a brother to him for years, and said, "Why'd you do it?"

Bret collapsed in his chair, closing his eyes and dropping his head into his hands. His face had aged a lot since Cam had last seen him, taking on lines that hadn't been there six days ago. "Fuck," he said wearily. "Money. It was money. My ass is in a big fucking jam, with some badass people —" He broke off, shaking his head. "I knew you'd figure it out. When we got the word this morning that you were alive and had walked out of those damn mountains, I knew. There was no way you wouldn't have poked around, examined the wreckage, no way you wouldn't have looked for the reason you went down."

Cam held his rage under control with an iron will. As much as he wanted to beat the hell out of Bret, literally tear him to pieces, he wanted answers more. Grief was waiting for him, he knew, grief for the loss of the friendship they'd had, but it would have to bide its time. "I thought it was Seth, until MaGuire told me about the transponder and radio. That was way too complicated, too involved, more than he could have done. You overplayed your hand."

"Yeah, I have a habit of doing that." Bret lifted his head, the expression in his eyes stark with regret. "It was an impulse. When Seth called that day, I saw a chance, and I was desperate so I took it."

"How'd you make yourself sick?"

"I'm allergic to cats, remember? I stay away from them, won't even date a woman who owns one. So I went to an animal shelter, picked a cat up and petted it, rubbed my face against it."

Cam *had* known Bret was allergic to cats, had known it for so long he didn't think about it; Bret was so careful in avoiding them that Cam had never seen him suffering from a reaction until the day he'd taken Bailey's flight in Bret's place. Even if he'd immediately thought of cats, he wouldn't have been suspicious, because allergic reactions happened.

"I didn't let myself think about it," Bret said tiredly. "I just did it. It was a way out.

The money from your life insurance for the business would have bailed me out of some big-time trouble. It was like . . . that was all I could think about, getting that money. But when Karen told me the plane was missing, all of a sudden it was real. I'd killed you. I'd murdered my best friend. It hit me, and all I could do was puke my guts out."

The odd thing was, Cam believed him. Bret was impulsive, tending to focus on short-term goals.

"I thought the plane would burn," Bret went on. "There's always a few gallons of unusable fuel left in the tanks. Even if there was some evidence left, I knew Seth would be the one suspected, because of that stupid fucking phone call, but other than that there was nothing to tie him to the plane. I didn't figure he'd ever be arrested."

"MaGuire said you're the one who pointed out that the plane hadn't taken on enough fuel."

"Yeah. I thought that if I was the one who pointed it out, no one would suspect me of being the cause." Bret rubbed his hands over his face, then met Cam's gaze. "What now?" he asked, standing up. "When I thought you were dead, that I'd murdered you, I did what I could to cover my ass. But you're too damn good a pilot to die easy, aren't you? I didn't know whether to laugh or cry when we got the word. I guess I did both. But I'll go along with however you want this to play out. I'll turn myself in, if that's what you want."

"That's what I want." Cam didn't bend. There was no going back, no letting years of friendship and good times soften him, because some roads you just couldn't travel again. "Attempted murder, insurance fraud . . . you'll do time."

"Yeah. If my ass isn't bumped off before then. Whatever." Bret had the look of a man who would never forgive himself. That was okay with Cam, because he'd never forgive him, either.

"One thing," he said.

"What?" asked Bret.

Cam punched him in the face as hard as he could, putting everything he had into it, rage slipping its leash like a cougar attacking. Bret's head snapped back and he crashed backward into his chair, overturning it and his wastebasket. He ended up sprawled on the floor amid the scattered trash.

"That's for almost killing Bailey, too," said Cam.

Of all the people Bailey had expected to see, Seth Wingate wasn't one of them. But there he was, standing on the doorstep of his father's house just before midnight that night.

She was packing — rather, she was searching for what few personal items of hers were left in the house, because Tamzin had emptied out her closet and thrown away all her clothes, as well as anything else she'd known for certain belonged to Bailey. The house had also been trashed. Bailey was so infuriated she was considering calling the police, but she was giving herself time to settle down before she did so.

The past few hours had been a complete upheaval. She still had a hard time accepting that Bret had tried to kill Cam, all for the insurance money, and if she had a hard time getting her mind around it she could just imagine how tough Cam was having it. Bret had seemed to be eaten alive with guilt, but that didn't change the facts. MaGuire had handled everything, even though he'd been as shell-shocked as everyone else. Bret had willingly gone with MaGuire to the police to turn himself in, but the legalities involved in dissolving the partnership and whether or not Executive Air Limo would survive were still up in the air. If it did survive, it would be simply as Executive Air Limo, because there wouldn't be any more J&L.

Bailey had some ideas about that, but again she wanted to think things through.

She also had to reassess her decision about managing the trust funds, now that she knew Seth hadn't been the one trying to kill them. On the other hand, once she discovered what Tamzin had done, she wanted to commit murder herself and wash her hands of the both of them. One decision that hadn't changed was that she didn't want to spend another night in this house that wasn't hers.

Logan and Peaches were at the house with her, as was Cam. They had come to help her pack, but there was precious little left of her belongings. Cam was white with rage, but they were both controlling it. Peaches was the one who was on the verge of a major temper tantrum, and Logan was keeping an eye on her as she stormed from room to room.

Now Seth was here, and even though she knew he hadn't tried to kill her, she didn't feel like dealing with his shit right now. She jerked the door open and stood squarely in the doorway, not inviting him in. Behind her, she heard Cam moving forward to stand just at her shoulder.

But Seth made no move to enter. Even though he was usually on his second or third bar stop by now, he didn't look wasted. In fact, he looked sober, which astonished her. He was dressed simply, in slacks and a pullover shirt, his dark hair trimmed and combed, his harsh face expressionless.

"A lot of people think I caused the crash," he said abruptly. "I just wanted to tell you that I didn't."

"I know," she said, so surprised she could barely speak.

Surprise flared in his eyes, too. He hesitated, then turned to leave. Bailey began to close the door, then stopped because he had stopped, his foot already on the first step down. He turned back.

"Who did it?" he asked. She could tell he hated having to talk to her, but he wanted to know. "Was it Tamzin?"

Tamzin? Tamzin was vicious and petty, but she wasn't organized enough to do something like that. "No, it was Cam's partner."

"Bret?" Seth was obviously taken aback. "Are you sure?"

"We're sure. He confessed," said Cam.

"Son of a bitch," Seth muttered. A mirthless smile touched his lips. "I guess Tamzin and I are more alike than I thought. She assumed I'd done it. I thought she had."

He took a deep breath. "You deserve to hear this. It hit me hard when I realized my sister automatically assumed I was a murderer. I took a long look at myself and didn't like what I saw." He met Bailey's startled gaze and gave a mirthless laugh. "I've gone to work at Wingate Group. In the mail room. Grant wants to see if I can stick it out."

Bailey held tight to the door. She had to, or her knees would have given way in shock. She didn't know what to say, so she blurted, "I'm going to give the management of the trust funds to someone else, probably a bank officer." She couldn't believe that Seth, of all people . . . had Jim been right in his reading of Seth, after all?

Seth's jaw tightened, and he glared at Bailey. "Don't," he snapped. "I want you handling them. I won't hate it so much if someone else is doing it, and I need you there as motivation. That was Dad's plan, wasn't it? I figured it out. He thought I'd hate you so much, hate you controlling my money, that I'd do whatever I had to do to straighten out my life. He was right, damn him. He was always right. He probably told you to use your own judgment about when to turn control over to me, didn't he?"

She couldn't do anything except nod.

Seth's mouth twisted. "He trusted you, and nobody could read people like Dad. So I'm going to trust him, trust that he knew what he was doing. You keep on managing the funds, so I can prove you wrong. One day you'll hand control over to me, then you'll be out of my life and I'll never have to see you again."

"I look forward to that day," she said honestly.

He looked past her and Cam, into the foyer. His eyebrows knitted together as he noticed the damage, the broken glass, the defaced walls. "What the hell happened in there?"

"Tamzin," Cam growled.

"Have her ass arrested," Seth said coldly, then turned and went down the steps, disappearing into the darkness.

Cam removed Bailey's hand from the door and closed it, then tugged her into his arms.

"Let's go," he said, kissing her mouth when she looked up at him. "There's nothing for you here. From now on, you're living with me."

Bailey smiled, trailed her fingertips over the bruises on his face. She felt absolutely no anxiety about that decision. "All right," she said, suddenly so happy she felt as if she could float off the ground. "Let's go. I'm ready."

ABOUT THE AUTHOR

Linda Howard is the award-winning author of many *New York Times* bestsellers, including *Drop Dead Gorgeous, Cover of Night, Killing Time, To Die For, Kiss Me While I Sleep, Cry No More, Dying to Please, Open Season, Mr. Perfect, All the Queen's Men, Now You See Her, Kill and Tell,* and *Son of the Morning.* She lives in Alabama with her husband and two golden retrievers.

We hope you have enjoyed this Large Print book. Other Thorndike, Wheeler, and Chivers Press Large Print books are available at your library or directly from the publishers.

For information about current and upcoming titles, please call or write, without obligation, to:

Publisher
Thorndike Press
295 Kennedy Memorial Drive
Waterville, ME 04901
Tel. (800) 223-1244

or visit our Web site at:

www.gale.com/thorndike
www.gale.com/wheeler

OR

Chivers Large Print
published by BBC Audiobooks Ltd
St. James House, The Square
Lower Bristol Road
Bath BA2 3SB
England
Tel. +44(0) 800 136919
email: bbcaudiobooksbbc.co.uk
www.bbcaudiobooks.co.uk

All our Large Print titles are designed for easy reading, and all our books are made to last.